Sugar Spinelli's Little Instruction Book

I don't always go by the book myself, so I admire a woman who can color outside the lines when necessary. After I saw Zeke Lonetree in the auction brochure, I figured a dark and mysterious type like him was bound to put a dent the size of a Cadillac in somebody's checkbook. I was looking forward to watching someone else plunk down a wad of cash for a change.

Then, to everyone's surprise, Zeke was pulled out of line. The editor-in-chief of that trendy fashion magazine *Cachet* phoned her bid in from New York City of all places, and took him right out from under our noses! I wish I'd thought to do that for Twyla. Ducky and I could have saved ourselves all that maneuvering. Oh well, live and learn. As Roy says, once your neighbor strikes oil, it's too late to buy his farm.

Dear Reader,

We just knew you wouldn't want to miss the news event that has all of Wyoming abuzz! There's a herd of eligible bachelors on their way to Lightning Creek—and they're all for sale!

Cowboy, park ranger, rancher, P.I.—they all grew up at Lost Springs Ranch, and every one of these mavericks has his price, so long as the money's going to help keep Lost Springs afloat.

The auction is about to begin! Young and old, every woman in the state wants in on the action, so pony up some cash and join the fun. The man of your dreams might just be up for grabs!

Marsha Zinberg
Editorial Coordinator, HEART OF THE WEST

Bachelor Father
Vicki Lewis Thompson

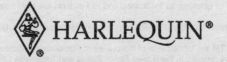

HARLEQUIN®

TORONTO • NEW YORK • LONDON
AMSTERDAM • PARIS • SYDNEY • HAMBURG
STOCKHOLM • ATHENS • TOKYO • MILAN • MADRID
PRAGUE • WARSAW • BUDAPEST • AUCKLAND

Vicki Lewis Thompson is acknowledged as the author of this work.

ISBN 0-373-82587-0

BACHELOR FATHER

Copyright © 1999 by Harlequin Books S.A.

Visit us at www.romance.net

Printed in U.S.A.

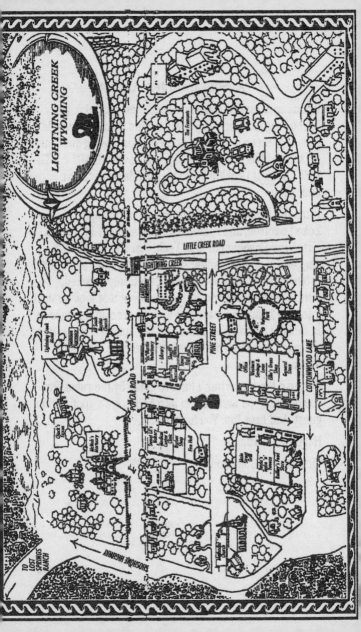

A Note from the Author

Wyoming is rugged country indeed. And rugged country breeds rugged men—my favorite kind. Imagine a whole passel of these drop-dead gorgeous guys being auctioned off to the highest bidder, and you have the HEART OF THE WEST series! I couldn't sign up for this project fast enough.

From the beginning, I had my eye on park ranger Zeke Lonetree, and lo and behold, I got him! Er, I mean *Katherine Seymour* got him. Yeah, that's it. Certainly *I* am not the one who spent days and nights in a secluded cabin with this bronze-skinned, beautifully muscled, tenderhearted love god with ebony eyes that look straight into your heart and make you want to scream *Yes, take me!* In this deal, *Katherine* gets to do the honors. I understand the rules. I'm the writer; she's the heroine. That lucky ducky.

Because I'm the writer, I have to abide by the rules. But you don't. If you want to slip into Katherine's spot, be my guest. And have fun. You lucky ducky.

Happy fantasizing,

Vicki Lewis Thompson

For Marsha Zinberg—editor, friend and classy dresser

PROLOGUE

I'M GOING TO DIE. The rapids pulled her under again. Through the churning bubbles Katherine saw a tree root. She grabbed at it, but fists of water punched her away. Fighting to the surface, she gulped in more water than air. Then the current took over again and slammed her against a submerged rock. She ignored the pain and tried to get a grip on the mossy, slippery surface.

No luck. The water closed over her head. Air. She needed air. But she was so tired. So very...no, damn it! Flailing her arms, she broke the surface again and choked as she tried to breathe.

"Here!"

Rescue! The possibility ran through her like an electric charge. Nearly blinded by the water pouring from her hair into her eyes, she struggled to turn in the direction of the voice. There...just ahead...a branch being held over the tumbling water!

"Grab it!" yelled the man.

She had one chance at this, she thought. One chance at life. As the river swept her toward the branch, she offered up a quick prayer and reached for the branch with both scraped hands. Contact!

But the river wouldn't let go. It tugged and pulled, trying to work her loose from her salvation.

"Wrap your arms around it! I'll bring you in!"

Following his orders took faith. She had to loosen her handhold to wrap her arms around the branch, and she was sure she'd be swept downstream in the process of getting a better grip.

But she wasn't. Inch by painful inch he worked her toward shore, until at last he could touch her hand. Once his fingers circled her wrist, she knew he'd saved her. Dizzy with gratitude, Katherine glanced up at the man who had just become the most important person in her life.

HE COULD HAVE MISSED HER, Zeke thought with a shiver. Headed back to camp with the string of trout he planned to cook for dinner, he could just as easily have cut through the trees instead of following the river. But an uneasy feeling he'd learned not to ignore had made him skirt the banks and check the rapids.

She'd scared the hell out of him. Adrenaline pumped through his system after he hauled her out of the water and she flopped facedown on a bed of wild grass.

He crouched beside her, his heart racing. "Was anyone with you?"

She gasped a few times. "No."

He swore. Although he didn't have to worry about looking for a drowning victim downstream, he wanted to shake this idiotic woman for traipsing around in the wilderness by herself. She'd almost paid the ultimate price.

But he'd saved her, and now he had to deal with the consequences of that. He'd deliberately left his cell phone at the ranger station, figuring he was off duty. Dusk was nearly upon them.

He leaned close to her. "Do you have a camp nearby?"

"No." Her breathing was steadier, but she didn't move from where she'd landed. "Lost my pack…in the water."

Zeke recognized a New York accent. Lord deliver him from greenhorns who thought Yellowstone was a slightly more rugged version of Disneyland. He sighed. "Then I guess you'll be spending the night with me."

CHAPTER ONE

Nine months later

WHAT A CIRCUS. From the porch of the main house, Zeke surveyed the crowded grounds of the Lost Springs Ranch for Boys. In all the years he'd spent as a kid on this ranch, he'd never seen the place so packed with people. But that was the idea—to get folks involved in this bachelor auction Rex Trowbridge, an alumnus who was now on the board of directors, had cooked up to raise money for the ranch.

Zeke longed to stay where he was, comforted by the familiar feel of the porch rail under his hand. But he had maybe five minutes before he had to walk out to the arena and climb up on the auction block where a gang of ranch alumni were gathering. The aroma of barbecued ribs filled the air, and fiddle music rose above the buzz from the crowd. Even CNN had shown up to film the action, so it looked like Rex would get the corporate sponsors the ranch needed to survive.

And Zeke wanted the ranch to survive. Lost Springs was his safe place, the haven his mind returned to whenever he felt rootless and alone. His thumb on the porch rail brushed over a small, crude carving of a lone pine. When he was ten he'd used his pocketknife to cut his mark into the wood, fully expecting to get in trouble for it. But he'd wanted to put his stamp on the place so that years later he could come back and find proof that Zeke Lonetree had been here.

He hadn't been punished for carving the tree into the rail. Every time he'd returned to the ranch he'd checked that nobody had sanded it down—to reassure himself that some things in life stayed the same. The thought of Lost Springs closing was more horrible than the thought of taking part in this bachelor auction, so he'd agreed to be here. But Rex had no idea how much it was costing Zeke. Walking up on that platform would be like slicing off a chunk of his soul and offering it to the buzzards.

A piercing whistle sounded above the hubbub, followed by shouted comments directed at Zeke from the auction block.

"Yo, Lonetree!" called Shane Daniels, one of the alumni who'd become a champion bull rider and a close friend. "We ain't got all day, son."

"Yeah, get your Native American butt out here!" yelled Chance Cartwright, who'd made good as a horse breeder and trainer. "All these women saw *Last of the Mohicans* and they want you bad."

Zeke groaned and wished he could treat this auction the way Shane and Chance did, as a big joke to be enjoyed. But both of them were used to being in crowds and rubbing elbows with the rich and famous. In fact, most of the guys on the block had high-profile, public positions, while Zeke's park ranger job in Yellowstone allowed him to spend most of his time the way he preferred—alone in the wilderness.

"Move it, Lonetree." Amos Pike, a toy manufacturer, motioned Zeke over to the platform.

Zeke took a deep breath and reminded himself why he was doing this. A phone rang inside the ranch house, but unfortunately it wasn't Zeke's job to answer it. He couldn't put off the inevitable any longer. Shane had given him a new Stetson for luck. With a sigh he tugged it low over his eyes and started down the porch steps.

"Zeke?"

He turned.

Rex, the guy responsible for his current misery, pushed open the screen door. He had a cordless phone in one hand with his thumb over the mouthpiece. "Come on in for a second," Rex said.

Zeke was delighted for any delay, but still he gestured halfheartedly toward the arena. "The guys want to get started."

"I know. We will in a minute. But it looks like you're being pulled from the lineup."

Hope lightened the heaviness in Zeke's chest as he followed Rex into the cool interior of the ranch house. "Pulled?"

"Yeah. Let me finish my discussion with this lady, and then you can talk to her."

Zeke listened to Rex's end of the conversation and figured out that someone was making a large donation in order to take Zeke off the block. He didn't understand what was going on or why, but he wasn't about to complain. He might still be obligated to a woman for a date of some kind, but at least he'd be spared the agony of walking the runway. He'd take it.

"Okay," Rex said to the person on the other end of the line. "That sounds great. I'll let you work out those details with him. And thanks again for your generosity, Ms. Rutledge. You'll be helping many young boys get a better start in life. Here's Zeke." Rex handed over the phone. "Way to go, stud," he murmured.

Zeke frowned in confusion as he took the phone and covered the mouthpiece. "I have no idea what this is about, Rex."

"Well, when you do, I hope you'll fill me in. My curiosity's killing me. Listen, even if you're out of the auction, how about hanging around, anyway? Some of the kids were hoping you'd give them an update on the wolves in the park."

"Sure." Still feeling bewildered, Zeke held the phone to his ear. "This is Zeke Lonetree."

"Ah, Mr. Lonetree. I'm Naomi Rutledge, editor in chief of *Cachet*."

Cachet. He'd heard that name somewhere, but he couldn't quite place it.

"The fashion magazine." She tossed her explanation into the silence as if she couldn't believe his ignorance.

"Oh." *Oh.* Katherine's magazine. A wave of dread washed over him. He hoped she wasn't tied into this bachelor-auction business in some way. He never wanted to see her again.

"Listen, I'll get right to the point. I believe you are acquainted with my senior fashion editor, Katherine Seymour."

Zeke closed his eyes. Surely it wasn't heartache he was feeling. He'd wiped that episode out of his memory months ago.

"Mr. Lonetree?" she prompted. "Does the name Katherine Seymour mean anything to you?"

He opened his eyes and cleared his throat. "We've met."

"Yes. So I understand. Well, she has some...personal business to discuss with you, so I would like—"

"Put her on. I'm sure we can handle it over the phone." Panic rose in Zeke's chest as he tried to fend off what he feared was coming.

"I'm afraid that's not possible. She's...unavailable."

"Is she okay?" The nature of Zeke's fear changed. He didn't want to get within two thousand miles of Katherine, but he didn't want anything bad to happen to her, either.

"She's fine. But she needs to see you, so I've arranged for her to fly out to Jackson Hole the last weekend in August. I presume that would be convenient to your place of employment."

"You can fly her anywhere you want, but I have no intention of—"

"The man I just spoke with assured me that you'd honor the terms of the bachelor auction and meet her there."

"You bought me for her?" Having a woman win him at an auction was bad enough. Having a woman procure him for someone else was ten times worse.

"I did nothing of the sort! *Cachet* is donating a generous sum to the Lost Springs Ranch for Boys, and in exchange I want you to meet Katherine in August and talk with her. It's a business arrangement. I'll even cover her expenses. Agreed?"

"Why are you doing this?"

"I'm not at liberty to discuss the reason. You need to take it up with Katherine when you see her. I'll mail you the particulars."

"Look, Ms. Rutledge, this is a complete waste of time for everyone. Katherine and I have nothing to—"

"I assure you, my donation to the ranch is *very* generous. I'm certain you wouldn't want to jeopardize that."

Zeke felt the trap closing around him, and he had no one to blame but himself. He'd acted totally out of character by making love to Katherine the night he'd saved her from the river. Then he'd made the further mistake of thinking the encounter had meant something to her. Months of her silence had convinced him otherwise. Now he was being summoned like some menial servant without being given any explanation. He longed to hang up on this bossy woman with the New York accent that reminded him of Katherine's.

But she'd practically said she'd withdraw her donation if he didn't go along with this ridiculous arrangement. He'd agreed to this damn auction to help the ranch, and now was his big chance.

"Do we have a deal, Mr. Lonetree?" she asked.

"We have a deal, Ms. Rutledge."

KATHERINE TOUCHED A FINGER to Amanda's cheek and guided the rosebud mouth to her nipple. As the baby nursed, Katherine stared at her in wonder. She couldn't believe that Amanda was nestled in her arms. So many times during the pregnancy she'd thought she would lose her. But Amanda had clung stubbornly to her chance at life, and Katherine had never known such joy as she felt now, holding her child.

"What a lovely picture you two make." Naomi smiled

gently as she walked into the hospital room dressed in her usual color scheme of black and white, her silver hair perfectly coiffed, her makeup flawless.

Katherine returned her smile. "Can you believe she's really here?"

"Not quite." Naomi walked over to the bed and leaned down to stroke Amanda's tiny head. "I didn't dare count on this, not with the problems you had carrying her." She finger-combed the baby's abundant jet-black hair. "I don't think this is going to turn blond."

"Probably not." Just her luck her baby's hair would forever remind her of that lusty night in the forest with Zeke Lonetree.

"She's beautiful, Katherine. I'm so sorry your parents didn't live to see her."

"Me, too." Her throat tightened, but as she watched Naomi tenderly smoothing Amanda's hair, she gave thanks that at least she had Naomi. "I guess this makes you a god-grandmother."

Naomi looked up, her eyes moist. "So it does." She cleared her throat and returned her attention to Amanda. "Although god-grandmother is a mouthful for a little kid. Maybe...she could just call me grandma."

Katherine's heart squeezed. "Of course she could."

Naomi gave the baby's hair one last stroke before turning to find a chair, which she pulled over to the bed. "And now that we've made it to this point, you and I have a few things to discuss."

"I plan on getting right back to work. If you have no objection, I'll bring Amanda to the office and set up a bassinet for her. I'm sure I—"

"I'm sure you can, too." Naomi laid her manicured hand on Katherine's arm. "But that's not what I want to discuss. I'm thinking of making some staff changes."

Katherine's breathing quickened. She was being demoted. Naomi might have seen her through this problem pregnancy with loving care, but she was the founder of *Cachet*, and she hadn't built the magazine into the industry giant it was by being soft. She'd decided to give Katherine's job to someone else because she didn't believe a new mother could handle the demands of being a senior editor.

Worst of all, Katherine dared not question the decision. When her parents died, Naomi had been her salvation, giving her a job at *Cachet* right out of college and promoting her regularly until she finally gained senior editor status. Katherine knew she hadn't worked up to capacity during the final months of her pregnancy, but Naomi hadn't ever complained. Under the circumstances, Katherine didn't feel she could beg for more consideration.

Feeling like a doomed prisoner, she gathered the courage to look directly into Naomi's eyes and take the bullet like a woman. "What sort of changes?"

"I want to train you to take over for me."

Katherine sighed with relief. She would work like a demon to justify Naomi's continued faith in her. "So you're going on vacation?"

"No, I want you to take over permanently."

Katherine's gasp dislodged Amanda's mouth. The baby's reedy cry of protest brought her attention back to the task and gave Katherine a moment to recover herself as she resettled Amanda at her breast. But her heart was still pounding when she finally glanced back at Naomi. "I...don't know what to say. I never in the world expected..." She stopped, at a total loss. Editor in chief. She couldn't comprehend it.

Naomi chuckled. "I can't go on forever, you know."

Katherine felt as if someone had just hit her over the head with the NYC phone book. "I guess I thought you would."

"And die in harness? Not this lady. Or worse yet, I could start losing my edge and have a staff who's afraid to tell me. No, I want to slip out of the top spot gracefully and leave someone I trust in charge."

"But what about Sylvia? Or Denise, or—"

"Darling." Naomi squeezed her arm. "You've been my choice ever since you were born."

"I have?" Katherine took a moment to digest that startling information. "No wonder you were so excited when I decided to work on the high school newspaper."

"It was all the encouragement I needed. Of course, I would have backed off if you'd chosen one of those other careers you talked about. I remember once you wanted to be an actress, and then there was your doctor-nurse period. And what was it you wanted to be when you were ten? A wilderness guide?"

Katherine smiled. "Yeah. Then I thought about all the bears I'd meet."

"Well, you made the right choice, both for you and for me. You've turned out to be a damned good writer and a highly competent businesswoman."

"Who got herself knocked up!" No matter how happy Katherine was about having Amanda, she was still embarrassed that she'd stumbled into motherhood by accident.

"Stress counteracted your birth-control pills," Naomi said briskly. "You couldn't have anticipated that." She gazed at mother and baby. "And don't tell me you're sorry, because I know you're not."

"No." Katherine dropped a kiss on the top of Amanda's head. "I'm not."

"So, are you up for some new responsibilities?"

The shock of Naomi's offer had lessened and now Katherine began to fully realize the scope of it—the confidence and the love that it implied. Her eyes filled. "You know I am."

Naomi blinked and looked away. "Good. Very good." She cleared her throat and glanced back at Katherine. "We only have one pesky detail to take care of."

A catch. Katherine wondered if she'd been premature in her gratitude. "What's that?"

"Amanda's father."

Katherine swallowed. It wasn't a comfortable subject.

Many times during the past few months she'd wished she could claim immaculate conception. After promising Zeke that birth control wasn't a problem, she dreaded telling him she'd been wrong. She'd rationalized postponing the call because she'd seen no reason to involve him if she ultimately lost the baby.

"You have to tell him," Naomi said.

"I know."

"He might just relinquish all rights to her."

"Maybe." Funny how little she knew about the man who had given her life twice, first by saving her from drowning and second by fathering Amanda. He was possibly the most gentle man she'd ever known, yet beneath that gentleness burned a fierce passion. Her heart still raced whenever she allowed herself to remember their moment of joining, when she'd felt somehow *claimed*.

The next morning, though, he'd been much more cautious and withdrawn. Plagued by her own insecurities, she'd suggested that maybe she ought to get back. Instead of trying to change her mind as some men might, he'd sealed himself off completely, which had convinced her there was no hope for a relationship.

"Do you feel anything for him?" Naomi asked.

Katherine looked up to find the older woman watching her closely. It was an important question. If she still had an emotional connection to Zeke, one that could potentially lead to a relationship, then she had no business letting Naomi train her as a replacement. She might not know a lot of things about Zeke, but she was absolutely sure of one thing—he would never live in New York. During their night together he'd made clear his love of the wilderness and his aversion to cities and crowds.

"I feel gratitude." Katherine glanced at the clock on the bedside table and decided it was time to switch Amanda to her other breast. She still felt a little clumsy handling the baby, but once she settled her in again, the tug of her small mouth felt perfect and right. "After all," she continued,

"Zeke saved my life, and he inadvertently gave me Amanda."

"I'm not talking about gratitude."

Katherine tried to be objective about her emotions regarding Zeke, but it wasn't easy. That night was like a blazing comet in her life, but her reaction to him had probably been born of many factors. She'd recently been dumped by Ken, she'd just been saved from drowning, and she'd never been stranded in the wilds with a man, especially a man as virile as Zeke. Maybe the fact that he was part Sioux had tickled her romantic fantasy. And maybe it was that look he gave her across the campfire, a look that promised so much pleasure...

"Katherine?"

She blinked and glanced at Naomi. Heat rushed to her cheeks. "Okay, he's very attractive, and I have some hot memories that are tripping me up a little. But he's apparently a real loner who wants nothing but wilderness surrounding him, while all I want is to work at *Cachet*."

"But what about your vacation last year? You didn't choose the Hyatt on Maui, don't forget. You opted for your personal little Outward Bound in Yellowstone. Maybe that yearning to be a wilderness guide isn't completely gone. Maybe you have a hankering for the great outdoors yourself."

Katherine smiled, more sure of herself now. "What I have a hankering for is a crisp set of galleys, a hot cup of espresso, and a bagel slathered with cream cheese."

Naomi beamed in approval. "Good girl. Although you'll have to go easy on the caffeine as long as you're breast-feeding."

"Decaf espresso, then." She noticed that Amanda had drifted off to sleep, her tiny hands curled into fists. "New York is what I know and love, and I've found my dream job. What could be better?"

"I can't imagine. So it's time to tidy up the situation with this man and get on with business. If he wants to surrender his parental rights, we're home free. If he wants partial custody, which I doubt, I'm sure you can work that out with him."

She made it sound so easy, Katherine thought. Something told her it wouldn't be quite that simple, but she tried to look confident as she nodded in agreement. "Right."

"Great. I've set it up so you can do exactly that."

Katherine stared at her. "Set what up?"

"He was part of a bachelor auction out in Wyoming, a benefit for a boys' ranch. I donated a chunk of money to the ranch in exchange for you spending a weekend with him in Jackson Hole at the end of August. You can tell him about Amanda then. She'll be two months old and should travel just fine."

"Naomi!" Katherine jerked, causing Amanda to startle awake.

"Or were you planning to tell him over the phone?"

"I—" Katherine paused to catch her breath and gently rock Amanda back to sleep. She should have expected something like this from Naomi. The woman had invented the term *take charge*. "I hadn't thought how I'd tell him, but..." She gazed at Naomi, still having trouble comprehending what her godmother had done. "You bought him for the weekend?"

Naomi waved a dismissive hand. "That's overdramatizing the whole thing. It's a business arrangement. I gave money to the ranch in exchange for helping my chief assistant tidy up her personal life."

"I can't imagine Zeke putting himself up for auction, let alone agreeing to spend the weekend with me simply because you paid the going price."

"I won't pretend that he was eager to comply. He tried to talk me out of it, said that the two of you had nothing to discuss. But when he realized that my sizable donation to the ranch depended on his cooperation, he gave in."

Katherine's chest grew heavy with despair. She'd been right about Zeke. He might have surrendered himself to a night of lovemaking, but he didn't want complications in his solitary life. Unfortunately, she was about to bring him a very large one.

"I still can't believe he was willing to take part in a bachelor auction in the first place," she said. "I've never met a more private man." ·

"He's an alumnus of the place. All the bachelors were. Quite an interesting story, really. They must have blanketed the media with invitations. Ours came quite a while ago."

"And you didn't tell me?" So Zeke had been raised on a boys' ranch. She hadn't known that. It made his lone-wolf image even more vivid.

Naomi regarded her with the same calm assurance that had kept her staff in awe of her for two decades. "You've been on an emotional roller coaster for months. Any mention of Zeke seemed to be stressful for you, and I was so afraid you'd miscarry that I decided not to bring this up. But it's worked out for the best. Going to Wyoming with Amanda is the right thing to do. You can clear the decks and then come home and settle into your new position."

"But Zeke doesn't want to see me. You said so yourself."

"He needs to see Amanda. You owe him that much, Katherine."

She gazed down at her sleeping child. Zeke's child. Naomi was right, but the thought of meeting Zeke again under these circumstances scared her to death.

"Your courage is one of the qualities that made me decide to turn over the magazine to you in the first place," Naomi said. "I'm not giving you anything you can't handle. You can do this."

Katherine lifted her head and looked into Naomi's eyes. "Yes, I can."

CHAPTER TWO

AUGUST TURNED OUT TO BE a wet month in the Tetons, and more rain looked likely as Zeke climbed into his battered king-cab pickup and headed for Jackson Lake Lodge on Friday afternoon. He spent the drive time singing "Ninety-nine Bottles of Beer on the Wall," because it reminded him of cookouts at Lost Springs and why he was putting himself through this. *Cachet's* donation would go a long way toward remodelling bunkhouses that no longer met the fire code, and Rex had already lined up a contractor for the renovation.

Naomi Rutledge had made it clear, however, that her check wouldn't be issued until after this weekend.

Zeke had never pretended to understand the thinking process of people who lived back East, but the whole deal was weird, even for New Yorkers. Painful though it had been, Zeke had combed through every moment of the night he'd spent with Katherine, searching for a clue as to what this could be about.

From the beginning, he'd tried to control his growing sexual awareness of her, which had been tough as their conversation grew more personal. He found out she'd broken up with her boyfriend, and to get her head on straight she'd decided to spend some time alone in the wilderness. She'd admitted that notion had been naive and overly dramatic.

Plucky, honest women appealed him, and this one seemed to be available. Eventually his desire felt natural and right, something to be seriously considered even though they'd just met. But while he was debating the issue, she'd made the first move. It had only been a light touch on his arm,

yet he'd felt his world shift. Then he'd turned to look into
her hazel eyes. That moment when he knew that she wanted
him as ferociously as he wanted her would be with him
forever. A moment like that could make a man feel like a
god.

This moment, however, when he was about to confront
her after nearly a year of silence, when he'd been summoned
to this meeting by her boss and kept in the dark about the
reason, made him feel like a toadstool.

He sang another chorus of the drinking song as he pulled
his beat-up truck in among the out-of-state cars and tour
buses parked at Jackson Lake Lodge. But he didn't have the
nerve to keep singing as he walked into the lounge where
they were supposed to meet, so the jitters he'd postponed
with the song struck with a vengeance. He'd always loved
this high-ceilinged room with tall windows facing Jackson
Lake and the jagged Tetons beyond. He hoped this meeting
wouldn't ruin the place for him.

Heart pounding, he scanned the room. He didn't see her.
Damn it, after all this, maybe she'd stood him up. Of course,
that would be a good thing. He didn't want to see her, anyway. Except that he'd gotten himself all worked up about
the prospect, and at least if he saw her, he'd find out the
answer to the mystery.

"Zeke?"

He wouldn't have bet that he'd recognize Katherine's
voice, but he didn't have to turn around to know she'd spoken his name. A flood of desire took him completely by
surprise as his body replayed the sensation of being deep
inside her. He turned to face her slowly, giving him time to
regain his cool. He knew she wouldn't be wearing rumpled
khakis this time, and he prepared himself for her city look.

But as he gazed at her, his brain stalled. When he finally
admitted what he was seeing, his knees almost gave way.

She looked more polished than she had a year ago, but
he barely noticed as his attention fastened on the canvas
carrier snuggled intimately against her chest. She supported

the weight of the carrier with one arm. With her free hand she cradled the head of a baby. A baby with very black hair.

While his mind shouted denials, his gut reacted with a primitive tug of certainty. *His.* He relived the dizzy ecstasy of being inside Katherine, of her warmth and a connection unlike any he'd known. When he'd finally poured himself into her, he'd experienced a sense of purpose he'd never felt with any woman. Maybe he'd known then, no matter what she'd said about birth-control pills. Maybe he'd known all along that this could be the only logical explanation for their meeting today.

"Her…her name is Amanda." Katherine sounded out of breath. "Zeke, I didn't mean for this to happen. Apparently the stress of nearly drowning short-circuited my system."

A girl. He noticed the baby's terry outfit was pink. He began to shake. A baby girl. Somehow knowing that she was a girl terrified him even more. She was asleep, her dark lashes creating a fringe above each cheek. She pursed her tiny mouth, then relaxed it again. Petrified though he was of this little bundle, he couldn't seem to look away.

"I didn't want to tell you over the phone. I realize this comes as something of a surprise." She paused. "Zeke, I wish you would say something."

With great effort he lifted his gaze and looked at Katherine. A frown creased her high forehead. How he'd enjoyed touching the smooth planes of her face as they'd lain side by side in his small tent, his battery lantern on low so he could see her while they made love. Her golden eyes had reminded him of a mountain streambed, the kind that he could stare into for hours. He might have even told her that. He knew he'd said things to her that he'd never said to anyone before, risked more than he'd meant to risk.

Her eyes brought him no joy today. All he could see was a woman who'd taken the best he had to give, then acted as if she could hardly wait to get away from him the next morning. Admittedly he wasn't good at expressing his feelings, but that morning he'd been trying to think how he could tell her what the night had meant to him. Before he had it figured out, she'd announced she'd better leave. He'd been half expecting her rejection. In his experience, caring too much almost guaranteed being discarded like an empty fast-food sack.

And now obligation was all that had brought her here to let him know they had a baby. He wanted to call Amanda an accident, but he knew she wasn't. At the time she was conceived, he thought he'd found his mate. That belief alone might have cancelled Katherine's birth-control pills. He'd seen people will their own death, so maybe you could will life into existence, too. Maybe he'd unconsciously done that.

He cleared his throat. "I think we should find a more private spot to talk about this."

"You're right, we probably should. But just let me say this. I'm not here to ask for anything—not child support or even for you to give Amanda your name. I take full responsibility for this baby. I understand how you want to live your life, and a child doesn't fit in very well. Now that you've seen her, if you'd like to relinquish all rights and never see either of us again, that's fine."

He stared at her, hurt tearing at his insides. She knew nothing about the way he wanted to live his life, but she'd use his loner status to justify closing him away from the baby because that suited her best. Anger and self-protection followed close on the heels of his pain as he threw up the walls that had sheltered his bruised heart all his life. He kept his voice low. "Is that what you came for? To have me sign off on this kid?"

"No!"

The baby's eyes opened and she started to whimper.

Katherine rocked her gently. "I mean, yes, if that's what you want, but if—"

"You could have hired a lawyer to put that in a letter and saved us both a lot of time." He took satisfaction from the distress in her eyes.

"I thought you deserved to see her."

"How considerate." He lowered his voice even more, conscious of others in the lounge starting to listen in. "You haven't seen fit to contact me in all these months, not even when you knew you were pregnant. Now you drop out of the sky, present this baby and suggest I give up my rights. That's a great idea, but I don't need three days in a plush lodge to work that out with you. Mail me the papers." He brushed past her and walked out of the lounge, refusing to allow the baby's wail to penetrate the thickness of the wall around him.

KATHERINE STOOD in the middle of the lounge in a state of shock, automatically comforting Amanda while she tried to assimilate what had taken place. Unless she'd misunderstood, Zeke had just agreed to the very thing that Naomi wanted, and for all intents and purposes, the visit had already accomplished its goal. She should feel jubilant, ready to celebrate before catching a flight back to New York.

Instead she wanted to cry. This was wrong, all wrong. Back in New York, she'd thought such a plan would be best for everyone, but after seeing Zeke again, she knew she didn't want him to sign some papers and disappear from Amanda's life.

When she'd walked into the lounge and caught sight of him there, his broad back to her, she'd felt an unexpected rush of delight. And awe. She'd forgotten just how big a man he was. His silky black hair seemed a little longer—it touched his collar in back now. But his stance was disturbingly familiar, and the faded jeans and blue flannel shirt could have been the same ones he'd worn that night. She suspected he had lots of similar clothes.

And he certainly fit the surrounding country with his massive frame and bronzed good looks. The rugged Tetons outside the window provided the perfect backdrop for a man in flannel and denim.

In spite of the anxiety she'd felt at presenting Amanda to him, she'd looked forward to the moment he would turn around, the moment she would once again be able to admire his warrior's face with those intense dark eyes. Until now she hadn't acknowledged to herself how much she'd missed him.

And now he was gone.

But maybe she could still catch him.

Grabbing up the diaper bag she'd set down, she clutched Amanda tight and hurried out of the lodge. She made it into the parking lot just as Zeke started to climb into an old gray truck. Calling his name, she started toward him as a light rain began falling.

He turned, but there was no charity in his glance. The forbidding look in his dark eyes almost made her give up and go back inside, but Amanda's warm weight against her body was all the motivation she needed.

"Please don't leave."

His expression was totally closed. "It's raining. Take her back inside."

"Come inside with me. We'll get some coffee. We'll talk." She was begging, but she didn't care. "I don't want you to leave like this. Surely you'll want to see her once in a while, and we need to—"

"Why?"

"Because she's your daughter!"

His laugh was harsh. "You say that as if it makes a difference. I happen to know being somebody's biological kid doesn't mean a thing."

So he'd been abandoned by his parents, she thought. He hadn't admitted that when they'd talked about neither of them having any family left. She took a deep breath. "You're right, it doesn't mean a thing to some people. I had you pegged differently."

His eyes hardened even more. "Up until ten minutes ago I didn't even know this baby existed. I wish you'd done us both a favor and kept it that way, but since you haven't, I'm going to leave here and pretend I never laid eyes on her."

"Zeke, please don't."

"It's the best thing all around. Now take her back in. It's raining harder." He climbed into his truck, started the engine and backed out of the parking space.

Katherine bowed her head over Amanda to shelter her from the rain and to hide the tears that threatened to fall. Naomi would be thrilled, she told herself, sniffing. A clean break. No strings. Lots of little girls grew up without fathers.

Amanda gurgled and waved her hand, bumping her fist against Katherine's damp cheek.

"Forgive me, sweetheart," Katherine murmured, not sure who she wanted to forgive her—Amanda or Zeke.

ZEKE STARTED OUT OF the parking lot, determined to get the hell away from the lodge as quickly as possible. But he made the mistake of looking in the rearview mirror.

Katherine stood there getting wet, her head bowed over the baby. They looked so hopelessly vulnerable, so in need of protection. Katherine was brave, but she had a reckless streak, too. That's what had nearly gotten her killed on her solo trek through Yellowstone. He remembered the stab of fear he'd felt when Naomi had called and he'd been afraid something had happened to Katherine.

Well, something had, and he'd been partly to blame for it. Would she do something foolish now just because he'd refused to talk about this baby business? He'd thought he was giving her exactly what she wanted by refusing to have anything to do with the kid, but his response seemed to have devastated her. Would he get some terrible message from Naomi Rutledge concerning Katherine and the baby's welfare?

With a muttered oath he slammed on his brakes. Slowly he backed the truck to where she was standing, pulled on the emergency brake and put the gearshift in neutral.

As he got down and rounded the truck, she was watching him cautiously, her eyes wide. She held Amanda with a protective grip. He'd been told that his size, combined with the features passed on by his Sioux ancestors, gave him a menacing air, so he deliberately relaxed his expression and unclenched his hands.

She had a large canvas diaper bag hanging from the crook of her arm. Vaguely he recognized Winnie the Pooh characters, although he'd been an adult before he knew anything about those stories. He gazed at her standing with her tiny baby, her storybook diaper bag, and an almost childlike uncertainty in her big eyes.

Damn it, he felt like rescuing her all over again. The woman kept getting herself in trouble, and he kept wanting to keep her safe. It was a bad combination. But he couldn't leave her standing here looking as if her world had suddenly stopped spinning.

"Let's take a drive," he said. "I don't feel like discussing this over a damn cup of coffee. I need to be doing something."

She peered at his old truck. "Do the seat belts work in your back seat?"

"Yeah." Then he realized that these days you didn't just decide to go for a ride with a baby. There were all sorts of rules and regulations. "Forget it. Just write me a letter when you get back to New York."

"No, I want to go for a drive with you. I brought her infant seat, just in case we did want to take her out somewhere with us. It's up in the room. Wait here."

She set the diaper bag down and hurried away before he could protest that this was all too complicated. He stood in the light rain waiting for her, the diaper bag by his feet. He'd always suspected babies were a lot of trouble, for a million reasons.

He was surprised by how quickly she returned with some contraption that she asked him to belt into the back seat so the kid was facing backward. All the baby would see was upholstery. It didn't look like much fun for the baby, but he remembered park visitors with similar child seats. He had to move some camping stuff to make room. Part of the reason he'd bought the king cab was to have a place out of the weather to keep his sleeping bag and small tent. The very tent, in fact, that Katherine had shared with him. The rain started coming down harder just as he finished.

"Let's get both of you in, then you can put her back there." He picked up the diaper bag.

"Okay."

He opened the passenger door, but it soon became obvious she'd have trouble getting in while Amanda was still strapped to her. He didn't want to touch her, but it was the expedient choice now that the rain was really sluicing down from the sky. Setting down the diaper bag, he put his hands around her waist and lifted her and the baby onto the front seat. His hands spanned her waist perfectly, just as they had when he'd lifted her on top of him and eased her down over... No, he couldn't think about that.

"Thank you." She didn't look at him.

He noticed the pulse at her throat throbbed and a pink flush tinged her cheeks. He wondered if his touch had anything to do with that. She might not want to maintain any permanent connection with him, but apparently he affected her. He'd bet she found that very inconvenient. Well, so did he.

"Watch your arms," he said. "I have to slam this to get it shut." He heaved the door closed, and by the time he climbed in, the baby was crying. He hoped to hell that wasn't going to go on very long. "What's wrong with her?" he asked.

"Just the loud noise of the door closing, I think." Katherine jiggled the baby and crooned to her. Then she lifted her out of the pouch and nuzzled her cheeks. "There, there, Mandy. You're safe. Don't be scared."

Zeke sat immobilized by her tenderness. For some stupid reason it made his throat ache to watch her cuddle that baby. You'd think he'd never seen a mother and baby before. To be honest, he hadn't been this close to many. Growing up on the ranch had meant being around lots of boys and young men. The couple who'd run the place had a daughter, little Lindsay Duncan, who now owned the place, but she was already a toddler by the time Zeke arrived.

Amanda's crying tapered off to small gasps and one hiccup. Then she quietly stared up at her mother with an unblinking gaze.

"That's my girl!" Katherine talked in a special singsong way and smiled at the baby. "Can you give Mommy a happy smile?" She tickled the side of Amanda's cheek. "Come on now, big smile. That's it. *Big* smile."

To Zeke's utter fascination, Amanda did smile, which seemed to make her cheeks look chubbier and gave her a double chin. It was the cutest thing he'd ever seen, and he knew cute when he saw it. Nothing matched a couple of tumbling bear cubs, or nothing had until now.

"Some experts say that a two-month-old isn't really smiling," Katherine said. "That it's just a reflex, or gas."

Zeke could tell from the more adult tone in her voice that Katherine was speaking to him, not Amanda. "Looks like a smile to me," he said.

"Of course it's a smile." Katherine lapsed back into her melodious baby talk. "We know a smile when we see one, don't we, Mandy? Yes, we do! Now, let's get you back in your seat." She lifted the baby from the pouch and handed her to Zeke. "Take her for a minute so I can turn around and get ready to lay her in there."

"Take her?" He pulled back as if she'd tried to give him a live grenade.

"Just for a minute."

"I don't know how to hold a baby!"

"Pipe down. You'll scare her again. Just support her head with your hand and the rest of her in the crook of your arm." She settled the baby into his arms and adjusted his hold. "Like that."

His body stiffened and his heart began to pound as he realized he had total responsibility for keeping this baby alive for the next couple of minutes. "I'm going to drop her. I just know it. Or squeeze her wrong and break something.''

''I doubt that.'' Katherine knelt on the seat and begin fiddling with the carrier in the back.

For the first time Zeke noticed what she was wearing—a long flowered skirt and a sleeveless blouse the color of young grass. The light material of the skirt stretched tight across her bottom as she adjusted the straps on the infant seat. Zeke tried not to pay attention.

He also became aware of two very pleasant scents replacing the smell of musty canvas that usually filled his cab. One was sweet and fresh, probably baby powder, but the other had a sexy tang to it. When he'd spent the night with Katherine she'd had no toiletries at all, let alone perfume. He'd even let her borrow his toothbrush. He'd loved the natural fragrance of her body, but this other was seductive in its own way. He liked it. He liked it way too much, in fact.

Amanda made a noise and jerked her small body.

He held her tighter. ''Don't do that,'' he instructed the baby.

She stared up at him.

He found himself staring back. Her eyes were a soft blue, yet Katherine's were hazel and his were brown. ''Why are her eyes blue?'' he asked.

Katherine answered as she continued to fuss with the seat. ''Because she's so young. The doctor said as she gets older they'll probably turn hazel, like mine.''

He continued to study the baby. Her skin wasn't as pale as Katherine's, yet not as bronzed as his. His skin-color genes and Katherine's must have combined into this shade, which was kind of nice. The thought of his genes combining with anyone's blew him away. Then he noticed the small dimple in her chin, a dimple just like…his mother's.

''Okay, hand her to me.''

Zeke was so afraid of dropping the baby in transit that the process of giving her to Katherine involved a lot of physical contact. And memories—the tickle of the downy hair on her forearm, the coolness of her fingers against his skin, the rhythm of her breathing.

While she strapped the baby securely in the seat, he faced forward and took several deep breaths himself, just to get over the dizziness of being so close to Katherine.

Finally she was back and buckled herself in.

He started the engine and turned to her. "We might be gone a couple of hours. Do you have what you need?"

"Yes. I have extra diapers and I'm breast-feeding. We'll be fine."

He wished she hadn't given out that bit of information. He didn't need to be presented with a picture of her unfastening her blouse and offering her breast to Amanda's little pink mouth. He'd be wise to get them both back to the lodge before that became necessary.

A car horn beeped and Zeke jumped. In his preoccupation with Katherine and Amanda, he'd totally forgotten his truck was sitting in a crowded parking lot blocking traffic. "Guess we'd better get rolling." Then he turned the key and ground the starter motor because he hadn't remembered the engine was already running.

Get a grip, Lonetree. Anyone who knew him would get a kick out of seeing him rattled, he thought. Among the other rangers, he was famous for never losing his cool. He'd faced bears, rattlers, even escaped convicts with calm detachment. But he'd never faced a situation like this one, and he had a feeling it was going to take every ounce of courage he could dredge up.

CHAPTER THREE

KATHERINE WATCHED the windshield wipers slap back and forth while she thought about what she'd done, running after Zeke like that. She'd have a tough time explaining herself to Naomi. She could just hear her godmother—*He was ready to give up all parental rights and you talked him out of it? Where was your brain, girl?*

Her brain had very little to do with it. She'd been operating on instinct, and right now her instincts told her this was right, for the three of them to be heading down the road together in the rain. Zeke had left the main highway to follow a narrow two-lane road with little traffic on it. Safe in the truck cab with Zeke, she felt cozy, almost peaceful. She hadn't felt that way for a long time, maybe not since the night she'd spent with him in his tent.

She glanced at Zeke and realized she'd never seen him at the wheel of a vehicle. He looked good there—competent and sexy. The day after her tumble into the river, they'd hiked to a ranger station, and another park service employee had offered to take her back to the Old Faithful Inn so Zeke could return to his campsite and get on with the solitary retreat she'd ruined.

And here she was again, invading his privacy. But for Amanda's sake, she'd brave it out and hope he'd be willing to accept some part in his daughter's life.

As if he felt her attention on him, he turned his head. "Should you check her? She seems too quiet."

"I'm sure she's asleep. She loves riding." His comment

made her smile. For the first month or so of caring for Amanda she'd had the same fears. She used to wake up twenty times a night and make sure the baby was still breathing. "Sometimes when she's fussy I bundle her up in her car seat, go outside and hail a cab, just so I can settle her down. It's worth the cost of a twenty-minute ride around town."

"You don't own a car?"

"Nope. Cabs are handier when you're in Manhattan. I don't live that far from the office. A car would be more of a nuisance than an advantage."

He frowned. "But don't you ever have the urge to get away from the city?"

"Yeah. That's why I came to Yellowstone last summer."

"Couldn't you have found someplace closer?"

"Well, sure. My parents and I used to camp in the Adirondacks when I was a kid, but that seemed too...tame. Besides, I'd been hearing about Yellowstone all my life."

"So you decided to tackle it alone."

"I like a challenge."

His jaw tightened. "I'd say you have one now, with your job and the baby."

And your stubbornness, she wanted to add, but didn't.

"And speaking of your job, what's Naomi Rutledge's stake in all this?" he asked.

Katherine decided that revealing Naomi as her godmother would only confuse the issue, so she stuck to the job situation. "She's offered to let me take over the magazine when she retires. Understandably she'd like my personal life to be under control before she does that."

He stared out at the rain-swept landscape. "That should be a no-brainer. I'll bow out of your life and Amanda's, like I said back at the lodge. Case closed."

"I think that's a mistake." She took note that his jaw now seemed carved in granite. He didn't appear to be the kind of man who would change his mind easily once it was made up. He'd given her Naomi's preferred response twice in a row, and she was no more ready to accept his decision than she had been the first time. But she wasn't sure she could explain why.

"I don't get it, Katherine."

A thrill ran through her. It was the first time he'd used her name since they'd met at the lodge, and the sound of it made a definite impact on her, reminding her of the way he'd said her name while they'd made love. "I'm not sure I get it, either," she said, picking at a loose thread in the stitching of the armrest. But she was beginning to suspect her behavior wasn't all motivated by Amanda's welfare. She'd been intrigued with Zeke a year ago. She still was. She'd told him the truth about liking challenges, and he certainly presented a huge one.

"Why didn't you contact me when you found out you were pregnant?"

At last—an easy question, one she'd been meaning to answer for him right away, but the sensual vibrations between them kept sidetracking her. "I had a very difficult time during the pregnancy," she said, glancing up. "The doctor said I was very likely to miscarry."

"All the more reason to—"

"I didn't see it that way. You were concerned about birth control that night, so I didn't think you'd welcome the idea that I was pregnant. There was no point in getting you involved unless there really would be a baby. I wasn't sure of that until the minute she was born."

His voice was tight. "That was two months ago. Did you forget to pay your phone bill? Or maybe you ran out of stamps. That can happen."

"I couldn't picture having a conversation about this over the phone. And a letter seemed even worse." She turned in her seat to look at him squarely. "Look, we got caught by a weird set of circumstances. I've tried to do what I thought was best. Maybe I've made some mistakes, but I—"

A loud bang interrupted her sentence and the truck lurched. Automatically she swiveled toward the back seat as Amanda started to cry and Zeke started to swear.

He eased the truck to the side of the road. "Sit tight. We have a blowout." He opened his door and cool rain blew in.

"Do you have a spare?"

"I think that was the spare that just blew." He climbed down and slammed the door.

Her heartbeat quickened. No spare. Before having Amanda, she wouldn't have been all that concerned, even if they'd had to walk back to civilization in the rain. But now she couldn't afford to be stranded.

Unbuckling her seat belt, she turned around and unfastened Amanda from her car seat to bring her up to the front. The baby wailed pitifully, her face scrunched up and her arms waving in the air. Katherine glanced at her watch and decided that the loud noise wasn't the only thing that had upset Amanda. She was due for some chow.

RAIN SOAKED ZEKE'S flannel shirt as he gazed at the hole in the sidewall of the left front tire and swore some more. He hardly ever drove the truck because he used park service vehicles when he was on duty. This afternoon when he'd started for the lodge, he'd remembered he hadn't fixed the flat after a nail had punctured it a couple of months ago, but it was too late to worry about it then.

He calculated the distance back to the lodge versus the distance to his little cabin. The cabin was closer. If he drove slowly, he might make it without damaging the rim too badly. Then he could call somebody from there.

Of course, that meant dragging Katherine and the baby to his cabin. He hadn't intended to do that, even though he'd been driving in that direction. He just happened to like this road, which was one of the reasons he'd decided to buy a couple of acres out here and put up a small log house. He had no neighbors within several miles, but he did have a phone, running water and electricity. Most of the time.

With one last disgusted look at the tire, he climbed back in the truck. "I think—"

"Close the door gently if you can, so you don't startle her."

He glanced at Katherine and caught his breath. Her green blouse was unfastened, although she'd modestly pulled it around her so that her breast barely showed. Somehow that made the whole picture more erotic to Zeke. Rain drummed on the roof of the cab, but he could still hear the soft sucking noises Amanda made while she nursed.

He pulled the door closed as best he could, knowing he'd have to open it and slam it again before they started driving. Then he stared straight ahead and tried to concentrate on following the path of an individual raindrop as it slid down the windshield.

He seemed to be having trouble getting enough air, and he cracked his window open a little.

A woman nursing her child was no big deal, he told himself. He lived among wild animals who raised their young that way, and this was the very same activity. Except it wasn't even close. A year ago he'd desperately wanted this woman, and she'd desperately wanted him. Now the result of their mating that night lay in her arms, the tiny mouth fastened to her breast. God help him, he wanted this woman still.

"Is the tire done for?" she asked quietly.

"Pretty much." He cleared the hoarseness from his throat and hoped she hadn't attached any significance to his husky tone of voice. He didn't want her to know how she affected him.

"Maybe somebody will come along."

"That's not too likely." He took a deep breath and let it out. He wanted to touch her, to cradle her breasts in both hands as he once had, to taste her. "Not many people use this road, and this isn't a good day for sightseeing."

"Zeke, please don't...don't leave me here and go for help."

He glanced at her in astonishment. "It never occurred to me."

Relief shone in her eyes. "Maybe I'm being silly. If I didn't have Amanda I wouldn't mind, but—"

"I wouldn't leave you." His pulse raced as he gazed into her eyes and saw the fulfillment she drew from nursing her child. No woman had ever looked so beautiful to him, so desirable as Katherine did now. Motherhood had given her a glow that he found almost irresistible. But he would have to resist.

"What are we going to do?" she asked.

For a moment he wondered if she was asking about the flat tire or if she wanted a solution to their much bigger problem. He didn't have one for it. But she probably was talking about the tire. "We'll drive on it," he said. "I have a cabin out here. It's not far. From there we can call a tow truck."

"You live out here?" She sounded quite interested.

"Yeah, when I'm not on duty at the park. It beats renting an apartment somewhere."

She nodded. "I can't picture you in an apartment. I imagine you clearing the land and building something out of logs, like Daniel Boone or Davy Crockett."

That made him smile. "Which is exactly what I did."

She gazed at him, her expression wistful. "That's the first time you've smiled since we met at the lodge."

"Yeah, well, this experience hasn't been a laugh a minute."

"I hate that it's so painful for you. She's a beautiful little girl, and I wish you could share some of the joy I feel."

"You're really happy about this?" All along he'd thought she was being a good sport for the baby's sake.

"How could I help being happy? Maybe I was a bit shocked when the doctor told me I was pregnant, but in about five minutes the shock wore off and I started feeling excited. A new life was growing inside me. That's a miraculous thing, Zeke."

He wondered if he'd have reacted that positively if she'd called to tell him right away. Maybe not, but he'd never know. Well-meaning though she might have been, she'd cheated him out of that sense of anticipation. "But what about your career? Isn't this messing things up for you?"

"It could, if I had a different boss, but Naomi gave me all the time off I needed to make sure this baby had a chance to survive. Now that she's here, I'm able to take her to the office with me, and when she's a toddler she can stay in *Cachet's* in-house nursery while I work." She paused. "My only regret is whatever trouble I'm causing you."

"You haven't caused me any yet." She'd caused him a fair share of heartache, but she'd protected him from any inconvenience so far. He wasn't sure he thanked her for that. "We wouldn't be stuck out on this road if it weren't for me."

"We wouldn't, but I would be. This tire would have blown on the way back home whether you were riding with me or not. And I probably would have decided to drive on it instead of hiking through the rain to the cabin."

"That makes me feel a little bit better." She glanced down at Amanda. "I think she's about finished. If you'll give me a moment, I'll burp her and put her back in her carrier so we can get going."

"Sure." He understood the message. He was supposed to stop looking at her and focus on something outside the cab so she could get herself together again. With some regret he did that, staring across a meadow to the misty forest beyond. Normally he could see the Tetons from here, but the clouds had moved in and completely covered them.

For once the landscape he'd grown to love didn't interest

him. He tried to ignore the rustle of clothing as Katherine buttoned her blouse, but it was pretty tough to ignore the happy little sounds she made as she talked softly to Amanda in the process.

He wondered if his mother had ever talked to him that way, with a singsong lilt to her voice. All he remembered were the frowns and the switches made of willow, and even those memories were hazy now. He'd only been three when she'd driven him to the entrance of Lost Springs and ordered him out of the car, but he still remembered everything about that moment—the clothes he'd had on, the smell of the dirt under his feet, the hawk circling overhead in a huge, cloudless sky.

"I'll burp her, change her diaper, and we're done," Katherine said.

Zeke took that as his cue that it was safe to look at her again. Sure enough, she was properly dressed now, with Amanda propped over her shoulder as she patted the baby's back. He'd probably never have the chance to watch her nurse Amanda again. Maybe that was best.

Amanda made a sound like a bullfrog. The magnitude of it startled Zeke. "Does that hurt her?"

"Nope." Katherine smiled. "It would hurt her if I let that gas stay in her tummy. Then she'd really scream. Listen, would you mind getting me the diaper bag from the back? This will just take a second."

He leaned over the back seat and hauled the multicolored bag up front. He placed it between them where she could reach it. "Want me to look away again?"

Katherine laughed as she placed Amanda on a pad on her lap and popped the snaps on the baby's pink jumpsuit. "Not on Amanda's account. She's a free spirit who doesn't mind in the least who sees her naked."

"Unlike her mother." After he'd led her back to his camp last summer, she'd made him hang a blanket between two trees so she could hide behind it when she took off her soaked clothes.

Her cheeks turned pink and she concentrated on untaping Amanda's disposable diaper. "I barely knew you then."

"You barely know me now."

She didn't look at him. "That's true, I guess."

"So why not make a clean break before this gets any more complicated? It's what you decided to do last summer, isn't it?"

Her movements stilled. "I thought that's what we both decided."

"Yeah, I guess we did." Wild horses wouldn't drag the truth from him.

She glanced up, her hazel eyes troubled. "But now there's Amanda."

"Look, I'll be glad to send you a check every month if that's—"

"No. I don't want money. I thought I made that clear."

"Then what do you want?" He watched the confusion in her eyes and believed that she didn't really know. "We can't make this turn out like a storybook," he said. "You can't wave a magic wand and turn me into the daddy who goes off to the office with a briefcase every day and then comes home to play patty-cake with his daughter."

"I know that." She popped open a plastic container and ripped out a moist towelette with an angry motion.

"So given that I'm staying here and you're going back to New York with Amanda, what kind of a real father could I be?"

"I don't have all the answers, Zeke."

"But you don't want me to sign away my parental rights to this baby."

She glanced up. "No, I don't. But you still have that option. If you decide that's the best thing for you, then by all means do it."

"I do think it's for the best," he said quietly.

"All right." She swallowed and leaned down to finish diapering Amanda. "Then I guess I'd better stop trying to change your mind." She snapped the baby's jumpsuit together again. "Hold her for a minute while I get organized to put her back in her seat."

He took the baby from her, and Amanda's tiny body felt a little less foreign to him this time. She stared up at him with the same concentration as before. Then she began waving her arms and kicking with her legs.

"Hold still now," he said, trying to keep his voice gentle. He didn't want her to start crying because he was too gruff with her.

She stopped wiggling and went back to her staring routine.

"That's better." He smiled in spite of himself. She was so serious-looking for such a little thing.

Then, to his total amazement, she smiled back.

Something stirred within him and his throat grew tight. He looked away from that endearing little smile and swallowed hard. "You about ready for her?" he asked.

"Yes." Katherine leaned over and lifted Amanda from his arms.

KATHERINE REMAINED SILENT as the truck rolled jerkily along the pavement, but the ride became more jolting when Zeke turned off on a dirt road. She kept glancing into the back seat, but Amanda slept through it all. As long as she was in motion, she was content.

But someday her needs would be much more than that, and Katherine wondered if she'd be enough parent for the little girl. So long as Zeke was a faint possibility on the horizon, she hadn't really contemplated the job of raising Amanda alone, even if Naomi had thought that was the logical decision. Now that Zeke had completely rejected fatherhood, Katherine realized that she'd unconsciously counted on him to have some influence in Amanda's life, no matter what she'd told Naomi.

Besides that, his rejection felt like a personal insult, both to her and her baby. She couldn't imagine how someone could look at Amanda and choose never to see her again. From the tender way Zeke had made love that night a year ago, Katherine had thought he had a soft heart. Apparently she'd been wrong.

The truck approached a wooden bridge that spanned a rushing creek and Zeke put on the brakes. "Damn, but that water's high."

"Are you worried about the bridge holding?"

"Not going across this time, but if the rain keeps up... Well, we'll just tell them to bring the biggest, baddest tow truck they have to get across the creek, that's all." He stepped on the gas and the truck limped across the bridge, the tires making a hollow sound on the boards.

Katherine turned to look back at the creek when they were on the other side. Brown water boiled only about a foot beneath the boards. The sight made her a little sick to her stomach as she remembered the helpless feeling of being tossed around in the rapids. Without Zeke she surely would have died that day. "Has the bridge ever washed out?"

"No, but I only built it two years ago, when I bought the property. I've never seen the creek running that high." He glanced at her. "Hey, don't worry. Forget I said anything. We'll be fine."

"I'm sure we will." Katherine faced forward again as they entered a grove of aspens, their white trunks shiny with rain.

"There it is, through the trees on the right."

She peered out her window and spotted the clearing between the glistening tree trunks. Behind the clearing rose a hillside covered with pine, and nestled against the hillside was the sweetest little log cabin she'd ever seen. It looked like something out of one of her history books in school, right down to the stone chimney and the small front porch. She almost expected to see a pioneer woman come out of the front door and wipe her hands on her apron as she waited for her visitors to arrive.

"It's charming," she said.

"Thank you." He sounded pleased with her response. He pulled the truck up beside the cabin, shut off the motor and glanced at her. "We can at least have a cup of coffee while we wait for the tow truck."

"Only if you have decaf. Everything I put in my stomach affects my breast milk, so I have to be careful."

His gaze warmed for a brief moment before he broke eye contact and cleared his throat. "Sorry. No decaf. Come on. Let's go in and make that call."

She strapped Amanda back into the baby sling and grabbed the diaper bag while he unlocked the cabin and came back out with a yellow slicker to hold over the two of them. When he helped her down from the truck, she was glad there was a baby between them. Once his hand closed over hers, she had the craziest urge to move right into his arms. As it was, they were plastered together under the slicker as they dodged puddles on the way to the front porch.

"It's really coming down," he said, shaking out the slicker. "Go on in. After I call, I'll see if I can't find something you can drink."

She stepped into the cabin and was greeted with the aroma of fresh-cut wood. The place looked as she had imagined—a single room with rustic furniture including a bed, a rocking chair, a table and two chairs. One corner contained a stove, sink and refrigerator. Another was partitioned off and was undoubtedly the bathroom. The room was neat but had no particular decorating touches, which didn't surprise her, either. Even without curtains, a tablecloth or a vase of flowers on a windowsill, the effect was still cozy and welcoming.

Zeke came in and closed the door behind him.

"It's very nice, Zeke."

"Simple." He walked over to the large window looking out on to the porch. The stationary center pane was flanked by two screened windows, which he'd left open, but now he closed them against the chill.

"Simplicity has elegance, too." Katherine said.

His grin was wry. "I wasn't going for elegance." He crossed to the wall phone hanging behind the rocker. "Have a seat," he said, gesturing to the kitchen chairs. "I'll call the towing company and then see what I have in the cupboard."

"I don't really need anything," Katherine said. It wasn't quite true. Her stomach was grumbling because she'd been too nervous to eat lunch. But she didn't want to bother him when she'd be back at the lodge in a couple of hours at the most. She'd eat then.

"Well, I'm going to have something." He picked up the receiver and started to punch out a number. He paused and clicked the hang-up button a couple of times. Then he clicked it again. Finally he replaced the receiver and turned to her. "Maybe you'd better reconsider having something to eat."

Anxiety added to the turmoil in her stomach. "What's wrong?" But she knew exactly what was wrong.

"This storm must be worse than I thought. It's knocked out the phone. Looks like we'll be here awhile."

CHAPTER FOUR

"HOW LONG DO YOU THINK the phone line will be out?" Katherine quickly calculated whether the baby's needs could be met for the next few hours. She always packed more than enough diapers, and she'd brought an extra terry sleeper. Food was no problem.

Zeke sighed and walked over to peer out the window. "No telling where the lines are down. Out here the telephone can be out quite a while before anyone notices or reports it. It serves mostly vacation cabins, which aren't used all the time." He turned toward her with a worried frown. "I should have headed back to the lodge and said to hell with the wheel rim. I'm sorry, Katherine."

"Don't worry about it." To her surprise, she wasn't sorry at all. If he'd been able to call a tow truck they'd have parted within a couple of hours. Now they had more time. She wasn't sure if that would change his mind about keeping some connection with Amanda, but it might.

"I could hike out to the road and try to catch a ride back to the lodge."

"That seems completely unnecessary." If he left, that would destroy any hope that he'd bond with Amanda.

"You'd be fine. You'd be safe here and there's plenty of food."

"I'd still rather you didn't leave us alone."

"You won't get washed away, if that's what you're thinking. We're much higher than the creek."

She was unwilling to admit why she wanted him to stay,

but she could offer him a reason he might accept, one that was also true. "I wasn't thinking of water, but speaking of that, did I ever tell you how I fell in the river in the first place?"

"I don't think we got around to that."

Because we had other things on our mind. She became aware that this one-room cabin put them in close proximity to a bed. Not that she would allow herself to get involved with him in that way again. They'd created enough problems for each other as it was. It was a beautiful bed made of peeled and sanded logs, a big bed, a soft-looking bed, a—

"How did you fall in the river?" he prompted.

She blushed and turned her attention away from the bed. She hoped she didn't have a telltale lustful expression on her face. "I was crossing the river on a log. A pretty fat log, too, so I shouldn't have had any trouble making it. Then I heard a snuffling noise behind me, looked over my shoulder and saw a bear at the edge of the river."

"What kind of bear?"

"A *big* bear."

He smiled. "I meant the breed."

"I didn't stop to ask him his pedigree. I just started scrambling across that log like a squirrel with its tail on fire, only I'm not as surefooted as a squirrel, and I fell in. As I headed downstream, I thought maybe it wasn't such a bad escape method, but then I couldn't stop myself and I kept going under, so I figured I'd probably drown. But at least that was better than being eaten by a bear."

He chuckled. "Far better."

"In my opinion." She liked making him laugh. She'd forgotten that she had that power. He'd told her that not many people got him to relax enough to laugh.

"For the record, I doubt you had much to worry about from that bear," he said. "He was probably after trout, not magazine editors."

"Oh, yeah? Maybe it was a grizz." She took her hands away from Amanda's sling and lifted them menacingly, curling her fingers into claws.

"A *grizz?*" He grinned. "Are you trying to speak the lingo, New York lady?"

He'd teased her with that label last summer. As the night had progressed, he'd switched to calling her *his* New York lady. His use of the term now sent a shiver of reaction up her spine, but she tried to keep her tone light. "I'm trying to tell you that I'd rather not stay in this cabin alone with Amanda when it's possible a bear could come along and bash down your cabin door."

"That's not going to happen."

"Do you or do you not have bears around here?"

"All right, there is a black bear that hangs around this area." He stroked his chin and his dark eyes sparkled. "And maybe she's been up on the porch a couple of times, but—"

"On the *porch?*" Katherine hugged Amanda tighter. "That does it. You're staying here with us until such time as we get escorted out of here by a burly guy driving a monster tow truck. Do I make myself clear, ranger man?" If he could toss out the nickname he'd given her that night, she could toss out his.

The laughter in his eyes faded, to be replaced with something more potent. "I don't know how long we'll be here."

"I don't care. I—"

"I do."

She met his gaze. "You really want us out of your life, don't you?" she said softly.

"Yes."

ZEKE TURNED AWAY from the pain flickering in Katherine's eyes. Sometimes the truth hurt, as he well knew. There was nothing more to say, so he'd better get some food on the table. Fortunately he'd done a little shopping the day before and had most of the basics.

He walked over to the kitchen cupboard and took down a can of tuna. "How about a tuna sandwich?"

"That's fine." Her voice held none of the playfulness from a moment ago, when she'd been describing her bear experience.

For a brief time during that conversation about the bear, he'd forgotten their situation and had found himself enjoying the Katherine he'd known a year ago, the one who had caused him to lower his defenses. He'd be wise not to lower them again.

"Can I help in any way?" she asked.

"I'll take care of it." He'd really done himself in this time, Zeke thought. Although he wasn't planning to tell Katherine yet, there had been times when the phone had been out for several days. He wasn't about to stay here with her for days, though. If necessary, he'd drive the truck the way it was. He'd rather have mega-repair bills than spend that amount of time here with Katherine and the baby. He didn't want to get in any deeper than he already was.

He put on some coffee and started working on the sandwiches while Katherine talked to Amanda in that cozy way she had. When she crooned to the baby in such an intimate tone he felt closed out, which might be how she wanted him to feel after the way he'd come across about the parental rights thing. But he knew himself, and being a part-time father would tear him apart. It was a situation guaranteed to produce misunderstandings and potential rejection. He had a very low tolerance for rejection, but he wasn't going to expose himself enough to explain that to her.

Rain pelted the window over the sink as he worked on lunch. He listened to it come down and thought about the creek bridge. Most likely the beaver dam upstream had given way, and if he wanted to get back across that bridge in the truck, he'd have to make his move soon. Obviously

Katherine wasn't going to let him go without her. He wasn't crazy about the idea of leaving her, either, although he thought she'd be safe enough, especially if he showed her how to fire his gun to scare off Sadie if she showed up.

But he doubted she'd agree to that procedure, and there was no way he could force her to stay behind. He decided to wait an hour. If the phone wasn't working by then, he'd suggest they drive the truck on the flat tire, get back on the main road and look for the nearest phone.

"Zeke?"

"Yeah?" He kept working on the sandwiches instead of turning around. The busier he kept himself, the better.

"I understand that you want to give up all your rights to Amanda and have no more contact with us, but I was wondering if...if you'd mind her knowing something about you."

A warning flashed in his brain. "Such as?"

"Well, that you love the outdoors, and you're part Sioux. Things like that."

The concept of Amanda being curious about her father hadn't even occurred to him. He'd been so focused on getting mother and baby out of his life that he'd forgotten Amanda wouldn't always be a baby. And kids wanted to know about their parents. He still wondered about his father and had done some fruitless research trying to find out who he was and what had happened to him.

"I could disguise the information so she wouldn't be able to track you down," Katherine said, "if that's what you're worried about."

He picked up the two sandwich plates and walked over to the table where she sat holding the baby. "Yeah, that's what I'm worried about." He also wondered how a grown-up Amanda would take the news that he hadn't wanted to have anything to do with her. Damn, but this was getting dicey.

"I think it would be better to give her some information rather than make you a big question mark," Katherine said.

"Maybe." He set down the sandwiches. "I made coffee, but I guess you can't have that. I suppose beer's out, too. I have orange juice and—"

"Actually, a beer would be fine. I have one once in a while when I'm afraid stress might have decreased my flow of milk."

His glance went immediately to her full breasts underneath the gauzy material of her green blouse. Fortunately he had the presence of mind to quickly look up again. He couldn't be caught staring at her. "I'll get you a beer." He walked over to the refrigerator and tried to ignore his memory's instant replay of Katherine poised above him, her breasts quivering with each upward thrust he made.

By the time he returned to the table with a foaming glass of beer in one hand and his mug of coffee in the other, he'd calmed himself.

"Thank you." She gave him a brief smile.

He realized that her smiles were in short supply this trip, too. He'd been proud of himself when he'd made her smile the first time after fishing her out of the river. She'd been so damned scared that she hadn't been able to stop shaking. He'd asked her country-bumpkin questions about life in the big city until at long last he'd coaxed her into smiling a little. That was the first moment he'd realized that he wanted more than a smile from her.

He'd never in a million years have guessed that such a moment could lead him to this. Silently he gazed at Katherine as she sat across the table from him. She'd taken Amanda out of the sling, and now she tucked the baby in the crook of her arm as she sipped her beer. A bit of foam clung to her upper lip and she licked it away with her tongue. An arrow of desire shot straight to Zeke's groin. He'd have to get her out of here soon.

He took a bracing drink of his coffee and realized how

much he'd hate to give up coffee if he were in her shoes. A mother's self-sacrificing behavior held a certain fascination for him, probably because he hadn't experienced any from his own mother. At least none he knew of. At Lost Springs they'd tried to convince him that his mother had been self-sacrificing when she'd left him at the ranch. It hadn't felt that way then, and it still didn't.

"So what would you like me to tell Amanda about you?" Katherine asked.

He picked up his sandwich. "Persistent, aren't we?"

"I figure I won't get another shot at this."

He paused, his sandwich halfway to his mouth. "Tell her I was a selfish son-of-a-gun who wasn't cut out to be a father." He bit into the sandwich.

"I'd like to tell her that you saved my life."

He glanced up.

"Without you I wouldn't be here now," she said quietly. "And neither would she. And I don't want to deliberately lie to her. You're not selfish."

He chewed and swallowed. "Sure I am. If I weren't, I'd want some sort of joint custody."

She gazed at him. "I don't believe that you're denying yourself that out of selfishness. I think..." Her voice trailed off as her expression softened.

He didn't want to ask what she was thinking when she looked like that. He'd seen that expression before, and he was no match for it. "You'd better eat that sandwich," he said a little too gruffly. "Keep up your strength."

Almost like an obedient child she picked up the sandwich, but having only the use of one hand, she fumbled with it. Some of the filling spilled out as she tried to maneuver it to her mouth.

She obviously needed some help so she could eat properly, but Zeke didn't want to volunteer to hold Amanda. Funny things happened to his insides whenever he ended up touching that baby. "Would you like me to get her seat out of the truck?" he asked.

Katherine glanced outside where the rain cascaded off the front porch roof in a continuous waterfall. "No sense in going back out in that until it lets up. But I could put her on your bed, if you wouldn't mind."

"She won't roll off?"

"She can't roll yet." Katherine pushed back her chair and stood, holding Amanda in both arms.

"Today might be her day to start."

"Not likely. I'll put her blanket and changing pad on your bedspread to protect it."

"I'm not worried about that. I just think it's dangerous to leave her there with no rails on the bed or anything." Zeke surveyed his little cabin for a better solution. "Hang on a minute. I think I have just the thing." He walked over to the fireplace and took the kindling out of an oval copper kettle he'd bought at a garage sale. He turned the kettle upside down and tapped it to get any scraps out, then crossed to the bed and took the spread off. Folding it, he tucked it into the kettle, letting the excess spill out and pad the sides.

Feeling proud of himself, he set it down next to the table. "How's that?"

"That's..." She looked at him and her eyes started to fill. She quickly averted her face.

He was crushed. "Okay. Stupid idea. Of course you don't want to put her in an old kindling kettle. I don't know what I was thinking." He stooped down to pull the bedspread back out.

"No, stop!" She sniffed and wiped at her cheeks with her free hand. "It's a perfect idea. I love it."

He stared at her, completely at sea. "Then why are you crying?"

"Because..." She swallowed. "Because, when you put that bassinet together, it was almost as if...well, you were acting like a f-father. And I didn't realize how m-much I wanted you to…oh, forget it.'' She choked back a sob and crouched down to lay Amanda in the makeshift bed.

Zeke stood there, hands clenched at his sides as he fought the urge to take her in his arms and tell her he'd do whatever she needed him to. He wanted to promise that he'd do his best to shield her and the baby from whatever disasters came their way, that he'd be the anchor she so desperately seemed to want.

But he'd be making empty promises. He couldn't follow her to New York and live in her world in order to keep those promises, and he doubted she wanted him to. He wasn't the sort of warm, easygoing man that women liked to have around on a regular basis, and Katherine had proved that by leaving last summer. So he said nothing and returned to take his seat at the table.

She fussed with Amanda for quite a while, and he figured she was getting herself under control. She'd had a hard time the past few months, he was sure. She'd said the pregnancy hadn't been easy, and from what he'd heard childbirth was no picnic, either, especially when you had to face it alone. He probably didn't want to know what she'd been through bringing Amanda into the world. He'd only have the urge to make it up to her.

''There.'' She sat down at the table again, clear-eyed. ''Shouldn't you try the phone again?''

''Yep.'' He got up and went over to pick up the receiver. ''It's still out.''

''Oh, well.'' She'd adopted a breezy air. ''I'm sure it'll be connected soon, and then we can get out of your hair.'' She started on her sandwich.

''I'm sure you'll be glad to get back to New York. You must be good at your job if Naomi Rutledge wants you to take over the whole magazine.'' Talking about her work felt safe—it reminded him of the distance between their very different worlds.

She swallowed a bite of tuna. "She blew me away with that news. Sure, we get along well, and she's been super through this pregnancy, but I never in the world imagined she wanted me to be her replacement."

"Sounds like a lot of responsibility." He'd hate being tied down like that.

"It is." She took another sip of her beer. "And I'm sort of scared, but the time I spent in Yellowstone last year has given me more confidence in myself." She glanced at him. "Up until I fell into the river, at any rate. That was pretty inept. But before that I'd been alone for almost two days and I really had time to think and evaluate my strengths and weaknesses honestly. I decided I was more capable than I gave myself credit for."

He shoved away his empty sandwich plate. "Time alone can be a good thing."

"I would expect you to think so. I don't hunger for that kind of isolation all the time, but I learned a lot during that trip."

Maybe that had been why she'd made love to him so eagerly, he thought. Feeling self-sufficient in the wilderness could give someone a real high. Add to that the adrenaline rush of nearly dying, and it was no wonder she'd wanted the earthy physical release sex could bring. It probably had nothing to do with him. Any reasonably decent guy would have served the purpose.

"I didn't know you were raised on a boys' ranch," she said.

He grew uneasy. "That's something you probably shouldn't tell Amanda. She could trace me in no time if she knew to start at Lost Springs."

She finished her sandwich and picked up her glass of beer. "You honestly don't think you'll ever want to see her? Not even when she's an adult and wouldn't require any caretaking?"

He picked up their plates and carried them over to the

sink. "Look, Katherine, I don't know the first thing about being a father. I never knew my own. The Duncans, the people who ran Lost Springs when I was there, were wonderful to all of us, but it wasn't the same as having your very own father and mother who had all your baby pictures and remembered when you said your first word and got your first tooth." He rinsed the plates. "I wouldn't have the foggiest idea how to treat a daughter, but you obviously do, so the best thing is for you to handle this alone."

"I guess you can't be any plainer than that."

He dried his hands on a towel hanging by the sink and turned back to her. "I'm trying to be as honest as I can, both with myself and with you."

Her smile was tremulous. "Same here."

"Then I guess we understand each other."

"I understand." She blinked, but there were no tears this time. Then she glanced down at the kettle where Amanda lay. "And I'll figure out some way to make her understand, too."

It was a sucker punch, and he felt it down to his toes. Amanda lay cradled by the green bedspread, fast asleep. As a kid he'd raised dozens of baby animals whose mothers were killed by predators or on the highway. As a ranger he was still doing it. Yet in all that time of nursing young wildlife, he'd never seen any creature look more vulnerable and in need of care than this tiny baby. And he was turning his back on her.

CHAPTER FIVE

SITTING IN A COOL CABIN in damp clothes gave Katherine goose bumps now that she didn't have Amanda to keep her warm. At least that's what she told herself. It couldn't be nerves, or the fact that without the baby in her arms, she began wondering what it would be like to hold Zeke again.

She looked for a thermostat on the wall and found none. She guessed that the fireplace provided the cabin's only heat, and she couldn't ask Zeke to build a fire when they could be leaving at any moment.

Picking up her beer glass, she left the table and moved around the cabin. She pretended to be interested in what she found, when her true motivation was to get rid of her jittery chilled feeling. She touched the log walls. "Did you peel the bark off yourself, or did you have some help?" She was pretty sure of the answer, but it seemed like a safe topic and she didn't like the sound of silence. She became far too aware of his body when they both stopped talking.

"I did it myself."

Of course he had. The original Lone Ranger. He might as well wear a black mask over his eyes and ride a horse named Silver. But even the Lone Ranger had Tonto. "So none of your friends from Lost Springs came over to help?"

"I invited them after I was finished."

"Oh." She gazed at the fireplace with its thick plank serving as a mantel. Something was carved into the front edge. She looked closer and saw that it was a tiny pine tree, all by itself. So Zeke had a brand, of sorts. The more she studied it, the more the carving irritated her. What right did he have to declare himself an island, especially when fate had given him a child?

And why was she being so noble about the whole thing and quietly accepting his decision to reject fatherhood completely? Naomi might think that was the best course of action, but Katherine would be the one trying to explain to Amanda that her father wanted nothing to do with her because he was a lone wolf with no ties and intended to keep it that way.

She turned toward the kitchen area, where he was straightening things up after their lunch. "I've changed my mind about something."

"Oh?" He hung the towel up and walked over to the table, but instead of sitting down, he placed both hands on the chair back, as if he needed to grip something while he heard what she had to say.

And he probably did, she thought. She had a tight hold on the beer glass herself. "I told you at the lodge that I didn't come here to get any money from you, and that's what I'd decided because I pretty much blamed myself for this pregnancy." She squared her shoulders. "But I'm not to blame. I took precautions. They just didn't work. So it's silly of me to shoulder all the financial responsibility. And besides that, if you send something every month, that will at least let Amanda know you care about her in some fashion."

He frowned. "I'll send it, but I wouldn't do it so she'd know I was thinking of her. In fact, I'd rather she didn't know where the money came from."

"Sorry." Katherine warmed to the fight. "You're overruled. And I'll tell you why. You just said yourself that not having your mother and father around when you were growing up left you unable to relate to a child. I don't want Amanda to have that problem. I want her to know that she has a father, and although he's emotionally unable to connect with her, he at least gives of himself in the form of a check every month.''

He looked like a cornered animal as his dark eyes blazed. "And I suppose you'd encourage her to write to me, and eventually you'd suggest that she come here for a visit.''

"Absolutely not! Do you think I'd take a chance with her fragile young ego? I wouldn't want her to get here and be brutally rejected.''

"I wouldn't—"

"Wouldn't you? Every single time I've tried to bring the two of you together, you've acted as if she has some contagious disease.''

"But she's a baby!'' he bellowed. "I've never been around babies! I don't know anything about them. I might accidentally hurt her. Or worse!''

Amanda began to cry.

Katherine glared at him and crossed the room to pick up the baby. "You certainly know how to scare her to death.''

"I didn't mean to be so loud, okay?'' He stalked over to the telephone. "This just proves my point. The less she knows about me, the better. I'll only create problems for her.'' He picked up the receiver and put it to his ear. "Damn it to hell.'' He started to slam the receiver into its cradle but caught himself and replaced it carefully.

Katherine swayed gently and kissed Amanda's cheek until her crying gradually subsided. "There, there, Mandy. It's all right.'' She glanced over at Zeke, who reminded her of a large caged animal as he paced back and forth in front of the window. Water still poured from the eaves. "We could be stuck here quite a while, couldn't we?'' Her belligerent mood hadn't eased any.

"No.'' His pacing ceased. "If you'll get her ready to travel, we'll head out.''

"Head out? What, you have a couple of mules stashed in a barn out back?'' She figured mules would suit his stubborn personality better than horses.

"No." He stared out at the rain. "We'll just drive on the rim."

"And ruin it."

"I don't give a damn if we do."

Katherine didn't much give a damn about his precious tire rim, either. But she didn't want to get stuck out there. "Is that a safe idea?"

He rounded on her. "Yes." His voice was carefully controlled, his gaze intense. "I may be *emotionally unable to connect* with that kid, as you said, but I would give my life to keep her from harm."

She caught her breath at the power in that statement. She had no doubt that he meant it, either. He might be a difficult man to get close to, but without hesitating, he'd put his life on the line for those smaller and weaker than he. She'd always suspected that if she'd missed the branch he'd held out for her that day, he would have dove into the water after her. Either he would have saved her or they both would have drowned, but he wouldn't have stood there watching her die.

And she still owed him for that. The anger drained out of her. "Zeke, I probably came on too strong about the money thing."

"I've always said I'd be willing to pay. I just don't want you building that into something more."

"Okay. I won't make it into something more."

"How soon can you be ready to leave?"

"I should probably feed her first, just in case it takes longer than we think it might."

"Fine. Let me know when you're ready to go." He opened the front door, letting in the scent of damp earth, and went outside on the porch as if he couldn't bear to be closed in the same little space with her for a minute longer.

ZEKE LONGED FOR A HORIZON to look at, but the forest was shrouded in gray and he couldn't see much beyond the clearing. He took a deep breath, drawing in the dank, loamy air. The chill felt good on his face. He didn't like the picture Katherine was painting of him, as if he were some weird recluse who couldn't relate to anyone.

It wasn't like that. He had friends. He interacted just fine with tourists at the park. But he had grave misgivings about ever being somebody's husband, and he sure as hell wasn't equipped to be somebody's father, especially if that person happened to be a tiny little girl.

He'd never been tiny. At three he'd looked six. He could still hear his mother telling him that he was too big, that he ate too much, that he was too loud. Apparently he'd been missing whatever a kid needed to make him lovable, or she wouldn't have dumped him off at the ranch. At least there in the midst of a gang of boys, his size had been a plus. He could watch over the smaller kids.

Women still made him feel awkward, though, like a bull in a china shop—except for the night he'd spent with Katherine. On his own turf, with the immensity of the woods surrounding them, he'd felt in tune with a woman for the first time in his life, and he'd allowed himself to hope that maybe he wouldn't live his life alone. Of course he'd been wrong.

And now this—having a daughter thrust at him with no mental preparation, and then being expected to say and do the right thing on selected holidays and summer vacations, all by himself with no woman to guide him... He couldn't deal with that.

Then there was the other problem. He was still attracted to Katherine. He could feel that attraction growing like a seedling reaching for the sun. She probably thought he'd escaped to the front porch because he was angry with her. In fact he was angry with himself for shouting and waking the baby, but he'd left the room because he wasn't sure what he'd do if he stayed while she unbuttoned her blouse again to feed Amanda.

He'd bought a couple of Adirondack chairs for the porch this summer, and he sat down in one while he waited for Katherine to finish getting the baby ready. For the first time he wondered why he'd bought two chairs. He'd ordered them from a catalog, and the order for two had been automatic in his mind. It just looked right to him, and yet he'd never brought a woman to the cabin until now, and when the guys from Lost Springs came out for the annual fishing trip, two chairs wouldn't be enough.

He shook his head and muttered a swearword under his breath. Katherine really had him going, making him question every damn thing about his life, including how many chairs he'd bought for the front porch. The sooner he got her and the baby back to the lodge, the better. Maybe he'd leave his truck there and rent a Jeep so he could head for some remote place and camp for a couple of days. Yeah, that's what he'd do. Some time alone would clear away the cobwebs.

The front door opened and Katherine came out carrying Amanda in the sling with the diaper bag over one arm. "We're ready."

He stood immediately. "Let me get the slicker." He managed to move past her without touching her and went inside to discover the cabin still held the scent of her perfume. He'd definitely have to go camping and let the place air out. Otherwise this reminder of her would probably keep him awake and fully aroused all night.

After grabbing the slicker, he went back out. "Give me the diaper bag and you can have the slicker," he said.

"What about you?"

A cold shower was exactly what he needed, he thought. "I'll just move fast." He handed her the raincoat and took the diaper bag. "Let's go."

She held the slicker over her head and started down the porch steps. He followed close behind. On the bottom step her foot slipped out from under her on the wet wood and she started to go down.

His brain froze with fear, but his body reacted, grabbing at her arm and hauling her back against him, baby and all. She lost her grip on the slicker and it fell to the mud below. The weight threw him slightly off balance and he staggered but managed to stay upright as rain pelted down on them.

Panting, she turned to him, her eyes wide. "I almost—"

He couldn't seem to let go of her. Her mouth was very close, pale and pink and wet with rain. Their bodies fit so that Amanda was pretty well shielded from the downpour, but they were still getting drenched. He barely felt it. "But you didn't fall."

"No. You saved me. Us."

He watched awareness replace panic in her eyes. Her glance drifted to his mouth, then rose again to his eyes. That subtle signal was all he needed. He lowered his head.

She made a soft sound as his lips found hers. He didn't know if she meant it as a welcome or a protest, but he didn't care. Just once. Then he would get her into that truck and back where she belonged, far away from him.

He remembered the shape of her mouth. And he remembered the sweetness, remembered the slight resistance followed by a yielding that made his blood pound in his veins. For one wild moment he considered taking her back inside. Then he forced himself to leave the temptation of her mouth. He lifted his head and looked into her eyes. They were glazed with desire, probably just like his. If he asked her to stay, she might do it. And then what?

"I thought you hated me," she whispered.

"I wish I could."

"Zeke..."

"We'd better go."

She nodded.

After releasing her, he leaned down and picked up the muddy slicker. She started toward the truck, her head down, her arm protecting Amanda as best she could. He tossed the slicker on the porch and followed her.

KATHERINE FOUGHT A NEW wave of desire when Zeke lifted her and Amanda into the truck. She loved the strength that allowed him to lift her to the seat in one smooth motion. That strength had saved her life once, and just now his strong grip had kept her from falling and quite possibly hurting Amanda when she went down.

And yet she'd felt the power in those big hands become the gentle caress of a lover. She'd never been touched with such tenderness as she had the night she'd spent in his tent. She doubted she'd ever be touched that way again, and she yearned for it so much that she was trembling. His mouth on hers had awakened her body instantly. She felt pliable, moistened...ready.

He'd had to slam the door again but Amanda seemed used to the noise and didn't start to cry. Katherine was thankful she had a baby to care for right now, a task to distract her from Zeke. Removing Amanda's wet terry outfit and replacing it with a dry one from the diaper bag kept her occupied as Zeke hurried around the truck and climbed in beside her.

"I have to slam this door, too," he said.

"Go ahead. She seems to be adapting." Katherine kept her attention focused on Amanda, who had picked this moment to become squirmy and vocal. While Katherine peeled the damp material away from her chubby body, she waved her hands and legs and made little crowing noises. When Zeke slammed the door, she jerked in response but didn't cry.

Zeke started the engine.

"Don't leave yet." Katherine spoke above the drumming of the rain on the metal roof of the cab. "I don't have her in the carrier."

"I know. I'm just getting the engine warmed up so I can turn on the heater. I don't want her to catch cold."

Katherine's hands stilled as she finally understood. He wasn't rejecting Amanda because he cared too little. He was rejecting her because he cared too much. He considered himself such an unfit father that Amanda was better off with nobody than taking a chance with him. The realization made her ache with regret for him and for Amanda. With this sort of beginning they'd probably never find each other.

Zeke turned the heater fan on low and tested the flow of air with his hand. "That's better. Are you about finished?"

"Yes." She quickly finished tucking the baby into her dry sleeper and snapped it up. "Can you take her—"

"Yeah, just a minute. Let me dry off as best I can first."

She waited while he rolled back his sleeves and took a clean bandanna from his hip pocket to wipe his damp hands and arms. Such big hands, such muscled arms. She remembered that the decision to make love had come before they'd entered the tent together, so that when he'd crawled in through the flap, he'd already stripped down to nothing. His massive body and bronzed skin had fascinated her, and she'd spent a long time just kissing him...all over.

"Okay, I can hold her now."

Katherine gave Zeke the baby without making eye contact with him. Then she turned around in the seat. The nubby upholstery was soggy from her rain-drenched clothes. "I'm getting your seat all wet," she said.

"It'll dry."

Amanda continued with her little experimental noises, crowing and gurgling in Zeke's arms, while Katherine positioned the straps on the carrier. Then Katherine heard a deep, male sound that sounded a little like "boo." Amanda gurgled some more, and Katherine heard a soft chuckle followed by another "boo." She was afraid to move. Zeke was playing with Amanda.

"She has a little dimple in her chin," Zeke said.

"Yes." Katherine cleared the huskiness from her throat. "Yes, she does. I'm not sure where she got it. Nobody in my family—"

"My mother had one."

She glanced over at him, but he was engrossed in Amanda and didn't notice her gaze. Her heart squeezed as she thought of what it must have been like for him—a small boy abandoned by his parents. She'd like him to tell her about it, but coaxing him to talk about that part of his life would take more time and trust than he was willing to give her.

"I'll take her now," she said.

He handed her the baby with great care, but she could tell he was already feeling more comfortable holding that tiny body. Katherine settled Amanda in the carrier and strapped her in tight. "Hang on, Mandy," she said. "We have a bumpy ride ahead."

"She'll probably just go to sleep," Zeke said.

"Probably." Katherine noticed the casual way he said it, as if he were already becoming somewhat of an expert on Amanda's habits. As she buckled her seat belt she wondered if he was aware that he was beginning, just a little, to behave like a parent.

"Ready?" He glanced over at her, his expression carefully neutral. But with a sharp intake of breath, his expression changed. He stared at her breasts and swore softly.

She looked down to discover that the rain had made the material of her blouse nearly transparent, and the cold had tightened her nipples under the lacy nursing bra. With the seat belt secured between her breasts, she was on display. She quickly crossed her arms over her chest. "Sorry."

Zeke swallowed and turned his attention to backing the truck around, but between his heavy breathing and hers, the windows were fogging up. Silently he switched on the defroster.

CHAPTER SIX

THE TRUCK HANDLED LIKE the tank Zeke had driven in the Persian Gulf War. That seemed appropriate, although he'd been in physical danger then, and he was in emotional danger now. Of the two, he'd been better prepared to deal with the war than this situation with Katherine. It was a damned good thing he'd decided to drive her back to civilization instead of waiting for the phone to be reconnected. Much more contact and he could predict what would happen.

Muscling the lame truck along the muddy road took all his concentration. He tried not to think about what he was doing to it in the process. Katherine sat silently beside him as they jolted along. He worked to make the ride as smooth as possible for Amanda's sake, but the baby didn't let out a peep, so she must have dropped right off to sleep.

The skies were producing a world-class rain, but it was a quiet storm with no thunder and lightning. He was grateful for that. Lightning was a ranger's nightmare, even in a wet forest.

This particular forest was mighty wet. The wipers cleared a fan of windshield glass only to have the rain obscure it again. Zeke leaned forward, watching for the first sight of the creek and the bridge. Once they made it over the bridge, he'd breathe a lot easier. If they made it past the creek, he could guarantee that he'd be free of her, and then he could start reconstructing his world.

Except it looked as if he wouldn't get over the bridge.

Zeke stepped on the brake and leaned heavily against the steering wheel.

"Oh, no." Katherine put her hand over her mouth.

Quietly he surveyed the swollen creek. The bridge had been ripped in half.

Katherine turned to him, her eyes wide.

He deliberately masked his despair, afraid she might misunderstand and think he was worried about their survival. He wasn't. The cabin would shelter them for as long as necessary. But the cabin wouldn't protect them from each other. "Guess we turn around," he said.

"And wait for the phone to be fixed?"

"Well, the phone is only part of our answer now. Even a tow truck couldn't get across that creek the way it is. The only way anybody could get in here today would be with a helicopter."

"So we have to wait for the creek to go down?"

"Yep. At least enough that a four-wheel drive can get through." He put the truck in reverse and searched for the best place to back it around, but the shoulders of the road looked very unstable.

"How long could that take?"

"Hard to say. Depends on how much more rain we get." He eased the truck back slowly, cranking the wheel as far as he could. The flat tire didn't help.

"Well." Katherine took a deep breath. "I was prepared for a few hours away from the lodge with Amanda, not a couple of days."

He figured Amanda would be the least of their problems. Her food supply was always available, and she didn't do anything but eat and sleep. Oh, God. Maybe she had some condition that required medicine every so often. He'd never even thought to ask. "What are you missing?"

"If we end up being here overnight, Amanda's going to run out of disposable diapers."

Maybe it was only his relief that the baby wasn't sick, but that struck Zeke as funny. He started to laugh.

Katherine got a haughty look on her face. "I'm glad you're amused. As a man who's never changed a baby's diaper, you can't be expected to understand the problem, I suppose."

"Disposable diapers," he said, still chuckling. "If that's the biggest problem we have in the next couple of days, we'll be doing great."

"Easy for you to say. You've never—"

"I'll make you a promise. If Amanda runs out of disposable diapers, I'll figure out a solution. Now, look over on your side of the truck and tell me what's happening with the right rear wheel. I'd like to back the truck up another foot or so if the area looks solid enough."

She turned in her seat. "I can't see real well, but I think it's okay. Start going slowly, and I'll tell you if it looks like it's starting to sink."

"Okay." He took his foot off the brake and gently pressed down on the gas. "How's—"

Her sharp cry of alarm made him jump. In his agitation he hit the gas instead of the brake, and the whine of a spinning tire told him they'd just slid hub-deep into the mud. He slumped back against the seat. Terrific.

"Zeke."

At the controlled terror in her voice he turned in surprise. This was inconvenient, but not the end of the world. Then he saw the bear peering in the window. "Sit still," he said.

Her face was chalky as she stared straight ahead, not looking at him or the bear. "I want to get Amanda up here with us."

"Don't. Chances are she'll go away if we don't do anything to interest her."

"H-how do you know it's a girl f-from just her face?"

"Because I know that face. Sadie has a den around here

someplace, although I haven't found it yet. But I've seen her with her cubs.''

"So she's the one who's...been on your porch?"

"Yep."

"Does Sadie look hungry to you?"

"Just curious. Take it easy, Katherine. I won't let anything happen to Amanda."

"I've heard that bears can rip open cars as if they were tin cans.''

"They have to be motivated. We don't have anything in here she wants."

"Except a baby!"

"She'd rather have candy. If you had a handful of chocolate, I might be worried. Now, turn your head slowly and look at me."

When she did, he gave her a reassuring smile. "You're safe, Katherine. So's Amanda. I promise." He didn't tell her why he could be so sure. If they had a real problem with Sadie, which he doubted, then he'd offer himself as a distraction while Katherine took Amanda to safety. It was a drastic solution and he didn't expect to have to use it, but it was a guarantee that mother and baby would survive.

He eased his hand across the space between the seats and took hold of hers. Her fingers were icy. He held her hand, moving his thumb up and down her cold fingers. "Trust me," he said. "This is my territory, and I don't allow my guests to be eaten by the bears."

"But we're sitting ducks, stuck in the mud like this, and even if we weren't, we couldn't outrun her with this flat tire."

"She'll go away eventually, and when she does, I'll dig us out of the muck."

She clutched his hand. "I don't want you to go out there, even if she leaves. She could come back."

"We can't sit in this truck forever." He liked having her hold tightly to his hand. He liked it so much he almost hated to tell her that Sadie was lumbering off into the mist and he had to go dig them out as promised. "Sadie's gone," he said. "And I'm going to see about the back tire."

She clutched his hand tighter. "Wait." After she turned slowly to look out the window, she sank back against the seat with a huge sigh, but she didn't let go of his hand. "I love the wilderness, but I have to admit I'm petrified of bears. When I was a little kid, a man in our neighborhood took a trip out west. He was killed by a bear. I overheard the grown-ups talking about it, and the details were seared into my seven-year-old brain."

He stroked the back of her hand with his thumb. He remembered how much he'd loved the texture of her skin and how much fun he'd had exploring every inch of it. "So why did you decide to hike through Yellowstone last summer? You must have known there would be bears in the park."

"That was part of it, testing my courage. Then when no bears showed up the first day, I relaxed and decided there weren't any around the area where I was. Of course I was wrong. And when that bear arrived, I was just as scared as I had been at seven. I hadn't conquered anything."

"That wasn't a fair test. When a wild creature shows up all of a sudden, most people are startled, if not downright frightened. Don't be so hard on yourself."

She turned her head to gaze at him. "It's just that I needed to succeed right then. I needed a chance to feel worthy. Instead I fell into the river, and caused…all sorts of problems."

Indeed she had. But for a few wonderful hours, she'd found that sense of worthiness in his arms. He was sure of that much, just as he was sure the feeling hadn't been enough to keep her there. And now she would go on seeking fulfillment in other parts of her life, with her child and her promotion at work. And he would try to forget her.

It wouldn't be easy. Right now her eyes looked the way they had when he'd decided to make love to her—the look that reminded him of a mountain streambed. He could sit here and stare into her eyes for hours.

"I didn't mean to hurt you," she murmured.

"I know." He squeezed her hand and released it. "I'm going to dig us out of here." Opening his door, he checked the footing before he climbed down.

"I'll help."

He looked around and she already had her door open. Considering how frightened she'd been a moment ago, he was stunned by her courage. But he didn't want her out there in case Sadie did come back. He couldn't predict exactly how the bear would react, no matter how matter-of-fact he'd been with Katherine. "Uh, actually I need you to sit in the driver's seat ready to gun the motor when I get us freed up."

"But—"

"There's only one shovel." He patted the wet seat where he'd just been. "Come on over here and get set. When I tell you, step down hard on the gas and keep the front wheels turned to the left. It won't be easy."

"I can do it." She closed the passenger door, startling Amanda awake. The baby began to whimper. Turning around toward the back seat, she started to comfort the baby with some soothing words and gentle pats.

"On second thought, never mind about driving us out," Zeke said. "You have your hands full. I'll—"

"Go dig," she said. "I'll handle things in here. If necessary, Amanda can cry for a little while. It won't kill her."

"You'd let her cry?"

"If I know nothing is majorly wrong with her, sure. Now, go dig. We're wasting time."

Spoken like a New York businesswoman, Zeke thought. He started to ask her if she had an appointment to get to. Instead he closed the door and slopped through the mud to the back end of the truck where he kept some tools in a metal box. Sure, they had to get back to the cabin eventually, but if it took them all afternoon, it didn't matter anymore. They might as well resign themselves to being marooned. But then, he was used to dealing with nature's whims and she wasn't. She was probably chafing under the restraint and thinking ahead to the problems this situation might cause at her office if it lasted through Monday.

The tire had sunk deep and the digging was hard work, but Zeke welcomed the labor. Big-muscle movement calmed him as it had always done. Once he'd hollowed out a trench in front of the tire, he collected rocks to line it. Finally he decided the job was about as good as he could manage. Walking behind the truck to get another vantage point, he called out to Katherine, figuring it would take her a while to stop fussing with the baby and get organized to drive the truck out.

The engine roared immediately, and before Zeke could jump out of the way, a geyser of mud coated him from head to toe. He swiped a hand over his face and spit the dirt from his mouth. That would teach him to underestimate her efficiency. At least the tire was free.

He replaced the tools in the back of the truck and used his bandanna to clean off some of the grime as he returned to the driver's side of the cab.

She was still in the driver's seat, and when she caught sight of him she jumped and her mouth formed a round O of surprise. She quickly rolled down the window. "What happened?"

"Well, I didn't get out of the way fast enough." He noticed Amanda wasn't crying anymore. Katherine was a whiz of a mother, all right.

"Oh, my." Her eyes began to twinkle and she pressed her lips together. "You look like you belong in a minstrel show."

"I'll bet I do. Care to scoot over now so I can drive us out of here and back to the cabin?"

"I'm here now. Why don't I just drive?"

"It's hard to handle with that flat."

"I can do it."

He recognized her need to be in control of something, even if it was only his balky old truck. No creature liked the feeling of being trapped, with no power. He shrugged. "Okay." He walked around and got into the passenger seat. "Go for it."

"I may not have a car in New York, but I know how to drive."

"I believe you." He gestured down the road.

With one last glance at him, she pressed her foot slowly on the gas. The truck moved forward, back on to the road, but the steering wheel jerked out of her grip. She grabbed it again, her jaw set. "I've got it."

"I see that you do." He made himself relax against the seat and gaze out the passenger window, although he flinched every time the truck lurched, knowing the strength it took to hold it steady on the road. Once he glanced over and saw a trickle of sweat roll down her temple, but he knew she wouldn't ask him to take over.

As she fought the truck and guided them down the road toward the cabin, he wondered what the labor room scene had been like. He'd heard that first babies could be the hardest to deliver. The idea of her delicate body wrenched with the pain of childbirth made him woozy, but he was sure she'd handled it like a trouper.

"Did you have any drugs?" He hadn't meant to ask the question out loud.

"Excuse me?" She gave him a quick, worried look.

"When you had Amanda. Did you take anything for the pain?"

"No. It's better for the baby if you don't, and I still think it was for the best, but partway into it I was ready for them to give me something. Turns out it was too late." The steering wheel jerked in her hands and she tightened her hold. "There's a window of opportunity when you can give the mother a painkiller, but I'd passed that window and had to tough it out. I'm glad now that I did, but at the time it was a little rough.''

He hated thinking of her going through that. ''Was anyone with you? Besides the hospital staff, I mean.''

''Naomi.''

''You should have called me, Katherine.''

''I—'' She fought the wheel as the truck forged over another rut in the world. ''The truth is, I didn't know you well enough.''

He smiled grimly. He'd imagined that he'd opened up his soul to her that night, that he'd allowed her to know him as nobody else ever had. Maybe he hadn't told her all the details of his life, but he'd loved her without holding anything back. He'd never lost himself so completely in a woman, but then, he hadn't told her so. And he certainly couldn't tell her now.

THE TRUCK WAS A BEAST, and wrestling with it gave Katherine great satisfaction. Her shoulders ached, but she was working out a lot of her frustrations, both physical and mental.

''Big rut up ahead,'' Zeke warned.

''Right.'' Katherine steered left, hoping to avoid it altogether, but the front tire caught the edge of the rut. Fearing they'd get stuck again, she gunned the engine. The jolt made her teeth snap together, and a searing pain shot up her right wrist. Tears pricked her eyes but she held on and kept going, determined that she wouldn't wimp out on this task.

''What's wrong?'' Zeke asked.

She gritted her teeth as her wrist started to throb. ''I'm…fine.''

''Don't give me that. Stop the truck.''

''No. I'll get us there.''

He reached over and turned the key. The truck lurched to a stop. ''Okay, what's wrong?''

She leaned her forehead against the steering wheel and fought tears. "Damn it, damn it, damn it! Can't I do one little thing right for a change?"

His arm came around her shoulders in comfort, but his tone was stern. "Tell me what happened, Katherine."

"I think... I might have sprained my wrist when we went over that big rut."

Zeke swore softly. "Which one?"

"My right one, of course! The one I need the most to take care of Amanda! I am the biggest screwup that ever existed!"

His arm tightened around her. "Hey, stop that. If you were the biggest screwup that ever existed, Naomi Rutledge wouldn't be asking you to take over her magazine, would she?"

"She might." Katherine swallowed a sob. "She's my godmother. She probably just feels sorry for me."

"Oh, yeah, I'm sure. The woman I dealt with isn't about to hand over her magazine to a screwup, not even her god-daughter. Now, let's trade places, and I'll get us home. Then we'll see about your wrist."

Katherine lifted her head and gazed at him through watery eyes. "And if I'm incapacitated, who's going to take care of Amanda?"

"I am."

CHAPTER SEVEN

ZEKE DROVE THE TRUCK as carefully as he could, knowing every jolt brought Katherine fresh pain. His stomach churned as he thought about her hurting, but he forced himself to stay calm. He had no problem with his own injuries, but when another creature was hurting, human or animal, he was in agony. That trait had eliminated a career in medicine, although in preparation for becoming a ranger, he'd taken some basic emergency training. He also knew from firsthand experience that once he iced her wrist and wrapped it in an elastic bandage, she'd feel better.

Amanda stayed asleep for the rest of the trip, but the rain was coming down as hard as ever by the time they reached the cabin. He opened the driver's side door. "Stay there. I'll help you inside."

"No, you get Amanda inside." She fumbled with the door handle with her left hand. "I can manage."

"Katherine…"

She turned to him, a fierce glow in her eyes. "Get Amanda. It's only my wrist. I can walk just fine."

He'd seen that same glow in the eyes of wild animals protecting their young, and he knew better than to argue. "Okay. But wait and let me help you down." He was out of the truck in seconds and splashing through puddles in his haste to get to her door. Once he opened it he held out his hand. "Let me take a look."

"I'm sure it's nothing." Gingerly she laid her hand in his.

"It's something." He lightly traced his finger over the delicate bone structure of her wrist. The swelling had already started. "Put your other hand on my shoulder," he instructed. "I'll try to lift you down without bumping your wrist. The door's unlocked. Go in and take a bag of peas from the freezer, wrap them in a towel and put that on your wrist until I get there."

"Zeke, I'm sorry. All I seem to do is cause you problems."

"It's my fault as much as yours. I knew the truck would be hard to drive. Now turn toward me so I can get you down from there." When she complied he fit his hands around her waist. He avoided looking into her eyes as he slowly lifted her down, taking care not to jostle her wrist. God, she felt so good, so warm within his grip. Every time he touched her was like coming home. But once her feet were on the ground, he released her immediately. "I'll meet you in there," he said.

"Do you think you can work the strap on the carrier?"

He glanced at her. "Go on. I'll figure out the strap." Once he was convinced she was on her way into the cabin, he turned back to the truck cab. "Somehow."

He climbed into the passenger seat, got to his knees and leaned over into the back seat the way he'd watched Katherine do it. Amanda was awake, waving her arms and chortling as if she found her view of the upholstery fascinating. Zeke studied the situation and figured out how she was belted in.

"Okay, kiddo, let's spring you from that contraption." He managed to unfasten the strap, but Amanda started kicking in excitement and got her legs tangled in it. "Great. Snafu right off the bat." Zeke worked to free her. "Hold still, now."

She seemed to kick and squirm even more vigorously.

Despite the chill in the air, Zeke began to sweat. He had to get her out of there so he could go inside and take care of Katherine's wrist. And the longer he took, the more worried Katherine would be. Finally his patience snapped. "Hold *still*, Amanda!"

She went rigid, at which point he was able to extricate her from the tangled strap, but as he hauled her into the front seat, she began to cry.

"Oh, hell." He cupped her against his chest and patted her back. "Now, stop. I can't take you in to your mommy while you're crying. She's got enough to worry about."

Amanda cried harder.

Zeke sighed and tried to think how Katherine had handled these situations. Of course if the baby was hungry, she was out of luck, but he didn't think that was the problem. He'd scared her by talking too rough. Maybe he could fix that mistake by trying some of the nonsense talk Katherine used.

He cleared his throat. "Oh, sweet little baby girl," he crooned. "Let's have a smile. Give Daddy a smile. Enough of the waterworks now. We have enough water coming down outside without you adding to it. Easy does it, sweetheart. I'm here, baby girl."

Amazingly, Amanda stopped crying.

"Thank God," Zeke muttered. "Lord knows how long I could have kept that up." Hunching over to shield Amanda from the rain, he climbed from the truck, grabbed the diaper bag and slogged through the mud to the porch.

Katherine was waiting at the top of the steps, shivering in her wet clothes, a bulky ice pack clutched around her wrist. "I'm afraid I have some bad news."

His heart beat faster. "Do you think your wrist is broken?" He quickly climbed the steps and ducked under the porch roof. "Because if it is, I'm hiking out to the road."

"No, I'm sure it's just a sprain. This is still critical, though. Your electricity seems to be out."

"Oh, is that all?"

"All?" She stared at him. "Lights, refrigeration, hot water?"

He shrugged. "We'll build a fire, light the lanterns and keep the refrigerator door shut as much as possible. No big deal. It'll be like camping."

"Oh."

He gazed down at her and suddenly was reminded of what had happened the last time they'd been in a camping situation together. His breathing quickened. "Or not." The huskiness in his voice probably betrayed his thoughts. "Let's go in and get your wrist taken care of."

KATHERINE DIDN'T WANT to admit how much her wrist hurt, but she took the over-the-counter pain medication Zeke offered without any argument. He'd settled Amanda in her makeshift bassinet, and she seemed to be content to lie there and suck on her fingers.

Zeke washed up at the kitchen sink and then brought a first-aid kit to the table, where Katherine sat resting her arm with the ice pack over it. Zeke pulled his chair close. "Okay, let's take another look." He eased the ice pack away. "Let's make sure it's not broken."

Katherine flinched. "I seem to recall that involves pain."

"Some, but I have to know. If you broke anything I'm not going to wait around for a tow truck. Breaks can get nasty if they're not taken care of quickly." He cradled her hand in his. "Tell me how this feels." He rotated her hand gently to one side.

She sucked in a breath. "Like you're shoving hot needles into my wrist."

"Good."

"*Good?*"

"Yeah. If your wrist was broken you'd be screaming at me to stop, not telling me how it feels." He laid her hand carefully back on the table and took a rolled elastic bandage out of the first-aid kit. "This won't feel wonderful, either. Try to distract yourself from what I'm doing."

"Yeah, okay." She looked away as he cradled her hand

once again and positioned the bandage against her palm. "I notice you don't have a television," she said, wincing as he wound the bandage securely.

"Or a radio," he added. "Which is lucky, because they wouldn't be working now, anyway."

"So how do you spend your time?" They were huddled so close that she became aware of the pattern of his breathing and the subtle scent of his body. Both were saturated with erotic memories.

"I hike."

She glanced out the window. "I guess you won't be doing that today."

"Guess not."

Damn, but it hurt to have him wrap that thing around her wrist. "So how do you spend your evenings?"

"You should know. You spent one with me."

Her head snapped around and she stared at him, but he didn't look up from his task. She wondered if he'd meant that to be as provocative as it sounded. Heat surged through her, and her voice was tight as she struggled to form a response. "I'd imagine that was unusual."

"Thanks a lot."

She'd say this for him, he'd taken her mind off her pain. "No, I mean..." What did she mean? "I didn't mean to imply you don't spend your evenings with women. I'm sure you—"

"Have a girl at every campsite? That's me."

Now that he'd broached the subject, damned if she didn't want to know about the other women in his life and specifically if he'd been involved with anyone since...since last summer. But she didn't know how to ask. "Okay, so you're a wilderness Romeo," she said, trying to sound flip about it. "But what do you do when you're alone?"

"I read. And sometimes I just sit, stare into the fire, and think." He secured the bandage and glanced up at her.

The look in his eyes made her quiver, and she wondered

if he was remembering that night by the campfire, how the conversation had grown quieter and quieter, the words further apart.

"I should probably rig up a sling for you," he said. "But first you need to get out of those wet clothes."

Uh-oh. That was exactly how she'd gotten into trouble the last time she'd been with Zeke. "I don't have a change of clothes."

"I'll get you something." He left his chair and walked over to a chest of drawers positioned against the wall at the end of the bed.

Katherine wasn't sure this was a good idea, taking off her clothes and putting on Zeke's. Too much intimacy was implied. Still, she was cold and wet, and when he laid a green flannel shirt, black drawstring sweats and heavy wool socks on the table, they looked invitingly warm and cozy.

Then she realized he was in the same wet condition, and his clothes were spattered with mud, besides. "You should change, too," she said.

"I will, once you and Amanda are all set. You can change in there." He tilted his head toward the bathroom. "Be careful of that arm, though. I'll be happier when it's supported by a sling."

She glanced up at him. "I don't know about the sling, Zeke. It'll be in the way when I nurse Amanda."

"We'll work around it when you're nursing her."

Deep inside, a coil of sexual tension tightened. Apparently he planned to be right there helping her when Amanda nursed. Her injury was knocking down the barriers between them at an alarming rate.

She stood and picked up the pile of clothes left-handed. "I should probably wash off my feet and ankles before I put on the socks. Will you be okay out here alone with Amanda while I do that?"

"Guess so."

"I'll hurry."

"Don't hurry so much you hurt yourself."

She grimaced. "Right." She headed for the bathroom. Once she closed the door she automatically flicked on the wall switch before remembering the electricity was out. But even in the gloom of a rainy afternoon she noticed the huge claw-foot tub that dominated the room. Decked out with a utilitarian showerhead and curtain, it still looked sinfully luxurious.

As she peeled off her damp clothes and washed up as best she could in the icy tap water, she imagined what a hot bubble bath would be like in that tub. Heaven. She wondered if Zeke ever took a hot bath. Certainly he did. Otherwise he wouldn't have installed such a thing in his cabin. It was an intriguing picture.

She was about halfway finished when Amanda began to cry. Gritting her teeth, she began working faster.

Then Amanda's crying stopped. She didn't usually stop crying by herself, so either Zeke had picked her up, or something was wrong. Immediately her imagination came up with a dozen possibilities that put Amanda in peril of her life. Zeke wasn't experienced enough to know if she was choking, or had the blanket over her nose, or…

Katherine jerked on Zeke's shirt and sweats, tied them quickly and hurried out the door to find him quietly holding Amanda in his arms.

He glanced up, a tender look in his eyes. Then he looked at Katherine's bare feet. By the time his gaze met hers again, all tenderness had vanished. "Didn't think I could handle it, did you?"

"I…" She paused and grimaced. "No. And I apologize. If you could please hold her a little longer, I'll go put on the socks." She turned back toward the bathroom, berating herself for stepping on Zeke's feelings at the very moment he was beginning to gain confidence around the baby. If she wanted him to form a relationship with Amanda, she'd have to back off and trust him.

ZEKE PACED BACK AND FORTH in front of the window, which worked off some of his frustration and seemed to keep Amanda from crying. But he didn't kid himself that he had any talent in that direction. When Katherine sprained her wrist he'd foolishly announced he'd take care of the baby. Oh, sure. And pigs could fly. Maybe he'd done okay with the smaller boys at the ranch, but he'd never been in charge of anybody this young, or this gender.

Katherine came back out of the bathroom with socks on her feet. "Zeke, I'm really sorry I reacted like that. You obviously had the situation under control."

As if to prove that wasn't true, Amanda began to fuss.

"I don't think so," Zeke said.

"She's probably hungry and needs to be changed." She hesitated. "If you're willing, I could show you how to change her."

He didn't think he had much choice. "Okay." He hoped it wouldn't be any more complicated than changing the oil in his truck. But as he glanced down at the squirming, fussy bundle in his arms, he decided it was probably more like deactivating a bomb.

He held her while Katherine used her good hand to arrange the necessary tools on the table. It all looked completely foreign to him.

"Okay, you can bring her over," Katherine said.

He walked up to the table, where she'd put a padded mat down. She moved aside and gestured toward it.

He started to put Amanda on the mat and paused with her suspended over the table. "Does it matter which end goes north and which end goes south?"

"Yes. Depending on whether you're right-handed or left-handed, her feet should be pointing in that direction."

"I'm left-handed." He turned Amanda carefully around and placed her on the mat with her head pointing right and her feet pointing left.

"You are?" Katherine glanced at him. "I didn't know that."

There was a lot she didn't know about him, he thought.

"Left-handed people are supposed to be very creative," she said. "That might be one reason you wanted to build the cabin all by yourself."

"As opposed to the fact that I'm antisocial?"

"I didn't say you were antisocial."

"You came damn close." He noticed Amanda watching him carefully. "Can she pick up swearwords, do you think?"

"You mean store them up for when she can talk?" Katherine smiled. "I don't know."

"I think I'll clean up my language, just in case. Okay, what's next?"

"Keep your right hand on her at all times. She can't roll yet, but I still like to make sure there's no way she can fall. Then just unsnap the legs of her sleeper."

"Right." His fingers seemed too big for the tiny snaps and he fumbled with the task. "Damn, these are tricky," he muttered, then remembered his new resolution. "I mean, *doggone*, these are tricky." He glanced at Amanda, who was staring at him as if he'd landed from another planet. "She's probably wondering if this is going to take all day."

"Actually, I'll bet she's fascinated by seeing a new face during this procedure. She's probably sick of looking at the same lady all the time."

He doubted it, but he appreciated Katherine's attempt to be encouraging. Finally he had Amanda's chubby little legs free. Next came the really dicey part. "Now what?"

"The diaper's held on her with those adhesive tabs. Pull them free and it will come off."

He followed her instructions, while Amanda gurgled at him. At least the baby wasn't screaming in agony, so he must not be doing so bad. Katherine stood very close to him, her shoulder touching his. When she moved he caught a whiff of her perfume. And he still wanted her as much as ever.

"Fold up the wet diaper and give it to me," Katherine said. "I'll throw it away while you start cleaning her up." She started to move away from the table.

"Hold it! I'm not doing this part without supervision."

"Just take the towelette from the container and wipe carefully in all the folds." She walked over to his trash container.

"There's a hell of a lot of folds here. I mean, a *heck* of a lot of folds. What if I'm too rough? What if she decides now's a good time to go again?"

"That's why you have a pad there." She returned to his side, a smile on her face. "At least she can't squirt you in the eye like a little boy might."

"They do that?" In spite of himself, he was fascinated by the habits of these uncivilized little creatures. In some ways they were like the wild animals he related to so well.

"Boys react just like a miniature fire hose, lots of times as soon as you take the diaper off. You have to be on alert the whole time."

"How do you know about this?"

"*Cachet* is very supportive of employees with children. They bring their babies to work, so I've been present at a couple of staff meetings where babies had to be changed before we could go on with the meeting."

"Oh." Although he was happy about the magazine's policy for Amanda's sake, he didn't enjoy being reminded about Katherine's perfect job.

"So, are you going to continue?" She gestured toward Amanda, who was kicking her legs and blowing bubbles.

"Right." He remembered that Katherine had really yanked to get one of the moist towelettes out of the container, so he took an end and pulled hard. About ten came out, all linked together. He had enough length to make a scarf. "Sh—sugar!"

When Katherine started to laugh, he glared at her.

"I'm sorry," she said, sobering immediately. "I guess you don't know your own strength."

"Can you stuff them back in?"

"It's not worth the effort. Just tear off one and throw the rest away."

"Okay. Whoops. We've got leakage."

"Well, now you have a purpose for those extra towelettes."

Once he had the puddle cleaned up, he started cleaning Amanda. He was sure he was doing it all wrong and she'd start crying any minute, but she didn't. In fact, the more he worked on her, the better he felt about doing it.

Katherine cleared her throat. "That's probably good enough." She gave him a clean diaper. "I only have four of these left."

"Then what?"

"Good question. Do you have safety pins around?"

"I don't know." He'd decided he should be able to put the diaper on without asking Katherine how it went, so he studied it for a minute, then studied Amanda.

"Maybe we can use dish towels."

"Maybe." He thought he had it figured out, so he lifted up one of Amanda's legs and shoved the diaper underneath that side. Then he lifted her other leg and pulled it into place. Except now the adhesive tabs wouldn't work unless he put her facedown. So he had the damn thing backward.

Lifting her legs one at a time again, he pulled the diaper out and turned it around. There. In no time he had her taped together and the snaps done up. He turned to Katherine. "How was that?"

Her eyes were warm and sparkly. "That was great. Thank you."

"And she didn't even cry."

"Why should she?"

"Well, because I'm big, and my voice is deeper and I figured I'd scare her."

"But you're gentle and slow with her. She senses you mean well."

"Yeah." He slid one hand under her head and the other one under her bottom as he lifted her off the table. "Animals are like that, too. Even wild ones can sense if you're trying to help them." He settled Amanda into the crook of his arm. He must have smiled at her, because suddenly she grinned back at him and waved her fists in the air.

"Hey, Mandy," he said softly.

She gurgled and waved her fists some more.

His heart swelled as he gazed down at her. She was beautiful. Whether he and Katherine had been wise or foolish when they'd made love didn't matter anymore. They'd produced Amanda, and that was reason enough to bless that night they'd spent together.

He glanced up at Katherine and caught her watching him with a tenderness that took his breath away.

"I knew you'd fall in love with her if you gave yourself a chance," she murmured.

little time to worry with the silverware." Concentrating on keeping his mind on his control, he slid the material under her arm and slipped behind her so he could tie the ends around her neck. But he kept getting her hair caught in the knot. "Lean you lift up your hair."

"Sure." She lifted her bandaged arm and tried to tuck her hair off her neck.

He hadn't expected the gesture to affect him like a jolt from a live wire, but it did. As she raised her arm, she lifted her breast and brought it into sweet prominence beneath her thin sweater.

CHAPTER EIGHT

ZEKE WAS AFRAID KATHERINE was right, and he was falling in love with Amanda. Not a wise move. She wasn't his to keep. But then neither were the wild baby animals he cared for and released when they were old enough to be on their own. He survived losing them, so he ought to be able to survive this.

"I should probably feed her," Katherine said, holding out her arms.

Zeke glanced at her bandaged wrist. "Let me rig up a sling for you first." He settled Amanda in her bassinet and she immediately began to cry.

"I'll feed her first," Katherine said.

Zeke hated hearing Amanda cry, but he put a restraining hand on Katherine's shoulder. "You need that sling. I'll fix it in no time."

She stilled under his hand.

He could feel the current running between them and took his hand away before his touch became a caress. "This won't take long." He took a pillowcase from the dresser and used his pocketknife to rip the sides open.

Katherine gasped. "You're ruining your pillowcase!"

"Doesn't matter." He walked over to her. "Bend your arm at the elbow."

She did as he asked. "I still don't think you should have cut open that perfectly good pillowcase."

"You need a sling for your arm more than I need that pillowcase, and with Amanda needing to be fed, we don't have time to come up with an alternative.'' Concentrating on keeping the process impersonal, he slid the material under her arm and stepped behind her so he could tie the ends around her neck. But he kept getting her hair caught in the knot. "Could you lift up your hair?"

"Sure." She slid her left hand behind her neck and lifted the hair off her nape.

He hadn't expected the gesture to affect him like a fist to the gut. Yet here he was, struggling to breathe as he gazed at that exposed, tender spot at her nape.

"Zeke?" She half turned toward him. "Is anything wrong?" Then she looked into his eyes. "Oh." Her eyes grew smoky with desire, and her lips parted.

"Turn around," Zeke said roughly. "Let me tie this. Amanda needs you."

Quietly she turned her back on him.

He fastened the tie with shaking fingers and hoped he had the tension right on her arm. His throat was tight with longing. "Go sit in the rocker," he said. "I'll bring her to you."

Her whisper of agreement sent chills of need up his spine.

Resolutely he walked to the bassinet and picked up the crying baby. A few hours ago her crying would have made him anxious, but he was beginning to understand it was her method of communicating. He didn't have to worry that something was terribly wrong every time she fussed a little.

He jiggled her and made faces, which sort of worked. Her crying was reduced to stray croaks of protest. But when he glanced over to see if Katherine was ready for the baby, all his cajoling stopped. Mesmerized, he stared at Katherine, her head bowed, the blond sheen of her hair catching the light from the lantern as she concentrated on the now-difficult job of unbuttoning her shirt. The process was slow, making it all the more erotic. Zeke's body throbbed in response as he watched her finish the task.

She looked up and started to speak. The words seemed to lodge in her throat as she gazed at him. Finally she spoke, her voice strained. "I can't figure out how to manage. Maybe I should take off the sling."

"We'll prop her on a pillow." He had no idea how he knew what to do, but somehow he did. Holding Amanda in the crook of one arm, he took a pillow from the bed and brought it over to her. "Hold your arm away from your body a minute." He knelt beside the rocker and tucked the pillow on her lap, providing a nest for Amanda. Gently he laid her on the pillow, and Amanda immediately starting nuzzling at the flannel material still draped modestly over Katherine's breast.

Katherine steadied her with her left hand, but she obviously had no way to move the flannel aside.

So Zeke did it for her. "Let me," he murmured. He trembled as he cradled the weight of her milk-filled breast. Then he carefully brought it toward Amanda's seeking mouth. When the baby took the nipple greedily, he kept his hand there as long as he dared, absorbing Katherine's warmth and the rapid beat of her heart. Amanda sucked steadily, and Zeke thought it was the sweetest sound he'd ever heard.

He glanced up at Katherine, but her lashes were lowered, as if she couldn't allow him to see the emotions swirling there. He understood. When his own needs became too great, he gently slipped his hand from under her breast, stood and went over to the door.

He had to remain there a minute until his breathing was under control and he could speak. "Call if you need me," he said finally. Then he went outside.

I NEED YOU. Katherine ached so much she wasn't sure if she could bear it. If Amanda hadn't been in her arms, she would have dragged Zeke over to the bed and demanded that he make love to her with all the vigor she knew he was capable of.

Yet making love to Zeke would be a huge mistake, putting her future in jeopardy. She could feel the danger, even without Naomi there to remind her. Naomi had sent her here to tidy up loose ends, not become more entangled.

The job Naomi expected from her required absolute focus. The two of them had made allowances for Amanda—her early childhood care could be handled right at the magazine. By the time she was in school, Katherine would have adjusted to her new duties and feel free to take part in whatever girlhood activities presented themselves with Amanda. Naomi had even hinted that she might be willing to take over as room mother or Brownie leader if the need arose. Naomi had everything mapped out, taking the demands of motherhood fully into account.

But she had not taken a love affair into consideration. For the first time Katherine wondered if Naomi had lovers. She'd divorced her husband years ago, and she was an extremely attractive woman. Now that Katherine gave herself time to think about it, she suspected Naomi did have love affairs, but obviously she chose appropriate men who would never interfere with her work.

Zeke was highly inappropriate. The passion would be too great, the distance too far, the needs too compelling. Loving Zeke could easily destroy her career. She might even be able to live with that, but she couldn't live with the prospect of sacrificing Naomi's hopes and dreams.

Still, she wanted Zeke to connect with Amanda, and that's exactly what he was doing. Unfortunately, with each step closer to Amanda, he came a step closer to stealing Katherine's heart. She desperately wanted Zeke to keep in touch with their daughter as she was growing up. But that would require her own participation. Somehow she'd have to make that participation friendly yet businesslike. Yeah, right. The task already seemed impossible. If she made love to him again, she might as well not even try.

When the time came to switch Amanda to her other breast, she gritted her teeth and managed by herself. Her wrist hurt whenever she used it, but she couldn't handle a two-month-old baby without using both hands. Naomi wasn't going to be happy about this sprained wrist, either. It would make her less effective at work.

Well, she couldn't do anything about her bum wrist now. What was done was done. But she could do something about Zeke.

He came back into the cabin just as she finished feeding Amanda. He brought in an armload of wood and the cool scent of wet pines. "The rain's stopped," he announced.

Katherine had been so absorbed in her thoughts that she hadn't noticed. "Do you think it's over?"

"Hard to say." He deposited the wood on the hearth and crouched with his back to her as he built a fire. "But even if it is, it'll take a day or so before that creek goes down enough to get a vehicle through."

She couldn't help admiring the flex of those strong shoulders as he worked. "But if the phone line is repaired, we might be able to have someone come out by tomorrow night?"

"It's possible." He stood. "Guess I'll go shower off some of this dirt and then we can think about what to have for supper."

"Okay." One night, Katherine thought to herself as Zeke walked into the bathroom. Surely she could make it through one night without giving in to temptation.

AFTER REMOVING KATHERINE'S underwear from the circular shower rod, Zeke stayed under the cold spray longer than he probably needed to rinse the mud off his body and out of his hair. He swore softly the whole time, using words he hadn't dredged up in years. He cursed unpredictable birth-control pills, the weather, his worthless bridge, flat tires and the fickle finger of fate.

But he couldn't bring himself to curse Katherine. She was as much a victim of this as he was. And she was still eager to escape. No matter that she caught fire instantly the minute he touched her—she longed to be far away from the fire itself. He sighed, knowing he wasn't the kind of guy to take advantage of a woman's weakness.

Turning off the shower, he stepped from the big tub and dried off briskly. He didn't realize until he was finished that he hadn't brought any clean clothes into the bathroom with him. Unfortunately for both of them, he'd have to go back into the main room of the cabin wearing only a towel.

He opened the door and glanced out.

Amanda dozed in Katherine's arms as she rocked back and forth, eyes closed. Maybe he could make it to the dresser and back to the bathroom without her being aware of him. But the continued rain had made the drawers stick. By the time he jerked and fought them open and tucked his pile of clothes under one arm, he glanced over his shoulder and found her watching him.

She cleared her throat. "Under the circumstances, it might be better if you didn't parade around here in a towel."

The unfairness of her implication that he was doing this on purpose irked him. "I live alone. I don't automatically think of protecting my privacy."

"I'd appreciate it if you'd start thinking about it."

"Would you?" He advanced on her. "Katherine, this is my house, and we're in the middle of the woods. Normally I don't even bother with the towel. So you see, I am making concessions."

Her cheeks grew pink.

He gestured toward the bathroom. "And maybe you'd better start thinking about the wisdom of flaunting your underwear in my face."

Her cheeks flamed, but her chin jutted defiantly. "You're the one who suggested I shouldn't sit around in wet clothes. What else was I supposed to do with them?"

He had to admit she had a point. He sighed. "Look, this is a small place. We can't get away from each other unless I pitch my tent out in the yard."

"There's a thought." A flash of humor softened her belligerent expression. "I don't mean that. And you're right, this is your house. It's just that…" Her gaze traveled over his bare chest, and when she looked back into his eyes, the hunger had returned to hers. Her voice was husky. "Please go put on your clothes."

He clamped down on his desire, turned and walked into the bathroom.

KATHERINE HADN'T MEANT to fight with Zeke, but no sooner had she vowed she could make it through one night than he'd appeared in front of her practically naked. She didn't think he'd done it on purpose, but that didn't change the surge of desire she'd had to fend off, was still fending off.

After Zeke returned, fully dressed, he moved around the cabin, taking care of the tasks that needed to be done. He made no conversation, but he made a lot of racket. It sounded like impatient noise to Katherine, and she didn't blame him.

As the watery light of afternoon faded, he lit two kerosene lanterns. Then he stoked up the fire and put on some bigger logs before getting a cast-iron kettle out of the cupboard, which Katherine assumed they'd use to heat dinner over the fire. He seemed pretty well equipped for the loss of electricity, she thought. It must happen often out here.

As she sat and rocked Amanda, lulling her to sleep, she thought of how different her life was from Zeke's. Electricity was essential in her world. It operated the elevators in her twenty-story apartment house, her answering machine, her personal computer, her microwave. Without those conveniences she wouldn't be able to exist comfortably. Without electricity, she wouldn't have any way to heat bathwater for her or Amanda.

And the forest was such a quiet place, at least when Zeke wasn't banging something or other, which he seemed to be doing pretty constantly this evening. Still, even his noise wasn't the same as the noise in her tenth-floor apartment, where traffic on the street below sent up a constant hum that she blocked out, just as she'd learned to block out the sound of doors closing and telephones ringing in other apartments. She lived in a beehive of people, while Zeke lived in almost total isolation.

She'd been so wrong to expect him to respond like a jaded urban guy when she'd shown up with Amanda. To think that he'd sit and drink coffee while they talked over their options was insane, she now realized. In her world that might have happened. Many men she knew hid their primitive urges under a veneer of civilized behavior. Zeke wasn't quite civilized.

And that was why making love to him had been such a transforming experience. But it would be selfish of her to do that again. Still, she had a hard time resisting Zeke's wildness. When they'd made love last summer, she'd fantasized they were creatures of the forest themselves.

"Is stew okay?" Zeke asked, turning from the cupboard to glance over at her.

"Fine. I like stew." She would have eaten anything he gave her, considering how rotten she felt about putting him in this untenable position.

Yet she had to remember that despite the pain she and Zeke had caused each other, the end result had been Amanda. She gazed down at her child, never tiring of watching her. Despite the clatter Zeke was making in the kitchen, Amanda lay quietly, eyes closed as she sucked gently on her fist. Gradually her body relaxed into sleep and her hand fell away from her rosebud mouth.

She was so perfect, Katherine thought, a lump of emotion lodging in her throat. So helpless, too. Amanda depended on her to make everything turn out right, and she was determined the baby's instinctive faith wouldn't be misplaced. Amanda deserved the best life Katherine could give her, and that's what she'd get.

Gradually Katherine became aware that the cabin was completely silent except for the crackling of the fire. She glanced up, expecting Zeke to have gone out for more wood. Instead he was standing by the fireplace gazing at her and Amanda. The minute Katherine saw him there, he turned and crouched down next to the kettle hanging over the flames and began to stir the contents.

"Is there something I can do?" she asked, pretending she hadn't seen that wrenching expression of longing on his face. "Set the table or something? Amanda's asleep."

He didn't turn. "Napkins and silverware are in the top drawer next to the refrigerator." His voice had a definite huskiness to it.

Oh, God, she should never have come here, Katherine thought. She should have overruled Naomi and sent Zeke a letter, just like he'd said. Then this man who had grown up an orphan wouldn't have any picture in his mind of the little family he'd created and yet couldn't be part of.

Except he could be a part of Amanda's life, if he'd allow himself to. When she was too little to send to Wyoming, Katherine could bring her. Sure, the contact with Zeke would be tough, knowing they had no future, but if she could survive this weekend, she could survive anything. And it would be better for Amanda, and better for Zeke, who was not going to forget this little baby, not judging from the look on his face a moment ago.

She eased out of the rocker and leaned down to lay Amanda in the makeshift bassinet. The arrangement made Katherine smile. Amanda fit inside the brass kettle perfectly. Another month and she'd be too big for it, but it was exactly the right size now. Katherine had left her camera in her room at the lodge or she would have considered taking a picture of Amanda to save for when she was older. Assuming Zeke would be a viable part of her life, that was.

She walked over to the kitchen area, but when she tried to open the drawer Zeke had indicated, she realized why he'd been making so much noise. All the drawers were swollen from the rain. The silverware clattered as she put some muscle into it and pulled hard enough to get the drawer open.

"I found a box of hot cocoa mix, if you'd like that to drink," Zeke said from his position by the fire. "I've already heated water for instant coffee."

"Cocoa's fine." Katherine set the table with Zeke's utilitarian white napkins and his stainless steel. There was something appealing about his uncomplicated life-style. She was beginning to appreciate that a minimum of possessions meant more time to do other things. Unfortunately one of the things she longed to do wasn't wise.

"If you'll bring me a couple of bowls, I'll dish this out."

"Sure." She opened cupboard doors until she found the bowls and took two out. Walking over toward the fire, she took a deep sniff of warm stew and thought what a cozy setup this was, having all the conveniences in one room. If they were a couple, this night in the cabin could be a lot of fun, she thought wistfully.

ZEKE SAT ACROSS THE TABLE from Katherine and tried not to think about sex. It reminded him of an exercise a professor had given during one of his college classes. Everyone was supposed to try not to think of a pink elephant. Nobody could think of anything else *but* a pink elephant.

Katherine used her spoon to point to her bowl of stew. "This is very good."

"Homemade's better, but this is okay in a pinch." The soft light from the kerosene lantern cast the same glow that it had when they'd shared a campsite. He'd cooked her trout that night, and she'd raved about that, too, he remembered.

She took another spoonful of stew. She'd nearly polished off the bowl. "I'm not fussy. As bad a cook as I am, I can't afford to be."

He'd guessed she wasn't much of a cook when she hadn't

leaped to take over his kitchen and whip up something amazing. Women who could cook, even if they'd sprained a wrist, usually liked to show off a little. "I was spoiled," he said. "Lost Springs had a great cook while I was there. I'm sure people expect boys in an orphanage to live on bread and water, but I swear Millie must have been Julia Child's clone. We ate like kings."

"What was life like there?"

"A boy's paradise. Dogs to wrestle with, horses to ride, cows to chase. We all had chores, of course, and the bigger kids were expected to take care of the smaller ones, but it was like never-ending camp, sleeping in bunkhouses with your buddies, going on roundup together, sleeping under the stars sometimes." *And sometimes you woke up crying because you dreamed about your mother driving away and leaving you with strangers.*

"And now the ranch is in financial trouble?"

"It was. The bachelor auction made a big difference."

"That's good." She picked up her cocoa and took a sip. "More stew?"

"No, thanks. I'm full and happy."

He deliberately avoided meeting her gaze. Now would come the tough part of the evening. They'd sat together like this a year ago, and after they'd satisfied their hunger for food, they'd begun to feel the pangs of that other, more erotic hunger.

Tonight would be worse, because he knew what awaited him in Katherine's arms. He wondered if sex with her would be that wonderful again, or if leftover adrenaline from her scare had made her more passionate that night. Well, unless she made a move toward him, he wouldn't find out. Damned if he'd take the blame for losing control and landing them in bed together again.

"I can't imagine you on an auction block," she said.

"I hated the idea. But I couldn't say no when everybody else was doing it. If they fell short of their goal I'd always wonder if it was my fault.'' He took a swallow of his coffee. ''As it turned out, I didn't have to go up there.''

''No.'' She hesitated, her shoulders tight. ''Maybe now you wish you had.''

He thought about that. At first he'd wished Katherine hadn't told him about the baby and had just stayed in New York, but now the idea of never seeing that little face, never touching that tiny body seemed unthinkable.

He glanced over at the kettle where Amanda lay sleeping. ''No, I'm glad you brought her out here.''

She sagged with relief. ''Thank you for saying that. All day I've been wondering if I made a terrible mistake. I thought maybe it would have been better if you'd never seen her. Then you wouldn't have any mental pictures, and that might be easier.''

''It would be easier. But not better.''

She toyed with her spoon. ''Zeke, couldn't we work out something where you could have contact with her? At least once in a while?''

Instinctively he threw up his barrier again. ''I don't think so, Katherine. I don't know anything about taking care of kids.''

''But you just said at Lost Springs the big kids were expected to take care of the small ones. You must have been a big kid at some point.''

''Yeah, but they were boys.''

She smiled.

He wished she wouldn't smile. Every time she did, his heart beat a little faster and his mouth went dry. When they'd made love in the tent, she'd been full of smiles. He was conditioned to expect pleasure to follow when Katherine smiled.

''Boys and girls aren't all that different,'' she said.

''Maybe not in New York, but out here we consider them a lot different. We even have separate bathrooms and wear different kinds of underwear, both of which are designed for those…differences.''

Her skin grew rosy. ''I didn't mean it like that. I meant that you can treat a little girl basically the same way you treat a little boy.''

''Is that so? I'm not so sure. On Saturday nights at Lost Springs, some of us would climb in the old ranch van and go to the Isis movie theater in town. And the big guys would take care of the little guys, which meant if one of the younger ones had to go to the bathroom in the middle of the show, one of the older ones would take him and bring him back. Just how would that work with a little girl?''

''To be honest, I hadn't thought of that. But it seems like a minor problem.''

''Maybe to you. Women have been hauling little boys into the women's room for generations. No man in his right mind would take a little girl into the men's room, at least not in this day and age.''

''You could figure out other things to do, outdoor things like hiking and camping. I think you and Amanda—''

''Don't do this, Katherine.'' He was beginning to panic. He knew a ranger who was a noncustodial father, and the guy's life was a nightmare. He had to face a little stranger every summer, and about the time he got reacquainted with his son, the kid took off for his mother's house to spend the next nine months changing into yet another stranger. And that guy had more social skills than Zeke, and his kid was a boy, which helped a lot, too. Zeke pictured himself trying to keep up with dolls and dresses and makeup. He couldn't imagine being able to cope.

''But—''

''I'm glad I had a chance to see her, but this is where it needs to end. Take her back to New York and raise her there. I'll send you money, but don't ask me to twist myself into something I'm not just to suit your image of what should be.''

She sighed and stood, gathering her dishes. "I'm not asking you to change anything about yourself, Zeke. Amanda would love you just the way you are."

"After growing up in New York City?" He picked up his bowl and empty coffee mug, along with the kerosene lantern, and followed her over to the sink. "You think she'd be happy spending time in this little cabin with no TV, no computer games, no friends to play with? Even you are mystified as to how I spend my time." He set the lantern on the counter. "You couldn't hack living here for days on end, so what makes you think Amanda will be excited about it? You'd be forcing something on her she didn't even want, Katherine."

She set her dishes in the sink and turned to him. "Everybody needs a father!"

"Yeah, well, everybody doesn't get a father." He dumped his dishes in with hers in an angry clatter. "Stop trying to make everything turn out perfectly for Amanda. The only way I can imagine her learning to like it here is for you to move in and raise her right in this little cabin. Are you ready for that?"

He was surprised that she didn't immediately reject his outrageous proposal. He'd meant it as a ridiculous suggestion, but she looked at him as if she might actually be thinking about it. There was a light in her eyes that hadn't been there a moment ago.

"Don't kid yourself." He started rinsing the dishes in cold water. "Don't think you could sacrifice yourself like that and be even slightly happy."

"Is it really me you're worried about?" she asked quietly, leaning on the counter. "Or would you be the one making the biggest sacrifice by allowing a woman and child into your world?"

The concept of having her and Amanda live with him was so stunningly beautiful that he couldn't speak. And because it would never happen, he put it out of his mind immediately. He scrubbed vigorously at the bits of stew in the bowls.

"It's okay, Zeke. You don't have to be afraid that I'll suddenly camp on your doorstep and ruin your peace and quiet."

He kept his attention on the dishes, cleaning them as they'd never been cleaned before. "By the way, you can take the bed tonight. I'll take the floor."

"Oh, no. I'll take the floor. I'm the uninvited guest."

He rinsed the bowls and started scouring out the sink. "Don't argue with the ranger, ma'am. I sleep on the ground a lot, so a blanket on the floor of a cabin is a step up for me. Besides, if I put you on the floor you'll toss and turn all night trying to get comfortable and keep me awake."

"I will not toss and turn."

"Yeah, you will." He looked up with a faint smile. "You did last time."

Her face filled with color. "I'm sorry. Why didn't you say something?"

"Are you kidding? I wasn't complaining, just stating a fact." His body stirred as he gazed at her. "Restlessness has its advantages, sometimes."

She swallowed. "I'll take the bed, then."

"Good."

CHAPTER NINE

JUST AS ZEKE WAS RUNNING out of tasks to distract him from his need for Katherine, Amanda came to the rescue by waking up. Thankful for the interruption, he hurried over to scoop her up from her bassinet. "Is she hungry already?" he asked, turning to Katherine.

"I doubt it. But I'll bet she wants her bath. I give her one every night about this time."

Washing the baby would take up some time, he thought. "Then let's heat water in the kettle and give her one."

"I guess we could use the kitchen sink," Katherine said. "Let me hold her while you get it ready."

Zeke carefully transferred a fretting Amanda to Katherine. While he filled the kettle and hung it over the fire, Katherine walked around the cabin and talked to Amanda in the sweet little singsong voice he'd tried to imitate out in the truck. Katherine was a whole lot better at it than he was. The sound of her voice seemed to soothe Amanda, but it had the opposite effect on him. Of course, anything Katherine did seemed to have a stimulating effect where he was concerned.

Too bad he couldn't take a bath so he could sleep better. He had a feeling he was in for a long, frustrating night. As he filled the sink with water from the kettle, steam warmed his face and neck. "This seems pretty hot. Should I add cold?"

"Probably. It should be lukewarm. After you add some cold, you can test it by sticking your elbow in."

"My elbow, huh?" He rolled up his sleeves, figuring he'd have to do it anyway when bath time came, added some cold water and dunked his elbow in. It was amazing how it registered the temperature of the water better than his hand. Still too hot. He added cold water a little at a time until he had it the way he imagined it should be.

"How about soap?" he asked.

"I have some liquid soap in the diaper bag. And you'd better have a couple of towels ready, too. And transfer the changing pad to the counter."

"Got a rubber ducky?"

Katherine laughed. "She's not quite at that stage."

Zeke flashed back to a time at the ranch he'd forgotten about, when he'd been put in charge of giving the smallest boys their baths. He'd loved the job and had gone so far as to whittle the kids toy boats they could play with. With a start he wondered if that long-forgotten experience had been the reason he'd bought the big tub for his bathroom.

Someday Amanda would be big enough to sail toy boats in her bathwater. And he had just the tub for that kind of fun, as it turned out. But he wouldn't be making boats for her or letting her play in the big claw-foot tub.

"I think we're set."

"This time I'd better abandon the sling so I can use both hands. You don't want to deal with a slippery baby one-handed."

"Keep the sling on." Without preamble Zeke lifted Amanda into his arms. "Let me do this. You can coach from the sidelines."

THIS WAS WHAT SHE wanted, after all, Katherine thought, although it felt strange having someone else give Amanda her bath. Zeke was definitely a fast learner, though. In short order he had Amanda's sleeper off and was working on her diaper.

He glanced over at Katherine. "So far, so good."

Amanda cooed and waved her arms.

"She knows what's coming," Katherine said. "She likes baths."

"Yeah, but she's never had one given by fumble fingers."

"Don't be silly. You're not clumsy." Quite the opposite, if she remembered correctly. *Adept* came to mind.

"I do a little better with bigger girls."

Katherine wondered if she'd just have to get used to being constantly needy until she finally left Zeke for good. She leaned against the counter. "We can't seem to avoid that subject, can we?"

"Pretty tough to avoid it when we're stuck together like this. And it's not as if we've never made love, so that barrier's been crossed."

"And we have the evidence to prove it." She saw that he was about to get the diaper off by lifting Amanda's legs one at a time again. When he'd changed her diaper before, she wouldn't have dared correct him and risk shaking his confidence, but now she felt he was less likely to give up the project if she made a gentle suggestion. "Try holding both ankles and lifting. That way you can slip the diaper out in one motion."

Zeke followed her direction. "I'll be damned—uh, doggoned. Big improvement." He gazed down at Amanda. "Smart mommy you have there, Mandy."

Too bad she enjoyed his compliments so much. She took the folded diaper he handed her. "If I'd been a little smarter, we wouldn't be here."

"You mean because you wouldn't have tried hiking Yellowstone by yourself?"

"Right." She walked over to the trash, deposited the diaper and came back to the sink. "Or I would have understood the intricacies of my birth-control pills and known we didn't dare make love that night."

Zeke put a restraining hand on the baby as he glanced at Katherine. "Oh, I think we would have made love."

"And knowingly run the risk of pregnancy? I don't think so."

"There are lots of ways to make love." His dark eyes were warm. "And we're both pretty smart, as a matter of fact. I'm sure we would have figured out something."

Her mouth grew moist and her body tightened. "Okay. Maybe you're right. But if we're both so smart, why can't we figure out a solution to this mess we're in now?"

"Oh, I think you have. You just have to be strong enough to carry it through." He regarded her quietly for a moment. "And now you'd better tell me how to do this so I don't drown our baby."

Her heart wrenched. He'd never used the term *our* before. "Well, you, uh—" A wave of emotion caught her by surprise and she had to clear her throat. "You hold her head and neck with your left hand, and—no, wait. I keep forgetting you're backwards."

"Watch your language. This little girl might be left-handed, too."

"Oops. Sorry. Let's say you're opposite from the way I am."

"That's better. So I should hold her head and neck in my right hand."

"Yes, and her bottom in your left." She hoped Amanda would be left-handed, as well as have Zeke's bravery and compassion, although she wasn't sure how much of that could be inherited and how much needed to be taught.

"Got her." He sounded nervous. "But she's getting squirmy."

"This is where your big hands help. Lower her into the water slowly and let her get used to it. Then slide your left hand out and use the washcloth on whatever you can reach. Don't worry about every nook and cranny."

"And there sure are a lot of those." Zeke eased her into the water.

"Oh, and I warn you she likes to splash. She'll be slippery when she's wet, so keep a firm grip on her."

"Okay, wiggly girl. Time to get clean." Zeke picked up the washcloth and Amanda started kicking. "Hey!" Amanda kicked harder, splashing water on Zeke's shirt. "Splashing is one thing. This kid's a motorboat."

"I probably should have told you to take off your shirt." Except Katherine didn't really want a shirtless Zeke walking around the cabin. She reached over and took hold of Amanda's flailing legs with her left hand. "Easy, baby."

Amanda stopped kicking and slapped both hands into the water, spraying Zeke's shirt again as she crowed loudly.

Katherine gave Zeke a look of apology. "She loves this, as you can tell. I usually put on my terry bathrobe when I give her a bath, so it doesn't matter."

"It doesn't matter, anyway." Zeke started washing Amanda as he grinned down at her. "Having a good time, aren't we?"

She grinned back and plopped her hands into the water again.

Zeke chuckled as he continued his gentle movements with the washcloth. "Gonna be a swimmer when you grow up, Mandy? Win a few medals?"

"Maybe she will." Katherine stood close to Zeke and basked in this moment of togetherness. "Swimming was my sport in high school."

"I didn't go out for a team until I was in college, but it helped put me through."

"You were in swimming, too?" He certainly had the physique for it, she thought. Massive chest and long, lithe legs.

"Yeah, I was. Small world, isn't it? So, do we do her hair and face?"

"I'll rinse another washcloth out in the bathroom sink for her face, so we don't get soap in her eyes. Be right back."

"Okay." Zeke sounded unconcerned, totally unlike the last time she'd left him alone with Amanda.

In the bathroom she found a clean washcloth, dampened it and wrung it out. The cloth would be cold, but better that than a soapy one. She'd started back into the main room of the cabin when instinct made her pause.

Without her there, Zeke had entered into a private world with Amanda. Katherine knew the feeling well—the coziness of a charmed circle that included only parent and baby. Zeke leaned over the sink, his shirt soaked as he cradled Amanda in his brawny arms and smiled down at her. He dwarfed the tiny baby, which only made the picture more poignant.

"Want a ride now?" he asked.

Amanda gurgled.

"Okay. A ride it is." He swirled Amanda gently in the water. "Whee," he said softly. "See, Mandy? Fun, huh? Now we'll go the other way. Whee. Don't worry. Daddy's got you."

Daddy. Katherine's chest tightened. Damn. In another second she'd start crying. She turned and went back into the bathroom and held the cold cloth against her eyes. Her dearest wish was coming true, and Zeke was building a relationship with his daughter. Katherine vowed then and there not to let her physical attraction to Zeke jeopardize that bond.

"Hey, Katherine! What's taking you so long? This kid's starting to wrinkle!"

Caught halfway between laughter and tears, Katherine turned on the faucet to disguise the tremble in her voice. "Be right there! Couldn't find the washcloth!" Taking a deep breath, she rinsed out the cloth again and left the bathroom.

ZEKE HELPED KATHERINE tuck a sweet-smelling Amanda into the copper kettle bassinet. He'd placed it next to the bed so that Katherine would have the baby handy during the night. While they stood together gazing down at her in her fluffy nest, she fought sleep and stared back at them.

Zeke thought how normal it would be to put his arm around Katherine at a time like this, but he didn't do it. He could talk to her, though. That was still allowed. "I never thought about it before, but baby animals are all sort of the same."

"How do you mean?"

"You have to think of how they see things. They're so small, and you're so big, that you have to be real careful that you don't scare them, or they'll never trust you."

Katherine glanced over at him. "That's true, at least for Amanda. I don't know much about animal babies."

"They're a lot the same. I thought taking care of Amanda would be more complicated, but she seems to be getting used to me."

"She's definitely used to you. Look, she's trying to stay awake, but her little eyes keep closing."

He enjoyed the low melody of Katherine's voice as she talked about the baby. He could stand here for a long time listening to Katherine and watching Amanda sleep. "She's been having too much fun. She doesn't want it to end."

"You could be right. Sometimes she fusses before she drops off at night, but maybe she likes the quiet of the woods."

"Maybe." He had an inspiration. "Since she's going off to sleep so easily, would you like to sit out on the porch for a little while? We can open one of the porch windows a bit so we'll hear her." He motioned to a couple of hooks by the door. "And I have an extra jacket you can wear if you think you'll get cold." During her moment of hesitation, he realized she might be wondering what he had planned for her on that porch. "We'll just talk, Katherine. I promise. Or sit and enjoy the crickets. It's peaceful out there."

The slight frown cleared from her brow. "Okay. That would be nice."

"Great." He crossed to the sink and grabbed a used dish towel. "Take your pick of those jackets. I'll wipe down the chairs." He felt like whistling as he went out on the porch and whisked the moisture off the Adirondacks.

She came out wearing his black nylon jacket. "Which chair?"

"Either one. Maybe you'd like the one closer to the door, in case Amanda wakes up."

"Good idea." She sat down, wincing when she knocked her sprained wrist against the broad arm of the chair. Then she leaned back with a sigh. "Great chairs."

"Thanks." He sat down beside her, and the feeling of sharing was all he'd hoped it would be. The damp, pungent scent of a rain-drenched forest settled around them and a cricket chirped nearby. "I figured a porch needed chairs."

"Definitely. And these are perfect. They make me think of the beach. When my parents were alive we spent a couple of weeks on Long Island Sound one summer. The beach cottages had chairs like this."

"I've never been to a beach like that. Never seen the ocean, for that matter."

"Never?" She turned her head to gaze at him. "Oh, Zeke, you would love it. The waves, and the ebb and flow of the tides, and walking barefoot along a deserted beach looking for seashells. It's your type of thing."

It might be, he thought, if he could share it with her. He pictured a dark-haired little girl squatting beside the surf, a pail and shovel in her hand. Amanda would love the ocean.

"Then again, maybe you wouldn't like it." Katherine faced forward again and her voice was more subdued. "I shouldn't make those assumptions after knowing you such a short time."

"You know me better than you think you do."

"I do?"

"Maybe even better than I know myself." He took a deep breath. Once he said this, there would be no turning back. "I'm willing to consider having Amanda come and visit me once in a while, Katherine."

She turned her head quickly toward him. "Really?"

"The idea still scares the devil out of me. Maybe I've learned how to change a diaper and give her a bath, but that doesn't mean I'll know what to do when she's two, or four, or fourteen. But I'm willing to try."

"Oh, Zeke." Her voice was husky. "That means so much to me. And it will mean the world to Amanda."

"I hope you're right." His declaration was almost worth it just to see the warmth and eagerness in her expression. "I still think there could come a time when she'd rather spend her vacation with her friends back in New York instead of out in the boonies with me."

"I doubt it." Katherine swept an arm around the clearing. "Look at all you have here. Only an idiot wouldn't feel lucky to be allowed to spend time with you here."

He thought of pointing out that she was itching to hightail it out of this paradise he'd brought her to, but he didn't.

She leaned back and gazed out through the trees where the clouds were giving way to a star-speckled night sky. "Listen to the wind in the pines. And the crickets, and the drip, drip, drip of rainwater from the eaves. The combination is hypnotic."

"I guess it is." He wasn't sure he'd have said that. The night was relaxing him, but he was far from hypnotized. The more he relaxed, the more he wanted to take her to bed.

"And the air smells so...so fertile."

"Mmm." He supposed she was only speaking poetically. After all, she was a magazine editor, and she had to come up with descriptions of fashion stuff all the time. She probably hadn't meant to use a word that made him think about sex. More specifically, sex with her. She had been fertile a year ago. No doubt she was again.

"Amanda will love coming here," Katherine said.

"But she'll be the only kid. That could be lonely."

"Maybe sometimes she will be. I was, too. But that can't be helped, can it?"

God, he must be insane. What he really wanted, now that he'd committed to this fatherhood thing, was to give Amanda a baby brother or sister. And this time he could be in touch with Katherine throughout the pregnancy, and he'd be there to watch the baby being born. After all, what difference would it make whether they set up this whole scheme for one kid or two? And to make love to her again, knowing that he was trying to get her pregnant—he grew hard just thinking about it.

Of course it was an impossible dream. He cleared his throat. "No, I guess it can't be helped."

She was silent for some time after that.

He sat and tried to become as hypnotized as she apparently was by the rhythm of the wind, the chirp of the crickets and the steady drip of the water. Instead the wind reminded him of Katherine's sigh of satisfaction, and the crickets sounded like the squeak of bedsprings. The dripping water beat in the same steady tempo that gave Katherine so much pleasure when he was deep—

"Do you think...you'll get married some day?"

No, not now. "Hard to say. If I did, the woman would have to like this isolated life-style. So far every woman I've been serious about has finally admitted she'd go crazy living the way I live, and we've broken off the relationship, so I may be out of luck. Why?"

"Your comment about Amanda being an only child. I started thinking about it and realized that you might get married and have other children, so she'd have half brothers and sisters."

"Would you like that?" He wanted her to say that she'd

hate it, that she never wanted another woman to lie with him the way she had.

"Well, I—suppose then Amanda wouldn't be by herself when she visited you."

He turned his head to look at her. "That isn't what I asked. Would *you* like me to get married and have other children?"

"I don't see what that has to do with anything. What difference does it make whether I would like it? If it would be good for you, and good for Amanda, then I—"

"Damn it, Katherine, stop being so civilized and reasonable. All right, I'll go first. You could do the same thing— find a New York stockbroker and have a slew of kids with the guy."

"Oh, I don't think—"

"Why not? You said the magazine office is set up for kids."

"Well, maybe, but men aren't beating down my door with marriage proposals. I'm not what you'd call a sexy woman."

He laughed.

"I'm not! Most men think I'm too tall, or too smart, or too skinny."

"Skinny? I don't think so!"

"It's true. I've been a skinny girl all my life, and I haven't even had much in the way of breasts until Amanda was born."

He gazed at her, remembering the pleasure she'd given him in the confines of his little tent last summer. Maybe her breasts were fuller now, but they'd fit his hands perfectly then, too. "You have beautiful breasts," he said. "I thought so before, and I still do." Even in the dim light from the stars he could see that her eyes darkened in response.

"So don't tell me you won't have any guys hanging around hoping you'll consider marrying them," he continued. He figured it was even more likely now, after the baby.

Pregnancy and childbirth had added to Katherine's womanliness in potent, yet undefinable, ways.

"Okay, maybe somebody might show up," she said. "And I suppose if I met someone and we decided to marry, I'd have to consider whether it would be good for Amanda to have a brother or sister. But we're talking a long time from now, Zeke."

He leaned toward her. "You know how long I'd like it to be? Amanda's welfare aside?"

"No. I'm not sure I understand your point."

His blood was heating up, and he couldn't seem to help it. "I'd like it to be never, Katherine. I don't want another man to touch you the way I have, to make you pregnant, to stand beside you gazing down at the little child you've created together."

She stared at him, her eyes wide, her lips parted.

He pushed on. "The only way I'd want Amanda to have a brother or sister would be if I made you pregnant again. That's selfish and unreasonable and exactly the way I feel."

Her breath came quick and shallow as she gazed at him. "I don't know how you do it," she murmured.

"Do what?"

"Make me want you more than I've ever wanted anyone. You don't even have to touch me. All you have to do is say something like that, and I'm on fire."

A shudder passed through him. He could take her inside now, and she would go. "But you don't want to be aroused, do you?"

She shook her head.

"Then I—"

A long, melancholy howl rose on the night air. He paused to listen.

Katherine's breath caught. "A wolf," she said, almost reverently.

"Yes." The howl came again. Then others in the pack joined in, creating a primitive chorus that gave him chills of pleasure every time. A pack had migrated down from Yellowstone, and although some people in the area weren't happy about it, Zeke was thrilled.

She rose from her chair and walked over to the porch steps, as if lured by the sound. "Naomi gave me the bachelor auction brochure to read. You helped bring wolves back to this area, didn't you?"

"Yes."

"That's something to be proud of."

"They don't scare you?"

She shook her head. "Bears are the only animals that really frighten me, and I'm sure that's from that horrible story I heard when I was a kid." She grasped the smooth post beside her and leaned against it as the wolves sent up another series of plaintive cries. Then she took a deep breath. "Magnificent."

Something shifted in the region of Zeke's heart. He hadn't meant to bring her to his sanctuary, yet it seemed at this moment as if she'd been destined to come. He knew she wouldn't stay, couldn't stay, but it seemed right that she was here now, sharing the magic of crickets and raindrops and a wolf serenade.

"Zeke, look!" She pointed to the night sky.

He pushed out of his chair and moved over beside her as a falling star streaked downward and disappeared into the trees, followed by another, and another.

She lifted her face in wonder. "It's a meteor shower, isn't it?"

Zeke gazed at her, more mesmerized by the expression on her face than the sparks of light blazing trails toward the horizon. "You've never seen one?"

"No, but I always wished I could. Oh, Zeke. This is beautiful. It seems as if it stopped raining just so we could see this."

"Yep, it does." He ached from wanting to hold her, but he kept his hands at his sides and allowed her to enjoy the show. From now on, meteor showers would be linked in his memory to the rapture on her face as she stared up into the night sky. Last summer she'd appeared like a meteor in his life, a flash of almost painful beauty that quickly disappeared. He'd worked for months to try to forget her. Now she was back, burning brighter than before.

And he would never, ever forget.

CHAPTER TEN

THE MAJORITY OF THE NIGHT threatened to ensnare Katherine, but she resisted surrendering completely. Standing here with Zeke as stars fell from the sky and wolves called to their mates wove a dangerous spell. The soft hoot of an owl echoed deep in the forest, and she recognized her susceptibility to that sound. It triggered a memory of nights spent in the Adirondacks with her parents, summer nights when she'd felt connected to the natural world and had dreamed of becoming a wilderness guide.

But she hadn't chosen that career path, and now her beloved Naomi was counting on her. She must not allow herself to fall in love tonight—not with the wilderness and not with the man. Although he stood quietly beside her, there was nothing calm about him. Heat and the pulse of unfulfilled needs bridged the space between their bodies. If she lingered, he would close that space.

A gust of wind swept across the porch as clouds began to edge out the cascading lights. Katherine smelled the pungent odor of rain on the breeze. It was her cue to break the spell.

"This has been fantastic." She forced weariness into her voice, although she was taut with the same emotions that ruled Zeke. She avoided looking at him. One glance into his dark eyes could be her undoing. "But I think I'll turn in. It's been a long day."

He cleared his throat. "Yeah."

A haunting note in his response tore at her resolve. But

for the sake of everyone—Zeke, Naomi, Amanda and herself—she had to be strong. "Mind if I get ready first?"

"That's fine."

She sneaked a peek at him. He was gazing out into the clearing, his jaw rigid. "I'll be fast," she said.

"Take your time."

He had amazing control, she thought as she left him standing on the porch. Most men would have pressed the issue on a romantic night like this one.

Once inside, she walked over to gaze down at her sleeping baby. Amanda looked snug as could be in her copper kettle. The fire had burned down to flickering embers, and Zeke had turned both kerosene lanterns low. With the cozy glow from the fire warming the room and sturdy log walls surrounding her, Katherine longed to snuggle into the shelter of Zeke's arms for the rest of the night. But if she gave in to that urge, she might not find the courage to leave.

She took off Zeke's nylon jacket that carried his woodsy scent, and hung it on the hook by the door. Then she crossed the room and turned back the covers on the bed. Zeke had probably made the bed frame, peeling the logs for the head and footboard the same way he had peeled and finished the logs for the cabin walls. It was a sturdy bed, just right for...sleeping.

Because she had no night wear, she decided to take off the socks and sweats and sleep in her panties and Zeke's flannel shirt. She also removed the sling from around her arm. But once she crawled under the covers, she discovered that Zeke's scent clung to the sheets, too. She should have been prepared for that, but she wasn't. There was no escape from the sensuous pull of this man whom she longed for and couldn't have.

The scent of him aroused her, but it held some comfort, too. As she drifted off to sleep she thought how strange it was that Zeke could make her feel so safe, yet so completely unsettle her at the same time.

THE FIRE WAS OUT and the air chilly in the cabin when Katherine awoke. At first she thought Amanda had caused her to come suddenly wide-awake, but when she leaned over the side of the bed to peer at the baby, she was still fast asleep.

Then she heard a moan. Sitting straight up in bed, heart pounding, she searched the dim cabin for the source of the sound. Zeke lay on the large rag rug near the fireplace, with a blanket over him. She could see no one—or nothing—else.

Then the moan came again, and she realized it was Zeke.

"No, no," he cried out softly, twisting his body under the blanket. "No, don't make me."

The desperate plea in his voice broke her heart. She couldn't imagine Zeke ever begging that way, and when awake he never would. But in the grip of a nightmare, all his pride was stripped away. As he moaned again, she wondered if she should wake him. She could end the nightmare, but then he'd know she'd seen him at his most vulnerable. For a man like Zeke, that could be worse than any nightmare.

"Please, oh, please." His voice was choked. "Oh, please. No. No-o-o-o."

Katherine couldn't stand it. Let him hate her for knowing too much, but she couldn't bear to let him suffer like this. Slipping out of bed, she picked her way around Amanda's bassinet and over to the fireplace where Zeke lay on his side with his back to her.

He cried out softly and muttered something that sounded like, "I'll be good. Don't, please."

Kneeling on the rug beside him, Katherine breathed in the charred scent of fireplace ashes as she put her hand on his shoulder. Such a powerful shoulder. Such a frightened man. She shook him gently. "Zeke, wake up. You're dreaming."

He jerked instantly awake and rolled to his back, nearly knocking her over. "What? What is it?"

She steadied herself by putting her right hand on his chest and noticed her sprained wrist didn't hurt quite as much now. She also noticed that she was touching bare skin, and wondered whether he'd left on any of his clothes. "You were having a nightmare."

"Oh." He put his hand over hers and exhaled slowly. "Yeah."

"I...are you okay?"

"Yeah." He gave her hand a slight squeeze. "Thanks."

His pitiful cries still echoed in her head. She couldn't make herself get up and leave him to fall asleep alone and maybe return to the same nightmare. Acting on instinct, she eased down next to him on the rug and pillowed her head on her arm. His warmth radiated out to her, taking some of the chill from the air.

For a while they lay there quietly. She could tell he was sorting his way through the nightmare as his heartbeat thudded steadily against the light pressure of her hand on his chest. If he went back to sleep, she'd slip away and return to bed. But right now, she believed he needed someone with him.

"I guess she was doing what she thought was best for both of us," he said at last as he began to gently stroke her hand.

Katherine waited, hardly daring to breathe for fear he'd stop talking if she became too intrusive. She had the feeling he might never have revealed his nightmare to anyone before.

"I thought it was because I'd been bad, and she was punishing me. But I guess she just couldn't take care of me anymore."

Katherine was sure he must be talking about his mother, but she didn't want to ask and ruin the moment.

"That gate looked huge, like it led to a giant's house, a

giant who would eat little boys. She told me to get out of the car. When I wouldn't, she yelled at me and dragged me out.''

Tears gathered in Katherine's eyes, but she remained silent.

''She told me to go through that gate and down the road, that someone would take care of me there.'' His voice dropped to a rough whisper. ''I thought they'd put me in a cage, fatten me up and have me for dinner. But I went. I had nowhere else to go.''

Katherine pictured a small, scared boy walking valiantly down a dusty road to his doom. She choked back a sob.

Zeke kept hold of her hand as he rolled to face her. He touched her damp cheek. ''I...I'm sorry. I shouldn't have—''

''Yes.'' She cleared her throat. She couldn't see his face very well in the shadows, but maybe that was best. The darkness might make him feel less exposed. ''Yes, you should have.''

''Katherine...I just...please let me hold you for a minute. I'm not going to...''

Silently she eased closer, wrapping her arms around him as he wrapped his around her. It was an embrace of comfort, not passion.

Zeke laid his cheek against the top of her head. ''I wish I could stop the dreams.''

''Maybe you can. Maybe telling me about it will help.''

His voice was low, subdued. ''The thing is, it came out okay. She was right. There was somebody there to take care of me, somebody who did a better job than she'd been doing. And it happened a long time ago. I should be able to forget about it.''

''You'll probably never forget about it, Zeke. Being left by your mother when you're small is the scariest thing to a kid.''

He took a long, shuddering breath. ''It was pretty scary.''

"When my parents died on the New Jersey Turnpike, I was eighteen, a nearly grown woman who should have been able to cope. But I was furious at them for months, thinking they never should have taken that trip, that it was somehow their fault that they'd died and abandoned me." She paused, realizing that it wasn't so easy for her to admit to weaknesses, either. "I have nightmares, too, sometimes."

Zeke rubbed her back lightly. "Eighteen is still pretty young."

His touch set off sensuous ripples within her, but she managed to keep her feelings pleasantly cozy, not overheated with desire. Now wasn't the time for that. "But I wasn't as young as you were. Do you know if your mother...if she's—"

His hand stilled. "Lost Springs was notified that she died a year after she dropped me off there. But sometimes I dream that she's come back, and I tell her about my job as a park ranger."

"I know." Katherine felt the tug of an old grief. "Sometimes I dream that my parents are alive, that it was all a mistake about the wreck. And they're so proud of me for becoming an editor at *Cachet*."

"Maybe they know."

"Maybe." Her throat tightened. "The hardest part has been this past year, when I was carrying their grandchild. And now she's here, and so beautiful. I want them to see her."

"I'll bet you do." His voice was rich with understanding.

"But having her helps, in a way. Because it proves to me that life goes on. My parents live on in Amanda."

He lay quietly for a moment. "I hadn't thought of it like that."

"You said your mother had a dimple in her chin like Amanda's."

There was another long silence. "She told me it was because I kept putting my finger there," he said finally. "She said if I ever stopped, she'd lose her dimple, so every chance I got I pressed on her chin."

Katherine smiled in the darkness. "That's cute."

"I'd forgotten about that until this minute."

"You see?" She snuggled against him, which felt good. Very good. She felt her resolve slipping. But Zeke would maintain control. He always did. "Nice memories might help balance the bad ones," she said.

"They might."

"I want you to have all sorts of nice memories with Amanda."

He didn't respond.

"You haven't changed your mind about having her visit, have you?"

The silence lengthened. "She might not want to be around me that much," he said finally. "I'm not a real lovable type."

Wrong. "Who says?"

"Well, think about it. If I'd been easier to live with, my mother would have tried harder to keep me."

"Oh, Zeke." Her heart ached at his implication that he didn't deserve to be loved. Instinctively she moved closer. "Your mother didn't leave because you had problems. She left because she did. Take it from me. You're very lovable. Amanda will adore coming to visit you."

"Mmm."

"You don't believe me. But I guarantee that time spent with you in this special place will be the highlight of her year."

"If you say so." His answer sounded neutral, as if he didn't much care one way or the other.

"Okay, now what's wrong? Did I say something to upset you?"

"No."

"I must have. Look, if I've said something insensitive, I'm sorry. I didn't mean to. I'm only trying—"

"It's not what you said." He carefully took her arm from around his waist.

"Then what's going on?"

"This." He took her hand and placed it against the cotton of his briefs, which bulged with his very hard erection. Then he laced his fingers through hers and drew her hand back up between them. His voice was strained. "I wanted to stay here snuggled together the rest of the night. I thought if I concentrated on something boring like laundry, I could keep control. But I think you'd better go back to bed, Katherine."

She ignited instantly, suddenly aware that she wore very little and he wore even less.

"I mean it." He paused, his breathing unsteady. "Unless…you've changed your mind."

She realized that was as close as he'd ever come to asking her to help him banish his demons, at least for tonight. A woman would have to be made of stone to reject the plea in his voice, and she was definitely made of flesh and blood. Warm, eager flesh and heated blood.

Slowly she lifted her face to his. "Help me change it," she murmured. "Kiss me, Zeke."

With a groan he covered her mouth with his.

SHE OFFERED OBLIVION, and he took it. When he kissed her, nothing else mattered, and he needed mindless pleasure, needed it so much he was shaking. Maybe she wouldn't love him forever, but she'd love him tonight. For a few hours she'd fill the hollow place in his heart, ease the familiar, constant pain he felt there.

She tunneled her fingers through his hair and her open mouth cradled his, inviting him deep. He grew light-headed and crazy with desire as he sank into the remembered richness of her kiss. Cupping her head, he guided her to her back on the braided rug. The scent of smoldering embers became an aphrodisiac, stirring his pleasure centers with year-old memories of a dying campfire and a passion-drenched Katherine in his arms. The cabin floor was no softer than the canvas-covered ground where he'd taken her that first time. There was something elemental about making love on an unyielding surface that suited the way Zeke felt about Katherine.

She'd wanted him desperately then, yet her needs seemed even more urgent now. And each little cry, each whimper soothed his battered heart. Maybe her desire for him last summer had been more than gratitude, more than a reaction to her close call in the rapids.

He unfastened the buttons of her shirt with trembling fingers and reached beneath the flannel to cup her warm breast. Her nipple was moist.

Need slammed into him with a force that made him gasp against her mouth. Lifting his head, he gazed into her shadowed eyes as he lightly squeezed her breast.

"Please," she whispered, easing herself free of the flannel shirt.

Heart hammering, he leaned down and drew her nipple into his mouth. With just the slightest pressure, warm milk pooled on his tongue. The sensation drove him wild, yet he hesitated, unsure if he could have what he sought.

In answer, she held his head and arched into his caress.

The blood rushed in his ears as he took the bounty she offered. So sweet, yet so maddeningly erotic. His groin tightened painfully as he licked and sucked, drawing equally from her warm, plump breasts.

Her breathing quickened, and her throaty moan told him she was responding as feverishly as he. He slipped his hand beneath the soft silk of her panties. She was bathed in passion, hot and ready. He nearly ripped the garment from her so that he could sink into that tropical paradise, but a scrap of sanity remained. Not yet.

Instead he caressed her there, paying homage to the throbbing nub that held the power of her release. When she quivered against him, he knew she was balanced on the edge, needing only a nudge.

He gave her that nudge. She gasped his name as the tremors took her, and he treasured the sound of it on her lips. He hadn't been a nameless wilderness fantasy to her, or an inconvenient problem when she gave birth to Amanda. She wanted him. *Him.*

Joy surged through him as he kissed her cheeks, her eyes, her mouth. He ran his hand over her quivering body. "I want to see you."

"Oh, Zeke." Her eyes fluttered open. "Childbirth... changes a woman."

He cupped her breast. "I know." His voice was thick with need. "I like it. Let me light the lantern."

"But—"

He silenced her with a kiss. "Please." Without waiting for permission he untangled himself from her and stood. It wasn't easy to leave her side when he was heavy with unsatisfied desire, but this might be the last time he made love to her, and he wouldn't be denied any part of the experience.

Moving as quietly as possible so he wouldn't wake Amanda, he lit the lantern and took a foil-wrapped package from the bottom drawer of his dresser. No matter how much he might want to give Amanda a brother or sister, he couldn't ask Katherine to go through that.

He set the lantern on the hearth, and the glow illuminated the most beautiful woman he'd ever seen. All that covered her was the small triangle of her panties, and soon that would be gone. He slipped off his briefs and knelt down beside her. "Katherine, you're so—"

"Please don't look too close," she pleaded, spreading her fingers over her stomach. "I have stretch marks. And my tummy's not flat like it was last summer."

"Lucky you." He drew her hands away and leaned down to kiss the faint white lines. "A warrior should show off her battle scars, not hide them."

"You're being nice."

"No." His voice roughened, and he realized seeing the stretch marks had created a different sort of frustration. He stroked his hand over her stomach, trying to imagine that she'd once carried Amanda there. "I missed everything about this pregnancy. I missed watching your body change, missed feeling the baby move, missed the moment when you opened your thighs and gave birth to our child." He looked into her eyes. "Don't hide the stretch marks, Katherine. I need to see them."

Moisture sparkled in her eyes. "I'm sorry," she whispered. "I'm so sorry, Zeke."

"It's over now." Yet as he eased away the panties covering her blond curls, he throbbed with the urge to start again, to plant another seed in her womb and watch the baby grow. Instead he picked up the packet from the hearth and ripped it open.

She watched his motions. "Zeke...what you said on the porch...about having another..."

He shook his head. "I was talking crazy." He finished sheathing himself and moved over her. "Just let me love you, Katherine. It will be enough."

CHAPTER ELEVEN

KATHERINE DIDN'T THINK one night of loving Zeke would be nearly enough, considering it would have to last her a lifetime. How she ached for him.

He gazed into her eyes. "It's only been two months. I don't want to hurt you."

She wanted him so much she could barely breathe, let alone talk. "I don't…think you will. But if you don't come to me soon, I might die."

"Me, too." He clenched his jaw. "But I'm going slow, just in case."

As he slid partway inside, the pleasure of having his solid length fill her again was so intense she shuddered with joy.

Immediately he stopped, his breathing ragged. "Are you—"

"In heaven? Almost." She cupped his face in both hands. "Give me all of you, Zeke."

With a groan he sank deep.

"Yes," she whispered as unexpected tears filled her eyes.

"I'm hurting you." He started to withdraw.

She wrapped her uninjured arm around his back and her legs around his hips, holding him tight inside her. Her voice was choked. "Don't you dare."

"But you're crying."

"Because it feels so good. I don't remember it feeling this good, Zeke."

He looked into her eyes for a long moment. Slowly he shook his head. "I don't, either."

"What's happened?"

He didn't answer, just gazed at her with those knowing eyes. "Loosen up," he murmured.

She relaxed her hold on him and he began to move. Oh, how he began to move. He spoke her body's language fluently—stroking, shifting, pausing, speeding up, slowing down. He seemed to take his cues from her, yet she spoke not a word.

And all the while he watched her face, her eyes, until gradually he'd tuned himself so perfectly to her that she lost any sense of separateness. His breath became her breath, his sweat her sweat, his body her body. And always he coaxed them upward, building the momentum, tightening the tension.

She'd never shared herself with another as she was sharing herself now. When the moment came, raining wonder all around them, her cry of completion mingled with his, and tears spilled down her cheeks at the unearthly beauty of what they had created together. And she knew what he was trying, without words, to tell her. Joy and sorrow mingled in her heart as she realized that something had happened, and they might never have the courage to face it. They'd fallen in love.

DAZED BY THE POWER of the moment, Zeke wondered if he'd ever find the strength to leave the magical shelter of Katherine's arms.

Then Amanda started to cry.

Beneath him, Katherine stirred. "I—"

"I know. She's hungry." He kissed the soft skin behind Katherine's ear before reluctantly easing away from her. "Go get back in bed. I'll change her and bring her to you. Then I'll build up the fire."

She sat up and reached for her panties.

"Don't," he murmured.

She glanced up at him and laid the panties aside.

"And leave the shirt off, too. I love to look at you."

Her eyes darkened and he wanted to make love to her again, this very minute, but Amanda needed attention. As Katherine stood, her breasts moving gently with the motion of her body, he wished he were a better artist so he could draw her. But paper and charcoal wouldn't capture her heat, or her delicious scent.

After a quick trip to the bathroom he picked up a squalling Amanda and cradled her against his chest. "Take it easy, Mandy. Your late-night snack is coming right up." He was impressed with how efficiently he managed to change her diaper, even when she continued to wiggle and cry. In no time he carried her to the shadowy bed, where Katherine had propped herself against the headboard with a pillow. God, he wanted to climb right in there with her. "Which side?"

"Let's start with the left this time."

"Good. Then I can help you when you nurse her on the other side." He laid the fussy baby carefully in the crook of her left arm.

"Thank you, Zeke."

"No problem."

Amanda nuzzled hungrily and Katherine helped her find the nipple.

Zeke stood there mesmerized by the sight of Amanda nursing. Now he knew the taste that little baby was experiencing. His mouth moistened. "I hope that I didn't...um, take more than I should have."

She smiled up at him. "No. I have plenty for her. But if you don't build up the fire pretty soon, I'll need some covers."

"Oh!" He'd been so entranced and so filled with heat watching her nurse the baby that he'd forgotten all about the fire. "Sorry." He hurried over to the hearth and soon had the blaze going again. Then he glanced at the blanket that had been tossed aside while they'd made love. Figuring he wouldn't need it now, he folded it and laid it on a chair. He might not sleep much, but he planned to spend the rest of the night in his own bed, starting now.

He brought the lantern over and set it on the bedside table before climbing into bed next to Katherine and Amanda.

She glanced over at him. "This feels a little like being at home with her."

He propped his head on his hand to get a better view of her. "You nurse her naked while a man watches you?"

She laughed. "Not hardly. I meant that I bring her to bed and nurse her there at night. But there's no man."

"Good." He was pretty sure there hadn't been anyone else in her life, but he liked hearing it all the same.

"And I wear a nightgown."

"Why?"

She glanced at him over the top of Amanda's head. "Because that's the kind of woman I am, I guess."

"I don't think so."

As she held his gaze, her eyes smoldered with passion. "You bring out a different side of me, that's for sure."

He needed to touch her, needed to feel her warmth, but while she was nursing Amanda, he'd use restraint. He slid his hand gently over her silken thigh. "Is it a different side, or the real Katherine?"

"I don't know." She sounded slightly out of breath. Then she looked down at his hand lying quietly on her thigh. "Zeke…"

"Don't worry. I won't do anything. But I need a connection." And this made a powerful one for him—his sun-browned hand resting against the creamy skin of her inner thigh.

"Oh."

"Does my hand there bother you too much?"

"It bothers me, but in a nice way."

He smiled at her. "Good." He hoped she felt the way he did, aroused but under control. He lay with his palm absorbing her warmth as he listened to the crackling fire and Amanda's little slurps and swallows. The baby patted her tiny hand against her mother's full breast. Remembering the pleasure to be found there made Zeke's mouth water and his groin throb. Control became a little tougher to come by.

When Katherine spoke again, her tone had become shy. "Nursing her has been a sensual thing for me. I've never admitted that to anyone."

"I'm the perfect person to tell."

"Yes." She stroked Amanda's cheek with her finger. "Wearing nightgowns and being proper is right for my apartment in New York, but I have to admit that being here like this...lying in bed with you while I feed her...seems even more right."

His chest tightened. "Dangerous talk."

"Don't be scared, Zeke. I'm not going to do anything stupid and wreck your life."

He chose his words carefully. He couldn't tell her that he wanted her to stay with him forever. He couldn't put that kind of burden on her. "I wasn't thinking about my life."

"Okay, I'm not going to do anything stupid and wreck all Naomi's plans for me at the magazine."

He lightly massaged her thigh, careful to keep his touch easy, both for her benefit and his. "We'll figure things out."

"I hope so. But I can't help thinking that the best thing for Amanda would be for her to have both of us, all the time."

The tightness in his chest moved up to his throat. He had to clear it before he could speak. "But that's not possible."

"No," she said softly.

Zeke knew there was nothing more to say. Tonight was all he'd have. Silently he watched Amanda nurse, and when Katherine started to switch her to the other breast, he helped arrange it along with a pillow to support the baby so Katherine's arm wouldn't have to take all the weight.

He longed to caress the moistened nipple Amanda had

just left, but he didn't dare. He was maintaining a precarious-enough hold on his control as it was. Lying here next to Katherine was torture, but a sweet kind of torture, and he wouldn't give up these moments for anything in the world.

He couldn't decide which was worse, his physical or mental frustration. But his physical frustration would be satisfied once Amanda went back to sleep. His mental frustration seemed doomed to continue for a long time, considering that Katherine couldn't run a New York magazine from the wilderness, and he couldn't be happy in a world of glass and steel.

SOMETIME DURING THE night, Katherine heard a crack of lightning nearby and waited for the rush of rain that would surely follow. When it didn't come, she snuggled against Zeke. Maybe the creek would go down enough for them to be rescued tomorrow. Not wanting to think about that, she reached for him and lost herself in the wonder of his touch yet again.

She awoke to a gray, misty light coming through the uncurtained window over the bed, and no sound of rain on the roof. Amanda and Zeke still slept. Moving quietly so as not to wake them, Katherine slid out of bed and put on her sweats, socks and shirt. Early morning had become her private time since Amanda's birth. The baby generally slept through the dawn hours, giving Katherine precious moments to herself, and she'd become greedy for them.

She turned to look at Zeke lying peacefully in bed. She could also use this time before Amanda woke up to make love to him one more time. But they hadn't slept much during the night, and if he had to get her and the baby back to civilization today, he needed his rest. She swallowed the lump in her throat. The moment of parting was inevitable, and when it came, she couldn't be a wimp.

The chirp of birds outside the window beckoned to her.

Tiptoeing to the door, she lifted the nylon jacket noiselessly from its hook before unlocking the door with slow, careful movements. She looked forward to a half hour on the porch all by herself to watch the sun come up and listen to the birds sing. Maybe it would help her come to grips with the decision she had to make.

Clean, cool air sifted into the room as she eased open the door, hoping the hinges didn't squeak. They didn't. She slipped outside, stepping onto the dew-covered porch floor. Her socks would get wet, but she didn't care. She started to close the door behind her as she gazed out into the clearing.

She stopped in mid motion and her hand tightened on the knob. The Adirondack chairs she and Zeke had sat in the night before were lying out in the yard. The arm was broken off one of them. She tried to make sense of what she was seeing.

Had there been a terrible wind in the night that had picked up the chairs and hurled them off the porch? Surely she wouldn't have slept through hurricane-force winds.

She glanced around. The birds still sang and the air smelled pure and sweet as sunlight slowly moved into the clearing, but the tranquillity she'd expected to find was gone. She stood on one leg and pulled off a sock, then repeated the process with the other leg. The boards were cold against her feet, but at least she wouldn't get the socks all muddy while she went out to retrieve the chairs.

Stuffing the socks in her jacket pocket, she started down the steps toward the first chair. Not wanting to cut her foot on a sharp rock, she watched the ground carefully. Then she gasped.

Imprinted perfectly in the mud at her feet was a giant paw print. Torn between horror and fascination, she studied the impression of a heavy pad and huge claws that had punctured awesome holes in the ground. Sadie.

ZEKE WOKE UP WITH a vague feeling that something was wrong. He sat up and looked over at the empty space where

Katherine had slept. Getting to his feet, he reached for his jeans as he surveyed the cabin in one quick glance. Katherine wasn't there, although Amanda was still asleep in her bassinet.

Damn, he'd wanted to be the first one out the door this morning, but it had been an eventful night and he'd overslept. He'd heard Sadie on the porch playing around with his chairs about four o'clock, but he'd decided not to risk alarming Katherine by trying to scare Sadie away.

Fastening his jeans, he walked over to the door and opened it in time to catch Katherine staring out toward the edges of the clearing, her whole posture reminding him of a deer scenting a predator. He was pretty certain Sadie was long gone, but sure enough, the chairs were tossed in the yard as he'd expected.

"Good morning," he said softly so as not to frighten Katherine.

She jumped anyway, whirling toward the door. "Do you see what she did?"

"Yep."

"Zeke, I have to get Amanda out of here. That bear could rip the door off its hinges if she decided to. Or break through the porch window."

"She could, but I doubt she'd decide to."

"Why not? What's the difference between that and what she did to your chairs?"

Leaving the door open so they could hear Amanda, he crossed the porch. "I've been wondering if she'd decide to come and play with those chairs." He walked down the steps and stood barefoot in the cool grass next to Katherine. "Now I know I have to bring them in at night."

Katherine gestured toward the upended chairs. "You call this *playing?*"

"Sure. If you're a bear."

She stared at him. "Then maybe if you're a bear it would

be even more fun to break into the cabin and maul the people inside."

"Too much work. Especially considering that it's the end of summer and she's had plenty to eat this year. If it had been a lean summer and she'd learned that cabins have food in them, then she might try that. But last night she was just being curious. I haven't had the chairs out there very long, so maybe this was the first time she's noticed them."

"You sound as if she's almost a pet!"

"No, not a pet. That's a dangerous fantasy some tourists have. I don't." He sighed. "Look, if it makes you feel any better, I have a gun in the cabin. I heard Sadie last night, and if she'd tried to get through the door or any of the windows, I would have used the gun."

Katherine's eyes widened. "A *gun?*"

"Yes. When you live out in the middle of nowhere like this, it's a good idea to have some form of protection. I keep it loaded and it's in the bottom drawer of the chest. In fact, if you want to learn how to use—"

"No!" She held up both hands and backed away from him. "I do not want to learn to use the gun. I don't even want to see the gun."

"Good Lord. It's just a tool, like any other tool."

"You can jolly well keep it to yourself, Zeke. What I want is to get my baby out of this place, where you need a gun to protect yourself from a prowling bear."

His patience was slipping fast. "Damn it, Katherine, I've never had to use that gun to protect myself from a bear in all the years I've lived and worked in this area. I never expect to have to use it, but you seemed so spooked I thought you'd want to know it's available."

"Well, I'm not comforted, okay?"

"Amanda's safer in that cabin than she is riding around in a cab in New York City, for God's sake!"

Katherine folded her arms. "Not with that bear around."

Suddenly he was tired of trying to convince her. "I'll go

see if the phone's working yet," he said. "If it is, then I'll hike to the creek and check that out."

"And what if the phone's not working and the creek's still full?"

He gazed at her in exasperation. "Maybe I'll figure out how to rebuild the bridge, and if that's not possible, I might decide to swim across with you and Amanda on my back."

"Now you're being ridiculous."

"This roller coaster ride we're on is getting to me, Katherine. Ridiculous or not, I'll find a way to get you back to the lodge. Something tells me it would be well worth the effort."

CHAPTER TWELVE

ZEKE FELT PERSONALLY affronted that Katherine didn't trust him to keep Sadie under control and Amanda safe. How could she think he'd let anything happen to that little baby? He stomped into the house and picked up the phone. If that was the way she felt, it was a good thing she wanted to spend her life in New York City.

The phone was still dead, so if he wanted to get Katherine and Amanda out of here, he'd have to figure out how to do it by himself. He pulled on his socks and boots and was reaching for his shirt when a soft cooing sound came from Amanda's makeshift bassinet.

He went over to investigate and found her wide-eyed and staring up at him. She waved her hands and crowed, clearly wanting to be picked up. He started to call for Katherine and paused. No, he could do this, at least up to a certain point.

"Mornin', sunshine." He crouched down and scooped the baby out of her nest. "Ready for another day?" As he cradled her in his arms, he smiled down at her, unable to resist that chubby face crowned by a shock of dark hair that proclaimed the Sioux blood flowing in her veins. She smiled back, and a warm glow surrounded his heart...until he realized his goal for the day was to get mother and baby back to the lodge. If he achieved his goal, he'd be giving up that smile.

He laid Amanda on the pad Katherine had left on the

table the last time she'd changed the baby. "Getting a little soggy in the britches, aren't you, kiddo?"

Amanda kicked her legs and started blowing bubbles at him.

This time he felt like a real pro as he unsnapped the pink sleeper and removed the wet diaper. The sleeper was also damp, so he decided to take everything off and start from scratch. Unfortunately when he looked in the diaper bag he found yesterday's sleeper, which Katherine had dried by the fire, but no diapers. As Katherine had predicted, they'd run out.

Again he started to call for Katherine but changed his mind. He'd started this project and he'd by damn finish it. "We have us a materials shortage, Mandy," he said. "But don't worry. When you've lived on a ranch full of boys like I have, you're used to running short now and again. We learned how to make do, which is how you and I will handle this temporary crisis. Right?"

Amanda crowed softly, almost as if she were having a conversation with him.

He pretended she understood everything he was saying as he cleaned her carefully with a towelette. "You know, my job as ranger makes a lot more sense now that I've met you. We always talk about saving the parks for future generations, but that was a hazy concept to me before. Now it's not."

Amanda smiled her toothless smile.

"Now I'm protecting the parks just for you." He leaned down and touched the tip of her nose with one finger. "Just for you, Amanda—" He started to add her middle name for emphasis and discovered he didn't even know what it was or if she even had one. Yeah, she probably had one. Katherine was too particular about details to leave that out, and she'd probably used Seymour for the baby's last name. Zeke hadn't admitted it to himself before, but that was another thing he resented—having no voice in choosing the baby's given name, let alone whose last name she'd carry. Fortunately he liked the name Amanda.

"Come on, sunshine." He could at least tag his own nickname on the baby, he decided, picking her up and settling her in the crook of his arm. "Let's go requisition you a diaper."

Her soft baby skin felt good against his bare chest as he walked over to a cupboard above the sink. He tucked her in a little closer, enjoying the sensation. With his free hand he opened the cupboard. "Let's see. We have a red and white stripe, a blue check and a yellow plaid." He glanced down at Amanda. "Which would you rather have? The yellow plaid? Good choice." He grabbed the dish towel out of the cupboard.

"Now we need something to hold this arrangement together. Let's go see what's in the junk drawer."

Amanda lay quietly in his arms, apparently enjoying the journey around the cabin as much as he was. He pulled out a drawer at the end of the counter and rummaged through it. "No safety pins, sunshine. Paper clips, but I don't think that's going to work. We have athletic tape in the first aid kit, but that won't hold a squirmy girl like you." He fished around in the back of the drawer. "But *this* will."

The baby gurgled happily.

Zeke grinned at her. "I knew you were the kind of gal who would appreciate the multitude of uses for duct tape. Now let's get you fixed up."

Back at the table he wasn't sure exactly how to fold the kitchen towel and he tried several versions before settling on one that seemed to cover the problem. Because he had to make sure he kept one hand on Amanda at all times, he ended up using his teeth to tear the duct tape. He was very careful to tape only the towel and not Amanda's delicate skin.

He gazed solemnly down at the baby. "Sunshine, I'm sorry to report to you that duct tape tastes like sh—uh, sheep dip. I guess. I've never tasted sheep dip, but I'm sure it's about as awful as this.''

She stared at him with such worried concentration that he chuckled. "But I won't make you taste it. I promise.''

Finally he had her snapped back into her dry sleeper. With a sense of great accomplishment, he picked her up and carried her outside, where Katherine was sitting on the porch in the unbroken chair.

Katherine glanced up, her eyes grave.

"I changed her," he said simply.

"Why, thank you, Zeke."

As he handed the freshly diapered baby down to her, he decided he'd never been as proud of an accomplishment in his life.

KATHERINE HAD HEARD AMANDA making her little morning noises and had started into the cabin when she noticed Zeke was already there, bending over the kettle. She'd backed quietly out of the door, retrieved the unbroken Adirondack chair from the yard and sat down on the porch to see what happened next.

She'd heard him talking to Amanda and wondered if he might be changing her. But there were no more diapers, and Katherine kept expecting Zeke to call her inside to figure out an alternative. Apparently he'd come up with one by himself.

Feeling a little out of the loop, she cuddled Amanda close. "How's my girl? Did you sleep well?" Damned if Amanda didn't look right past her and up at Zeke, as if the baby were fascinated with her new friend. Katherine acknowledged her jealousy with a touch of shame.

Zeke stood nearby, almost hovering. "Do you... need any help?"

She'd created some distance between them by fighting with him about Sadie. Maybe she'd make it easier on both of them if she maintained that distance. "Thanks, but I'm used to working around my bum arm now," she said.

"Then I guess I'll see about fixing the other chair."

"Okay."

He went into the cabin and emerged a short time later carrying a hammer and a handful of nails. As Katherine watched him walk down the steps and out to the overturned chair, she wished he'd thought to put on a shirt and spare her the sight of all that glorious muscle. But the sun that caressed his bronzed back so lovingly had started to warm the clearing and he probably didn't need a shirt.

Unbuttoning her own shirt, Katherine used the broad arm of the chair to take some of Amanda's weight off her injured arm. The baby sucked eagerly. Maybe it was only Katherine's imagination, but Amanda seemed more content and less prone to fussing ever since Zeke had started helping to care for her.

The hollow sound of a hammer blow drifted from the far side of the clearing. Katherine looked up and discovered Zeke had taken the repair project a distance away, probably so the hammering wouldn't disturb Amanda. Yet he was still close enough that she could see the flex of his back muscles and the bulge of his biceps as he drove another nail into the arm of the chair.

A pair of jays chattered in an aspen tree and a squirrel darted out on a pine branch near the porch. There was no end of other visual diversions for Katherine, but she couldn't seem to avoid the pull of Zeke's lithe movements. He embodied all the reasons a woman took up the art of man-watching.

She shouldn't watch him, though, she told herself. Torturing herself by admiring his body glistening in the sun was stupid, considering that she was determined to leave here today. Maybe she'd overreacted about the bear. In her heart she knew Zeke wouldn't let anything happen to Amanda. But Sadie could serve as a convenient wedge to pry Katherine and Zeke apart. Without something to fight about, they might find their inevitable separation impossible to tolerate.

Even with something to fight about, leaving would be the hardest thing she'd ever done, Katherine thought as she gazed across the clearing. God, the man sure knew how to drive a nail. She couldn't tear her attention away from Zeke until he finished the job and hooked the claw hammer in the belt loop of his jeans. Just as he picked up the chair and turned toward her, she lowered her head and concentrated on Amanda again. She hoped he hadn't caught her staring.

He brought the chair up on the porch and set it beside Katherine's. "Now that chair has some character." His manner seemed to dare her to refute that and make more disparaging remarks about the bear.

She decided to avoid the subject. "Did you check the phone?"

"Yeah." He unhooked the hammer from his belt loop and laid it on the arm of the chair before he sat down. "Still out."

Katherine tried to be discreet as she shifted Amanda to her other breast, but she had the impression Zeke noticed every little movement she made. If he was as fascinated by her as she was by him, then he would notice. "Do you really think you can fix the bridge?"

"Depends on how far down the creek is." Turning away from his quiet, but thorough, study of her as she nursed Amanda, he leaned back in the chair and focused his attention on the woods beyond the clearing. "I'll take a little hike down there after we have some breakfast and check things out."

"And leave us here?" She hadn't meant that to sound quite so panic-stricken. Except for the bear, she'd do fine here by herself. But Sadie had her a little spooked. "What I mean is, I'd like to go along. It's a beautiful day. Maybe I could help you."

"You don't have the shoes for it, Katherine."

"I could manage."

He propped his elbow on the chair and rested his chin on his hand as he gazed at her, his dark eyes growing warmer by the minute.

Conscious of that glow, she tugged her shirt to cover more of her exposed breast. "I really can manage. The shoes will be fine."

He shook his head. "If you're worried about Sadie, the chance that she'll come by in the hour or so I'm gone is practically nonexistent."

"You're probably right." She was feeling sillier by the minute. She was letting this darned bear turn her into a coward. "Never mind."

He continued to study her. "On the other hand, if that bear came by and scared you, I'd never forgive myself. Maybe your shoes will work."

She sent him a grateful look. "Thanks, Zeke."

He watched Amanda nurse for a while.

Katherine felt the heat of his gaze but didn't think she could very well ask him to turn away. After all, Amanda was his daughter, too, and after today he wouldn't be seeing her for some time. It was just that she'd never been so conscious of the little slurping and swallowing sounds Amanda made, or of how often the baby patted her hand against Katherine's breast, drawing Zeke's attention there.

"What's her middle name?" Zeke asked quietly.

"I didn't tell you?"

"No."

"I'm sorry. It's Lorraine. My mother's name."

"Amanda Lorraine. That's nice." He paused. "I suppose her last name is Seymour?"

Katherine caught a slight challenging note in the question. "Well, yes. I had to decide, for the birth certificate, and I wasn't sure if you wanted anything to do with—"

"I understand."

The way he cut off her explanation didn't sound particularly understanding. She remembered the little pine tree carving on his mantle that indicated a certain pride in his family name of Lonetree despite, or maybe even because of, his difficult childhood. She wondered if he was beginning to feel possessive toward Amanda. "Maybe you'd like to discuss hyphenating her last name," she said.

"Maybe." His glance strayed from her for the first time in several minutes as his attention shifted to a point over her right shoulder. "Stay still."

Her pulse jumped. Oh, God. The bear. "What?" she croaked.

"Two deer, a doe and a buck. They're only about thirty yards away. You'll need to turn to see them."

She let out a long sigh. "I thought it was Sadie."

"She only comes in the late afternoon and evening. I've never seen her around here in the morning, and most animals are creatures of habit. Now just turn slowly to your right and you'll be able to see them on the edge of the aspen grove."

Katherine loved deer, with their liquid brown eyes and graceful carriage. Amanda had begun to drift off to sleep but she continued to nurse sporadically, so Katherine kept her tucked against her as she eased around.

Sure enough, the deer grazed only a short distance beyond Zeke's truck. The buck had a fine set of antlers. He raised his head, looked around regally, then stared straight at Katherine before lowering his head to graze again.

"They're beautiful, Zeke. They look tame enough to pet."

"Fortunately, they're not. That would be dangerous for them."

As if to prove Zeke's point, the deer lifted their heads in response to a slight breeze blowing toward them from the direction of the cabin. In seconds they'd bounded off into the woods.

"I guess they caught our scent," Katherine said, gazing after them.

"Yep. They have to use all their senses to avoid predators, to find food...to mate."

The resonance in his voice triggered a response in Katherine. She turned her head to find his gaze focused on her like a laser. Her movements had dislodged the shirt somewhat, and Amanda picked that moment to doze off, releasing Katherine's nipple. Heart pounding, she pulled the shirt over her bare breast. "Whereas we've evolved past that need," she said.

"Have we?" His dark gaze grew intense. "Maybe I've been around these animals so long I'm growing to be like them. I find your scent...irresistible." He gazed at her a moment longer, then stood, looking out at the clearing. "Irresistible," he murmured, almost to himself.

His stance reminded Katherine of the buck that had recently left the clearing with his doe. When Zeke turned, a haunted expression on his face, she expected him to bolt, too, away from her.

Instead he paused in front of her chair. Slowly he leaned down, bracing both hands on the chair's wide arms, effectively imprisoning her there. "I know you have to leave." His dark eyes searched hers.

"Yes." She expected him to push away and leave her to her frustration while he dealt with his. His kiss caught her off guard.

She gasped in surprise. With a murmur of need he deepened the kiss, urging her to relax back into the chair, to accept the sweet pressure of his lips, the gentle thrust of his tongue. The bristle of his morning beard was rough against her skin, but she didn't care.

Dazed and aching, helpless to do anything but respond, she lifted her mouth, opening to his invasion. He kissed her greedily, tasting, nipping, delving again and again as his breathing grew ragged.

Finally, with a groan, he drew back, the muscles in his arms bulging as he gripped the chair arms and stared at her with eyes black as midnight. His voice was hoarse and his chest heaved. "If I don't get you out of here today..."

She was shaking. "I know."

He shoved himself away from the chair. "After breakfast."

ZEKE DIDN'T RECOGNIZE himself anymore. His famous control had disappeared. The minute Katherine walked into the cabin he wanted to put that sleepy baby in her bassinet and take her hot-blooded mother to bed. But once he did that, he could forget about getting her out of here today. And the sooner she left, the sooner he could start to heal.

So instead of seducing her, he got a small fire going and whipped up oatmeal in the cast-iron pot. In a separate pan he heated water so he could make coffee for himself and cocoa for Katherine. In the midst of all that, Katherine announced she needed to change Amanda's diaper.

"So soon?" he asked, turning from where he was stirring the oatmeal in the pot. There was another reason to get Katherine back to the lodge today. The dish towels wouldn't hold out much longer.

"I'm afraid she's ready again." She laid the baby on the changing pad and started unsnapping her sleeper. "Besides, I'm dying to find out how you—" She paused and began to laugh.

"What's so funny?" He realized he sounded a little defensive, but he couldn't help it. He was new at this, and besides, he'd run into a supply problem. "I thought it was a pretty good job."

"It's a wonderful job." She sounded as if she were trying to control herself, but her efforts weren't very successful. She kept bursting out with new giggles. "I just never would have thought of—" she tried to disguise another fit of laughter by clearing her throat elaborately "—of duct tape."

"I couldn't find any pins, and I didn't think paper clips would hold."

"Well, this duct tape holds like crazy. She may be welded into this yellow plaid diaper for life."

Zeke was quite certain he could manage his invention a whole lot better than Katherine was doing. "Here, you stir the oatmeal and I'll change her." He leaned the spoon against the side of the pot and crossed to the table. "And you'd better put the sling back on your arm, too."

"All right." Katherine's hazel eyes sparkled with merriment as he approached. "Maybe next time you might want to use a teensy bit less of that tape, though."

He looked into her eyes and forgot all about diapers. "How come you always look so damn kissable?" He realized he sounded downright cross, and maybe he was.

She matched his irritated tone. "It's not like I'm trying to be attractive, Zeke. I mean, look at me—no makeup and clothes six sizes too big, for heaven's sake." She moved aside but kept her hand on the baby's tummy until he put his next to hers. Then she stepped back.

He started working at the duct tape. Maybe he had been a little overzealous in his application of it. "You know, when I made love to you a year ago, you weren't trying to be attractive, either." He glanced over at her. "Maybe pure, unadulterated Katherine is what turns me on."

She rolled her eyes. "Men are forever saying things like that. Then some beauty queen strolls by and their tongues hang out."

He went back to his task, made more difficult because Amanda had decided to start kicking and waving her arms. "I can't speak for the guys you know in New York, but I go in for earthy, not flashy. When you stroll by in that flannel shirt, my tongue's dragging the ground."

She didn't answer right away. When she spoke, her voice was subdued. "You're forgetting that's not the real me. Ninety percent of the time I look nothing like this, even though it's pretty much all you've seen. After all, my job involves putting out a fashion magazine."

"Good point." Depressing point.

Her voice gentled even more. "But it's good for a girl's ego to have a man say he likes her just the way she is. Thank you for that."

"Don't mention it." He struggled with the tape. "You'd better put on your sling and then go stir the oatmeal. It's no fun when it starts sticking to the pan."

"Right."

Feeling in need of a mood elevator, he leaned down and kissed the baby on the nose. "Hey, sunshine. Looks like somebody thought you needed industrial-strength diapering this morning."

Amanda gurgled at him and patted his face.

"Don't worry. I'll get you out of this sooner or later." He wondered if he could talk Katherine into strapping duct tape over her sweats. The stuff would make a terrific chastity belt. Finally he got the diaper off and turned to Katherine, who was vigorously stirring the oatmeal. "Would you please get me another dish towel? They're on the top shelf of the left-hand cupboard."

She leaned the spoon against the lip of the kettle and went over to handle his request. She had to stand on tiptoe and strain to reach the towels, even though she was a fairly tall woman. If she lived here, Zeke thought, he'd move the cupboards down a foot. But of course she'd never live here, so they could stay where they were.

"You don't have a whole lot of these," Katherine said as she handed him the red-striped towel. "It won't matter if we can get back to the lodge today, but if we can't for some reason, then—"

He took the towel. "If I can't take you back today, we'll have bigger problems than a shortage of diapers." He glanced at her. ''The longer we stay in this cabin together, the tougher it'll be when you leave.''

''You don't have to tell me that. We'll make it out.''

Zeke gazed at her standing there, her cheeks flushed, her eyes bright as a mountain meadow. ''We'll see.''

CHAPTER THIRTEEN

TWO HOURS LATER, KATHERINE stood with Zeke on the banks of the turbulent creek. If anything it looked more impassable than it had the day before. Little of Zeke's bridge remained, so repairing it had only been a pipe dream.

Katherine glanced over at Zeke. He had insisted on carrying Amanda in the baby sling, arguing that he was more surefooted in his hiking boots than she was in her city shoes. He'd been right about that. She'd slipped twice but hadn't fallen down...yet.

"What do you think?" she asked, although his frown pretty much said it all.

"Let's follow the path downstream a ways. There's one wide spot where it's always more shallow. Before I built the bridge I used to take the truck across there."

"But the creek wasn't running this high, I'll bet."

"No." Zeke glanced up. Heavy clouds had begun to gather in the west. A hawk glided on the steady wind blowing the clouds in their direction.

"You think it's going to rain again, don't you?"

He nodded. "How are your feet holding up?"

"Fine," she lied. She'd crammed her shoes on over his heavy socks, which made them too tight, and she was afraid she'd rubbed more than one blister on each foot. But she'd been determined to come with him, both for the comfort his presence brought and for the chance to assess the situation firsthand. If he decided to bring the truck through, she wanted to have some idea of whether they'd get stuck in the process.

"Then let's go." He started down the trail winding beside the creek.

If she'd had hiking boots she would have thoroughly enjoyed herself, but her hiking boots were back at the hotel and her feet hurt. Still, she drew pleasure from the Christmas scent of the pines and the merry chatter of birds, squirrels and chipmunks. A red fox with a spectacular plume of a tail ran across their path, and three deer disappeared through the trees like tawny shadows.

She wished she could relax into the peaceful scene as she'd been able to do so often as a child in the Adirondacks. Instead she couldn't help worrying about how Zeke would get them back to the lodge today. In fact, she wondered when she'd ever get back to the lodge, and New York seemed a million miles away.

Naomi had booked her to return Monday so she'd be at her desk bright and early Tuesday morning to approve the next issue's layout and make assignments for the Milan show. Besides that, a feature on a new designer was due by— In her preoccupation she tripped over a tree root and barely missed falling.

Zeke turned quickly. "You okay?"

"Fine." She managed a smile.

"Your feet hurt."

"Not much."

"You're limping."

After making such a fuss about coming and insisting that her shoes were fine for the trip, Katherine wasn't about to admit to her problem. "Yes, because I just stubbed my toe on that tree root. Go on. I'm right behind you."

"We're almost there." He turned and continued along the muddy path.

Katherine took a deep breath and followed him. That's what she got for ignoring the beauty around her and worrying about some future problem. That was a lesson she'd thought she'd learned during her solo hike last summer, but apparently she needed more teaching. Good thing Zeke was carrying Amanda, who seemed totally happy with the arrangement, too.

"Here's the place," Zeke called out.

Katherine came up beside him and surveyed the rushing creek. "It doesn't look a lot better, to be honest. And how would you get the truck here?"

"There's a wider path that cuts through the trees. We can take that back to the cabin, now that we're here." He adjusted Amanda's weight against his chest as he gazed out over the creek. "The water's gone down some since early this morning. See where that debris is hanging from that low branch?"

Katherine looked where he was pointing. "Yes."

"That's where it was a few hours ago. If it doesn't rain again, it'll go down some more by this afternoon. We could probably make it."

"If it doesn't rain."

"It might not."

Katherine wouldn't have wanted to bet on it. Yet Zeke seemed to think they had a chance of driving out of here this afternoon. And that's what she wanted, of course. The woods were beautiful, and Zeke...well, Zeke was indescribable. But she had to get back to New York.

"I guess we might as well start home," he said. "I—oh, God, look at that." He stared upstream.

"What?" Katherine strained to see what he was looking at with such a worried expression, but she couldn't figure it out.

"There. On the branch coming toward us. A mother raccoon with her babies."

Finally Katherine saw a cluster of brown fur clinging to a flimsy branch. Eventually she differentiated a nose and tail and gradually made out the babies, perhaps four of them, riding precariously on the mother's back. "Will they be okay?"

"Maybe not." Zeke started unfastening Amanda's sling. "Downstream there's a waterfall. I don't think the babies could survive that. Hold Amanda for me."

Katherine took a sleeping Amanda and put on the sling, but she didn't like the looks of this. "What are you going to do?"

"Wade in and see if I can pull the branch over next to the shore, so the mother can climb off."

"Zeke, that water's really moving." Katherine didn't want the baby raccoons to drown, either, but she was more concerned about keeping Zeke in one piece.

"I'll be fine." He started down the embankment, hanging on to the trunks of saplings as he went.

Katherine tried to tell herself that Zeke did this sort of thing for a living and he would be fine, but when he put his foot into the water and slipped, she cried out.

"Don't worry!" he called over his shoulder as he righted himself and started wading into the stream.

She worried, anyway. Rushing water had nearly killed her once, and she didn't trust it. As Zeke got in over his knees, she held her breath. He might be a big man, but the current was powerful.

Amanda stirred and started to fuss.

"Not now, baby," Katherine said, jiggling her. "Mommy has to watch out for your daddy, who is doing something brave and foolish, I'm afraid."

Zeke staggered in the swift water, and Katherine's stomach churned. Finally he reached a point that must have satisfied him, because he stopped and looked downstream, waiting for the branch to come by.

"What if they bite you?" she called.

"They don't usually carry rabies," he called back.

Rabies. She hadn't even thought of that. She'd only been concerned that he'd be wounded, not that he'd contract a potentially fatal disease. "Maybe you should just come on back, Zeke."

"They're almost here."

Amanda started crying in earnest.

"I can't feed you now, sweetheart," Katherine said, her attention glued to the drama in the middle of the stream. "Daddy's trying to save some baby raccoons, and I'm hoping I don't have to try and save Daddy."

The branch drifted slightly out of reach as it was about to pass Zeke, and he moved toward it, nearly going down and causing Katherine's stomach to flip-flop again. But he stayed upright and grabbed the very tip of the branch. Katherine was barely breathing as the mother raccoon stared at Zeke and hissed. Katherine half expected the animal to lunge for his throat. After all, she didn't know this tall creature holding the branch was trying to save her babies.

The rush of water and Amanda's crying made it difficult for Katherine to hear, but once in a while she thought she heard the low murmur of Zeke's voice. She edged to the right for a better view, and sure enough, she could see that his lips were moving. He was talking to the raccoon.

Her heart pounded as he slowly edged back toward shore, dragging the branch with the raccoons on it toward safety. All the while he kept up his steady, soft monologue. When he was ankle-deep in the water, Katherine began to breathe easier. She spoke soothingly to Amanda and the baby settled down a little.

Finally he dragged the branch through the shallow water and anchored it against the embankment with some large rocks. The mother crouched on the branch and followed every movement he made. At last Zeke stood back. "Okay, the gangplank's down whenever you're ready."

"Good job," Katherine said, feeling proud and immensely relieved. But when he turned to climb the embankment, Katherine noticed him wince and saw that his jaw was clenched. Fresh fear shot through her.

"What's wrong?" she said.

He glanced up at her. "When I slipped out there I turned my ankle wrong. But I'll be okay."

"You sprained your ankle?" If it hadn't been such a horrible possibility, she would have laughed. First her wrist and now his ankle. A couple of gimps.

He climbed to the path beside her, his breath coming in jerky gasps and his face pale. "I think so. But I'll be okay." He turned, breathing heavily, and stood with his hands on his hips while he watched the mother raccoon. "She's going. Okay, there, take it easy. That's it."

Katherine was glad to see the raccoon scramble safely to shore and disappear into the underbrush. But she was afraid Zeke had paid a hefty price.

He sighed and turned back to her with a wan smile. "Mission accomplished."

"I'm glad, but I don't like the fact you hurt your ankle."

"I'll just walk it out on the way back." His eyes reflected pain, yet he managed a grin. "Unless you want to carry me."

"I wish I could. But I'll at least take Amanda." She expected him to argue with her.

"Okay, if you don't mind."

"Sure, no problem." She glanced away so he wouldn't see the concern she knew must be shining in her eyes. It was just a slight sprain, she told herself. Nothing to be worried about. He'd probably be able to walk it off, like he said.

But she didn't really think so, not from the way he was favoring it as he started down the path. They'd taken no more than ten steps when the first drop of rain fell on Katherine's nose.

ZEKE KNEW HE HAD A BAD sprain, had known from the minute it happened. But there was no use saying that to Katherine when there wasn't a damn thing to be done except limp home. He'd considered trying to fashion a makeshift crutch before they started the hike back, but then he'd taken a look at the clouds and decided against it. Besides, Amanda was fussing and needed to be fed soon.

He wondered if he'd still be able to drive with his sprained ankle. Well, he'd just have to. That was assuming it didn't rain any more today and raise the creek again. Then the first few raindrops fell, and he began to accept the inevitable.

How ironic. It looked as if he'd be closed in the cabin with Katherine for at least another night, but judging from the pain in his ankle, he'd be in no condition to make passionate love to her. Just when he thought this situation couldn't get any worse, it did.

As the rain came faster, he stopped and turned back to Katherine. "If I thought this would blow over, I'd say we could wait it out under a tree. But I think we'd better keep going."

"Me, too." As she pulled the lapels of her jacket closer around Amanda, the baby started squirming and crying. "And Amanda's quieter when I keep moving."

"I'm going to feel like a jerk if either one of you comes down with a cold because of this."

"Hey, I begged you to come along, so it's my fault, not yours. And breast-fed babies are pretty resistant to colds." She licked away a raindrop that had landed on her upper lip. "I've been rained on before. How's your ankle?"

He wondered how he could possibly think about sex at a time like this, but the motion of her tongue when she'd licked away the raindrop had caused a reaction in his groin. "I'll live."

Katherine jiggled Amanda as she gazed up at him. "I'd better warn you I'm a complete dunce when it comes to first aid. I never can remember when you're supposed to heat something or when you're supposed to ice it down."

He had a momentary image of her tending to his injury,

her gentle hands on his skin. Nope. Bad idea. "Don't worry. I'll be able to handle it myself. How are your feet?"

"Probably in better shape than your ankle. Let's go."

Gritting his teeth against his increasing pain, he set out again. He must have torn something in there for it to hurt so damned bad. At least the raccoon family had made it, though. He'd think about that while he was walking, to take his mind off his ankle.

He remembered the day the ranch had inherited some baby raccoons when a mother was killed out on the main road. He and four other lucky kids had been allowed to raise a baby raccoon as a pet. Saving that little family today had been sort of a tribute to Stinky's memory, and the warm feeling that gave him took away some of the pain.

Not enough, though. By the time the cabin came in sight he was feeling dizzy from it. He stopped to catch his breath as the world wobbled a little.

"Zeke?" Katherine peered up at him. "You don't look so good."

"I'm okay." He fished in his pocket for the house key and handed it to her. "Go ahead and get Amanda out of the rain. I'm sure she's hungry."

"No, we're going in together." She took hold of his arm. "You can lean on my shoulder if you want."

He was beginning to see little white spots in front of his eyes. "That's okay. Go on. I'll be right there."

"Nope." She gave his arm a little pull. "I'm not going without you."

"Katherine, I think I—" The world went black.

THE NEXT THING ZEKE KNEW, someone was trying to take off his pants. And they were damned determined about it, too—pulling, puffing and cussing a blue streak. It wasn't helping the pain in his ankle one bit, either. He slowly sat up, propping his hands on the floor behind him, and came face-to-face with Katherine.

She stopped tugging on his pants. She'd only been using one hand, which explained a lot of her awkwardness. "You're conscious! Oh, thank God!"

Nearby, Amanda fretted in her bassinet.

He tried to figure things out. The last he remembered he was outside. "How did I get into the cabin?"

"I dragged you." She looked a mess, her hair soaked, mud streaking her face and the front of her shirt.

"Dragged me? With a sprained wrist? Katherine, you should never have tried to—"

"I was supposed to leave you out there?"

"Maybe not." Even though she was wet and covered with mud, she was the sexiest-looking woman he'd ever seen. "I guess I passed out."

"You went down like a felled tree." She resumed pulling at his pants.

The movement hurt like hell, but he kept his tone light. She was only trying to help. "What are you doing?"

She glanced up. "You need to get these off."

"Why?"

She frowned impatiently at him. "I don't know much about first aid, but in every movie I've ever seen, when the hero gets hurt, the heroine undresses him and puts him to bed. Besides, you're all muddy and you shouldn't get into that bed in muddy clothes. And besides *that*, your ankle is swelling, and if I don't get these jeans off soon, you'll never get them off without cutting them. These look sort of new and I didn't think you'd appreciate having them cut up."

"I don't have to get into bed."

"Are you kidding? You just passed out. You should be in bed." She gave another yank and the jeans came free. She took them to the door, opened it and tossed them outside before coming to stand over him. "I got your floor all muddy, too, but that can wait. Take off your shirt and I'll help you into bed."

He wished he could be pain-free enough to enjoy this.

Then Amanda's fussing became more demanding and he realized Katherine had postponed taking care of the baby to tend to him. "Look, I appreciate what you're trying to do, but I can manage from here. I'll bet you haven't fed Amanda yet."

"No, and I'm not going to until you're in bed and we've done...well, whatever is necessary to that nasty-looking ankle. Take off your shirt. It's all muddy from where I dragged you across the yard and up the steps. I'll get a towel to get some of the dirt out of your hair."

He finally decided the best way to restore some calm to the situation was to do as she asked. She seemed to have a program in mind, and it had to proceed in order, beginning with him climbing into bed.

He glanced over at the bassinet. "Sorry, Mandy. Guess you'll have to get in line." He unbuttoned his shirt and took it off as Katherine returned with a towel and knelt down behind him.

"You really need your hair washed." With her left hand she began rubbing the towel briskly over his hair and scalp. "But we'll have to take care of that later. This will get the worst of it."

He thought of mentioning that she was working on the wrong end of him. While she was concentrating on getting the mud out of his hair, his ankle seemed to be swelling more every second. But the sensation of having her rub his head felt good, especially when she swayed close enough that her soft breasts jiggled against his shoulders. To hell with his ankle.

"There. That's better." She stood and walked around to peer down at him. "Now, do you think you can stand, or do you want me to help you?"

He was beginning to get in the swing of this. Certain things could make a guy forget he was in pain. "I might need some help."

"Okay." She crouched down beside him. "Put your arm

around my shoulders. When I count to three, I'll start lifting. Put your weight on me and on your good ankle.''

"I will." He put his arm around her, and she slipped her arm around his waist. Nice. Her smooth cheek was only a breath away. He watched her clench her jaw in concentration and a wave of tenderness swept over him at her earnest attempt to render aid.

"Here we go," she said. "On three. One, two, *three*." She gripped his waist and heaved.

He could tell she wasn't terribly familiar with helping people to their feet, and his bulk threatened to topple them both until he put some of his weight on his bum ankle. With a soft grunt of pain, he rebalanced himself and leaned fully on Katherine. The feel of her warm body almost made up for the sensation of someone cutting at his ankle with a chain saw.

"I'll bet it hurts," she murmured.

"Some."

"Let's get you over to the bed."

He allowed her to guide him there, where she'd already folded back the sheets and propped up one pillow as a backrest. She turned him and eased him down to a sitting position. Before he took his arm from her shoulders, he fantasized pulling her down with him. He might really screw up his ankle with a stunt like that, but his ankle wasn't much of a consideration. Amanda was, however. Her fussing had turned into an outraged wail. She needed Katherine to feed her.

"Let me lift your legs for you so you don't strain that ankle any more than necessary," she said.

"All right." He couldn't remember ever allowing someone to baby him like this. The few times he'd become injured he'd always handled the problem himself or made do with a quick trip to the emergency room. No one had ever fussed over Zeke Lonetree. And damn, but it felt nice.

She held both feet carefully as she maneuvered him fully onto the bed. "Okay, now what?"

He leaned back with a little sigh. Maybe relaxing on a comfy bed wasn't such a bad idea. "I'm fine now. You can feed Amanda."

"I know there's something more we should do with your ankle. Or is it too late?"

He grinned at her. Propped in bed with his weight off his ankle made him feel a lot feistier. "Yeah, it's too late. I think we'll have to amputate."

"Don't even joke about a thing like that. What can I do for you?"

"Well, if we elevate it with a pillow, that will probably help with the swelling."

"Makes sense. If you'll hand me the other pillow, I'll fix it up for you."

Despite the pain when she lifted his ankle, he enjoyed her hands on him way too much. The brush of her bandaged wrist reminded him that she'd probably suffered some pain dragging him into the cabin, yet she'd done it. She obviously cared about him, which made the chemistry between them even sweeter. But he tried to seem unaffected by her touch. He didn't want her to think she was arousing him and stop these gentle ministrations.

She stood back and surveyed him. "Done. What else?"

"I don't suppose the freezer's cold enough to keep anything frozen."

"Nope. I checked that right after I dragged you in here."

He smiled at her. "I thought you didn't know anything about first aid?"

"Well, duh. That's what you did for my wrist. I was pretty sure I should use some ice for your ankle if we had any. But we don't."

"Then I guess you've done all you can for now."

She gazed at him doubtfully. "Aspirin? For the pain?"

He shook his head. "Go feed the baby."

"Okay." She glanced down at her mud-spattered shirt. "Mind if I borrow another shirt and change first?"

"Be my guest. Why not let me hold her until you get ready?"

"Oh, Zeke, she needs changing and she's hungry and squirmy. I don't think—"

"Let me give it a shot. My ankle's not in great shape, but there's nothing wrong with my arms. Maybe I can settle her down some."

"Well, if you want to try, that would be very nice." She hurried over to the bassinet, picked up Amanda and held the baby away from her muddy shirt as she brought her over. "Hey, Mandy, don't cry. Daddy's going to hold you for a while until I get cleaned up. Be a good girl."

He discovered he liked the way Katherine said that—*Daddy's going to hold you*—as if Amanda should feel honored. Actually he was the one who felt honored to be able to hold her, even fussing the way she was. He cradled her against his chest and started telling her about his pet raccoon Stinky. Sure enough, she stopped crying and acted as if she were hanging on every word.

While he told his story, he was aware of Katherine opening not one, but two dresser drawers.

"So you really do have a gun in there," she said.

He interrupted his story to answer her. "Yeah. If I were a horse you could shoot me and put me out of my misery."

She paused beside the bed, a red-and-black shirt in her hands. "Does it really hurt that bad?"

"No," he lied. "I'm kidding."

Her forehead creased in worry. "Could it be broken?"

"No. Just a sprain." Except that he knew certain types of sprains could be as painful and take almost as long to heal as a broken bone. If he hadn't started out with that kind, he'd probably created it by walking on it all the way back to the cabin. "Now go change your shirt before Mandy gets bored with my stories."

"Be right back."

After she went into the bathroom, Zeke returned his attention to Amanda. "Okay, where was I? Did I ever tell you about the time that Stinky got loose in the ranch house kitchen? No? Well, I thought the cook was going to fix raccoon stew after that little episode. But it wasn't my fault. I'll tell you a secret. It was Shane Daniels who almost got Stinky barbecued. You'd like Shane. He's..."

Zeke paused as he wondered how his buddies from the ranch would react to the news about Amanda. One thing was for sure, they'd have kicked his butt if he'd refused to have anything to do with his daughter. Parenthood was pretty sacred to those guys, for obvious reasons. It was pretty sacred to Zeke, too, which was why he'd originally thought he'd rather be no parent at all than a half-assed one. But now that he'd agreed to stay in touch with Amanda, he'd just have to figure out how to be a decent father under crummy circumstances.

Amanda began to wiggle and whimper.

"I'm sorry, sunshine." He brought his attention back to the baby in his arms. "I'll bet you want me to finish the story. It was like this. Shane decided to play a joke on the cook. And that's when all the ruckus started."

CHAPTER FOURTEEN

KATHERINE KEPT THE BATHROOM door open a crack so she could hear Zeke's tales of Stinky while she washed the mud off and changed into a clean shirt.

His raccoon stories charmed her tremendously. So that's why he'd been so determined to make sure the raccoons survived. She wondered if he'd tell Amanda those stories again when she was old enough to understand them. And if Amanda would come back to New York demanding to have a raccoon for a pet.

Katherine tried to imagine what Zeke would look like by that time, closing in on forty, maybe with touches of gray in his raven-black hair. Instinctively she knew he'd only become more attractive as he grew older—his type always did. Some woman was bound to come along who fancied herself a pioneer lady ready to live in Zeke's wilderness with him.

It would be heaven. Katherine glanced guiltily in the bathroom mirror as the traitorous thought glowed like neon in her brain. She couldn't allow herself to think such things. Naomi was offering her the top job at a prestigious magazine. Anyone who turned that down would be foolish, not to mention incredibly ungrateful. Besides, Naomi would be crushed, and Katherine could never do anything to hurt her generous and loving godmother.

She nudged off her muddy shoes and peeled off her socks. Sure enough, blisters. She left the socks off. While giving her hands one last wash after handling the socks, she wondered if a soak in the icy water would be almost the same as ice on Zeke's ankle. Once Amanda was fed she'd see about that.

She ran a comb quickly through her damp hair and looked at her bandaged wrist. In order to get it somewhat clean she'd had to saturate it with water and it was soggy and uncomfortable, but she couldn't worry about that now. She left the bathroom as Zeke was winding up a story about Stinky's adventures with a ranch dog named Shep. After taking another dish towel from the cupboard to use as a diaper, she walked over to the bed, amazed at how quietly Amanda lay in Zeke's arms.

He glanced up at her. "You look good in red."

And you look good in bed, she thought. "Thanks. I'll take her now."

"She's a good baby, isn't she?"

Using her left arm, Katherine lifted Amanda and carried her over to the table to change her. "I think so. I don't have much basis of comparison except for the babies of employees at *Cachet.*" She unsnapped the sleeper. Good thing she'd washed the spare plus the soiled dish towels and dried them by the cooking fire before they left on the hike.

"I'll bet the other babies cried more than she does."

"It seems that way." She'd used considerably less duct tape on this diaper, so it wasn't such a struggle to take off. "Other mothers have told me that it's just luck when you get an even-tempered baby. I think it might also be because I keep her on a regular schedule and make her feel as secure as possible."

"Or maybe it's because of me." He sounded downright smug about it.

"You?" Katherine placed a restraining hand on Amanda and turned toward him. "What, you passed on some calm-and-peaceful genes?"

"In a way."

Amanda had apparently run out of patience. She started to wail like a little banshee.

"Even Amanda disagrees about that." Katherine taped up the diaper and snapped Amanda into her suit as quickly as possible, considering the soggy and unwieldy bandage on her wrist. Then she picked her up and started over toward the rocker as Amanda continued to cry.

"Would you pull the rocker over here and talk to me while you feed her?" Zeke asked above the hubbub.

Katherine paused for just a heartbeat. "Sure." As she dragged the rocker closer to the bed, she wondered if he realized how revealing his request was. Her strong, silent mountain man was beginning to enjoy having company.

Because she didn't want to buy trouble, she positioned the rocker so that she was on an angle from Zeke's direct view. She knew the sight of her nursing Amanda aroused him, so she'd keep herself out of sight as much as possible.

Sitting down in the rocker, she worked at the buttons of her shirt. The wet bandage really was more clumsy than a dry one, and Amanda's squirming and crying didn't make things any easier.

"If you'll come over here, I'll unbutton that," Zeke said.

Oh, no, you don't. If he unfastened those buttons, she'd become just as aroused as he was by the process. "Thanks, but I've got it now." With a sigh of relief she gave her breast to Amanda and silence settled over the cabin.

"You can't blame her," Zeke said. "She started getting hungry back on the trail. She's had to wait a long time."

"I don't blame her." Katherine leaned her head against the back of the chair and rocked slowly while she listened to the rain. Nursing Amanda was one of the most satisfying experiences of her life, and it frustrated her almost as much as the baby when she couldn't do it on schedule.

This recent crying jag was about as bad as it ever got. Amanda had suffered no bouts with colic or unexplained illnesses. When the two of them were free to do their thing, the baby was a joy to care for. The pregnancy had been difficult, but the doctors had assured Katherine she didn't have to worry that she'd always have difficult pregnancies. The next one would probably be a breeze, they'd said.

Except there wouldn't be a next one. If all her children could be this wonderful, Katherine was a little sorry she wouldn't have any more. Although she hadn't admitted the fact to Zeke, she didn't want to have another man's child any more than he wanted her to.

Then she remembered Zeke's comment that if Amanda had a brother or sister, he wanted to be the one to father the baby. A thrill of awareness ran through her at the thought that Zeke would entertain such an idea. Of course it was crazy and she'd never follow through with it, but making a child with Zeke had been an outstanding experience.

She glanced over at him. He was watching her, a glow in his dark eyes that almost made her believe he could read her mind. Silence could be erotic, she realized, especially when it was filled with soft sucking sounds from the baby she and Zeke had created. She'd better start making some conversation, as Zeke had originally requested.

"So why do you think Amanda's temperament is all your doing?" she asked.

"Simple. It's her Sioux blood."

"And Sioux babies are all even-tempered? Come on, Zeke."

"I don't mean Sioux babies in particular. Traditionally, Native American babies had to be quiet and well-behaved. During warfare between the tribes or against the white man, a crying baby could alert the enemy."

She had no trouble picturing Zeke as a warrior—in some ways he seemed like a throwback to those days. "Yes, but that was a long time ago, and it was probably mostly conditioning after they were born, not some innate part of their makeup."

Zeke grinned. "You're probably right. But it sounded good, didn't it?"

"Sure did. It's good copy, as we say in my job. Naomi's already suggested that Amanda would make an exotic runway model with her coloring."

Zeke frowned. "A model? Don't they have to starve themselves to stay skinny enough for the camera?"

"If she inherits my metabolism she won't have to starve herself. And I think she'll be beautiful enough to make it."

Zeke still looked doubtful. "Sure, she'll be beautiful enough, but what kind of a life is that?"

She loved his parental assumption that his daughter would be gorgeous. Even more she loved his concern for Amanda's future. "Well, there can be a lot of pressure, but a lot of money, too. And if she has any interest in acting that's a logical step from modeling."

"You mean be a movie star?"

Katherine gazed down at Amanda. "You never know."

"So many movie stars seem to have messed-up lives."

"But not all of them." Katherine glanced at him. "If Amanda grows up with lots of self-esteem, she could handle herself in that world. But then I want her to grow up with lots of self-esteem no matter what she decides to do with her life."

"Which is where I come in."

Katherine nodded. "I think so. When I brought her out here I was confused about that. Naomi had convinced me I could raise Amanda without you."

"You could."

"Maybe. But I don't want to." She met his gaze. "And I hope you don't want me to, either."

He took a deep breath and looked into her eyes, as if making some sort of pledge. "No, I don't. Not anymore."

AFTER KATHERINE FINISHED feeding Amanda and was tucking her in for her nap, Zeke noticed how chilly the air is the cabin was. He'd been so engrossed in watching Katherine nurse the baby, he'd been oblivious to the temperature, but now that she'd buttoned her shirt, he could concentrate on something besides the temptation of her breasts.

He surveyed the small pieces of wood left on the hearth. Not enough for a decent fire. Throwing back the covers, he gritted his teeth and swung his legs to the floor.

Katherine glanced up from where she was crouched next to Amanda's bassinet. "What do you think you're doing?"

Zeke fought dizziness as he stood, balancing himself by holding on to the headboard of the bed. "We need wood."

"Get back in bed." She checked the sleeping baby once more and stood. "I'll take care of the wood."

"I feel dumb having you do all the work." Using the mattress to steady himself, he started toward the dresser. "I'll just put on some sweats and another shirt."

"No, you won't." She stepped into his path, blocking his way.

"Katherine—"

"You should see yourself." She crossed her arms and planted her feet more firmly. "It's freezing in here and sweat's popping out on your forehead. Now, I want you to give up this macho routine and go back to bed before you pass out again."

He had to admit he didn't feel so great whenever he put the slightest weight on his ankle.

"Get back to bed and stop being ridiculous."

"Katherine, I—"

"If you don't start moving, I'm going to kick you in your bum ankle, ranger man! My goodness, what an ego you have. Nobody can do anything but you. Now get going."

He gazed down at her. She was so adorably belligerent it was hard for him not to smile. Figuring she wouldn't appreciate that, he set his mouth into a tight line and nodded. Turning, he sat down on the mattress again.

"That's better. Do you have a bucket around here?"

"Under the sink."

She walked over to the sink, opened a bottom cupboard and took out the bucket. "As long as you've moved yourself, I want you to soak your foot and ankle in cold water while I'm busy getting the wood. And wrap a blanket around your shoulders so you don't catch cold." She tipped the bucket under the faucet and started filling it.

"Yes, ma'am." While her back was to him, he allowed himself a grin. "At least you didn't tell me to soak my head."

"That's not a bad idea." It was a good-size bucket and she had to use both hands to lug it over to the bed. "But we'll start with your foot." She set the bucket down slowly, so the water wouldn't slosh out. "Put it in there."

"My foot isn't going to fit all the way in. It's too big."

"Do the best you can to cover your ankle."

He braced himself against the shock and dipped his toes in. Damn, the water was cold. But she'd come up with a good idea. The sooner the swelling went down on his ankle, the sooner he'd be able to take care of things around here. Muttering a few curses, he immersed his foot as far as possible.

"Well, now you're shivering."

He glanced up at her. "No j-joke."

"That's partly because you don't have the blanket fixed right." She reached around him with both arms, practically embracing him as she adjusted it. "You'd think somebody with Sioux blood would know how to wrap a blanket around himself."

"Very funny." Her close proximity and her tantalizing scent were really getting to him. He'd just about decided to grab her and kiss that smart mouth of hers when she stopped fiddling with the blanket and stepped back.

"Good. You've stopped shivering."

He wanted to tell her that was because his foot and ankle were completely numb and he was getting an erection from all her fondling. He thought better of it. "You sure have been bossy recently," he said.

"If you'd stop trying to be Superman I wouldn't have to boss you around." She surveyed him. "You need a sock on that other foot."

"If you say so."

"I do." She walked over to the dresser and took out a pair of wool socks. She laid one on top of the dresser and came over to kneel in front of him.

"I can put on my own sock, Katherine."

"Oh, be quiet. This is faster." She rolled the sock over his foot and up his calf.

He loved every second of the experience. He'd never realized before how sensitive that area of his body could be.

"There." She stood and put her hands on her hips. "Now I'll get the wood. After that I'll build us a fire and make you some hot coffee and me some cocoa. Then I'll fix us something for lunch. How about that?"

"Sounds good, Superwoman."

She lifted both eyebrows. "Hey, I'm not the one who passed out in the yard and then thinks he can do all his normal chores. I'm just taking care of business."

"And your wrist needs to be rebandaged."

She hesitated, looking at it. "Nope. First I'm getting the wood."

"Then take my gloves. They're in the pocket of my heavy jacket. In fact, you might want to put the jacket on, too."

She walked over to where the jackets hung and took down his heaviest one. It dwarfed her. Then she pulled the leather gloves out of the side pocket as she headed for the door. "See you in a few minutes. With firewood."

"Okay." Zeke's heart swelled as he watched her go out the door dressed awkwardly in his clothes. What a loving, bossy, vulnerable, sexy woman. He didn't regret a single moment he'd spent with her, and he wouldn't want anyone else to be the mother of his child. Thank God he'd pulled her out of the river that afternoon. He couldn't imagine a world without Katherine in it. And as that last thought sank in, he caught his breath.

No doubt about it, he was in love with her.

LEAVING HER FIRST THREE loads of wood by the door, Katherine carried the fourth stack into the cabin and set it on the hearth. She was enjoying herself, she realized with some regret. She liked building fires and walking in the woods and sitting on the porch gazing up at the night sky.

She took off Zeke's gloves and stuffed them in the pocket of his coat before hanging it up. Then she glanced over at Zeke. "Firewood's in."

He watched her, a soft expression on his face. "Thanks."

The warmth in his eyes beckoned her, and she had the biggest urge to walk over there and into his arms. Instead she turned, knelt by the hearth and began stacking kindling and pinecones to start a fire. As the kindling began to crackle she reached for a piece of the wood she'd brought in. With great satisfaction she put the wood on the fire. They would be warm tonight because of her.

She placed the fire screen in front of the blaze and stood. "Now for some lunch. How's your ankle?"

"I think the swelling's gone down some. It's probably time to wrap it with an elastic bandage. Then we'll redo yours."

Katherine glanced down at her wrist. "Do you have more of these?"

"Several. Sprains are common in the woods."

"No kidding." Walking over to the bed, she crouched down to peer into the bucket. "I think I could wrap your ankle for you. Let me get the first-aid kit and a towel to dry you off." She started toward the bathroom.

"And after you wrap my ankle, I'll change the bandage on your wrist."

She laughed. "This is beginning to sound like an episode

from *General Hospital.''* When she returned, she handed him the kit while she knelt down to take his foot from the bucket and dry it. His toes were starting to wrinkle, but the swelling didn't look nearly as bad around his ankle.

"We really are quite a pair of cripples, Zeke."

"Yeah, but put us together and we're awesome."

She thought about that as she dried his foot, being careful to get between his toes. They were awesome together. Where one of them had a weakness, mental or physical, the other one seemed to fill the gap. With parents like that, a kid could have it made. But she wasn't sure Zeke would be able to do his share of filling in gaps when he lived clear out in Wyoming. She wondered if telephone calls would help. Probably not much.

"I think my foot's dry," Zeke said gently.

She realized she'd been continuing to rub his foot as she considered the problem. "Oh." She glanced up at him. "Sorry."

"It felt sort of good."

"Oh," she said again, aware of a light in his dark eyes. She glanced away, afraid to hold his gaze for long. "We'd better get your ankle horizontal again and wrap it."

"Right." Laying the first-aid kit behind him, he took the blanket from around his shoulders and tossed it across the end of the bed.

His chest muscles flexed as he did so, and Katherine suddenly became aware that he wore nothing but his briefs and the sock she'd recently put on him. The sight of his bronzed body was potent medicine. She needed to get this first-aid business taken care of, and fast.

Before she could reach down to lift his feet, he swung them up to the bed and laid his ankle on the pillow. Then he reached into the first-aid kit, took out the rolled bandage and tossed it to her. "Wrap away."

She caught the bandage and frowned at him. "You need to take it easy lifting that ankle."

"I don't like feeling like a damned invalid."

"As if I didn't know." She unfastened the clip from the bandage and sat down on the bed near his feet. "If I remember right, I wrap your instep and then wind this up around your ankle."

"That'll work. Make sure it's tight enough." He leaned back against the headboard and crossed his arms over his chest.

And did he ever look yummy posed like that, she thought. Time to get busy and then get the heck off the bed. "I'm going to prop your foot on my knee. Let me know if anything I do hurts too much."

"Okay."

"I'll bet you won't. You're such a macho type." She worked gingerly to wrap the end of the bandage around his instep.

"I wasn't exactly the macho type last night with that nightmare."

She stopped wrapping and glanced up at him. It was the first reference he'd made to it today. "That dream took you right back to being three years old. Not many little boys of three are macho."

He gazed at her, his dark eyes gentle. "I appreciate the fact that you didn't bring up the subject again. Some people might have pestered me for more details."

"I figure it's up to you when you want to talk about it."

"Thank you."

"You're welcome." She dared not look into his eyes any longer. She leaned over her work again. His skin was still cool from soaking in the water, although she could feel warmth when she lightly touched the swollen part of his ankle.

As she unrolled the bandage around the puffy part she had to cradle the weight of his calf in her other hand. Man, did he have muscles. And a sexy kneecap. He didn't have a lot of body hair, which was probably due to his Sioux heritage. Touching the back of his leg reminded her of the delicious texture of his bronzed skin…everywhere. She'd explored it thoroughly in the lantern light the night before. She didn't have a lot of experience with men, but she knew instinctively that making love to Zeke was an exotic experience by anybody's standards.

"That might be just a *little* too tight."

A quick look told her he was clenching his jaw against the pain, and when she inspected her wrapping job, she quickly started undoing it again. "I am so sorry." In her agitated state while daydreaming about Zeke's body, she must have pulled the bandage tighter and tighter. She winced when she thought of how that must have hurt him. "That was stupid of me."

"It's okay, Katherine."

"It's not okay." She started rewrapping, not looking at him. "You wouldn't be in this fix if I hadn't come into your life in the first place. Now you have all these problems like what to do about Amanda, and on top of that you sprain your ankle, and I can't even take care of it properly for you."

"I'm not sorry you came into my life."

"Yeah, well, being not sorry is a long way from being glad, and I don't blame you. Your life was going fine until—"

"I'm glad you did, then."

That brought her head up. "You are?"

"Yes."

"That's…nice." Oh, God. Whenever he looked at her like that she began to tremble. She swallowed and went back to her work. Her fingers shook as she attached the metal clip to the end of the bandage.

"There. You're done." She eased his foot off her knee and onto the pillow. Then she stood up and tossed the covers over him, more to get his body out of sight than to keep him warm. The fire was heating the room up nicely. At least she told herself it was the fire that was causing her skin to feel so toasty. "Ready for some coffee?"

"After we do something about that bandage of yours."

"Oh." She glanced down at the damp, grungy-looking elastic and had to admit it felt icky. But she wasn't sure it was wise for her to be close to him at the moment. "Later."

"If you wait, then Amanda will wake up, and I'll bet you'd like a clean bandage before you deal with her again."

He was right about that. And there was no way she could wrap it properly by herself.

Zeke patted the mattress next to him. "Come on. Let's take care of this so you can forget about it for a while."

"Let me put another log on the fire first." She walked over to the fireplace and spent a fair amount of time tending to the blaze, hoping in the process her reaction to Zeke would lessen. It didn't.

"Hey," Zeke called. "The fire's perfect. Come on over here and get your wrist taken care of."

"Now who's the bossy one?" But she went over and sat on the bed.

He cradled her hand gently and started unwinding the bandage. "If you wouldn't try to act like Superwoman, I wouldn't have to boss you around."

"Ha, ha." She tried to be nonchalant as she sat with her hand in his, but she was having a lot of trouble. His body heat seemed to reach out to her, drawing her closer. She deliberately held herself away from him.

"How does your wrist feel?" His breathing was slow and steady as he unwrapped the elastic. Apparently he wasn't bothered by being so close to her.

"It's a little sore. Not bad." She didn't know how anyone could keep from reacting to his gentle touch. All he was doing was taking a bandage from her wrist, yet it felt like a caress.

"There. It's off. Looks pretty good. Not much swelling."

"No." She gazed at her wrist. "Sort of wrinkly and white."

"That's because you left the wet bandage on so long." He held her wrist loosely and examined it. "Looks better."

"I'm sure I'll live." But his touch was driving her insane, reminding her of how it felt to have his hands all over her body. If he placed his fingers over the pulse in her wrist, he'd know what he was doing to her.

He took a new bandage from the first-aid kit and with calm precision started wrapping it around her wrist. "Amanda's sure sleeping soundly."

"Yes, she is." She wondered if he heard the quiver in her voice. She felt almost feverish. The minute he finished wrapping her wrist, she would get up and start lunch. There were lots of reasons why making love was a bad idea, starting with his injured ankle and ending with the possibility of two broken hearts.

But he seemed to be taking forever. She remembered what he'd said about scent being a part of the mating process. He must be right, because as she sat breathing in the sheer maleness of him, she grew damp and aroused.

She decided to try talking to dispel the tension growing within her. "So, what do you want for lunch?" She'd meant the question to sound bright and cheerful. Instead, a husky note had betrayed her. The question sounded downright suggestive.

He glanced up from his wrapping job, his gaze unreadable. "What are you hungry for?"

His expression gave no indication that he'd meant anything sexual by that remark. Yet heat burned in her cheeks as she thought of the answer she wanted to give. "I guess we should make it something easy."

"Good idea," he said softly, and broke eye contact so he could return to wrapping her wrist.

She wanted him so much she was afraid she might start drooling. Time for a little joke. "If there was such a thing as a wrist-wrapping contest, you'd get the prize for technique, but you'd never win in the time trials."

He finished the last couple of turns with deliberate care and reached for the clip to hold the end in place. "Got an appointment?"

"Yeah. I'm supposed to have lunch with this ranger I know."

"Sounds important." He closed the lid on the first-aid kit, but he didn't release her hand. Then he caught her gaze with his as he brought her hand up and placed a soft kiss in her palm.

As she stared into his dark and mysterious eyes, she almost forgot to breathe. Her heartbeat thundered in her ears. "He'd hate it if I...stood him up," she whispered.

"Then don't."

CHAPTER FIFTEEN

ZEKE KNEW MAKING LOVE to Katherine again wasn't a good idea. It would probably make his ankle hurt now and his heart hurt later. But he couldn't seem to help himself.

He slipped his hand up through her hair and cupped the back of her head. When his mouth touched hers, her lips were already parted, inviting him to kiss her the way she loved to be kissed. She clutched his shoulders and he thrust deep with his tongue. Her moan of delight aroused him as nothing else could. As nothing else ever would.

And so he would make love to her now because he had no choice, and he was no longer willing to give her one, either. They might part, they might live in different worlds for the rest of their lives, but she was his mate, and they were born to be joined together in a basic, primitive way. To deny it would be like trying to stop the orbit of the earth.

He couldn't seem to get enough of her mouth, but he wanted so much more. The buttons on her shirt slipped from their holes as if nothing would stand in his way now. When the shirt was open he reached for her breast. The weight of it in his hand felt so good he couldn't help the growl of satisfaction that rose in his throat.

He hadn't realized his connection to her would intensify now that she'd borne his child, now that she nursed that child with the breasts that he loved to caress. The emotion he'd experienced after their first night together had been strong, but it paled in comparison to what he felt for her now. She'd become completely, gloriously female, which made him feel more a man than ever before in his life.

He eased his thumb across her nipple, bringing forth moisture. He was the man who had made her pregnant, he thought triumphantly, the one who had caused her breasts to fill and her body to grow ripe with their daughter. He'd created a place for himself in her life no one could ever take away. He was the only man who could have given her Amanda.

Stroking his thumb across her nipple, he drew back a fraction from the sweetness of her lips. "I need you," he murmured.

"What about...your ankle?"

"We'll work around it."

"I shouldn't let you..." She sighed gently and arched her back in pleasure as he continued to stroke her breast. The lapels of the shirt fell away, revealing the dusky rose contrast of her nipples against her milk-white skin. "This is selfish of me."

His breath caught at her beauty. "No. I want you to give me memories. I'll need them."

Her eyes fluttered open. She gazed at him, her lips parted, her breathing shallow and quick. "So will I," she whispered.

His body tightened in anticipation, yet when she pulled away from him and stood, he thought perhaps he'd lost her. But when she walked to his dresser and pulled out the bottom drawer, he knew he'd won...everything.

She placed the condoms on the bedside table and stepped back. Then she slowly took off her shirt and let it drop to the floor.

He was dazzled. He'd never been able to see her like this, standing before him in the full light of day. The gray light coming through the window outlined her body, making her seem to glow.

She untied the string holding the waist of the sweatpants.

Instead of pushing them down, she allowed them to slide sensuously to her feet while she kept her attention focused on him.

His erection began to throb as he realized she was being deliberately provocative. "Am I getting…a show?"

Her voice was shy but her actions were not. "I think you deserve one." She stepped gracefully out of the sweats.

"Thank you," he said, his huskiness revealing just how grateful he was. She was no longer hesitant about revealing her body to him, stretch marks and all. He considered that a gift.

As she stood before him wearing only natural light, he allowed himself the pleasure of a long, leisurely visual trip back up that magnificent body as he anticipated running his hands over her again. He moved over to make room for her, oblivious to any pain in his ankle.

"Be careful, Zeke."

"I don't feel a thing. Come here."

Her gaze was hot, but she moved slowly as she knelt on the bed beside him. "You need to let me be in charge," she said.

His heart beat faster. "Is that right?"

"Yes. You're injured."

"According to you, injured people need to take their clothes off."

"That's right." Her smile tantalized him. Then she glanced down at his cotton briefs, which barely contained him. "And that's what I intend to do."

He'd never had an experience like it. As she peeled his briefs down, she showered him with light, yet intimate, kisses. Her hair swung forward and tickled his heated flesh, and he thought he might go crazy from the feathery sensations created by her hair and her lips.

When she had him so worked up he thought he might explode, she paused in order to work the briefs down over his ankles. In the process her nipples brushed against his knees, and his pulse skyrocketed again. He had to fist his hands to keep from grabbing her and pushing her down to the mattress, no matter how much his ankle screamed in protest.

"I'm so afraid I'll hurt you," she murmured.

His voice was strained. "Trust me. I wouldn't care."

"Then you're having a good time?" She tossed the briefs aside and glanced at him.

He gave her a lopsided grin. "As if you couldn't tell."

Still moving carefully, she eased back up the bed and wrapped her warm fingers around his erection. "I can tell. I just like to hear you say it."

He groaned. "I'm having the time of my life. I—" He groaned again as she took him into his mouth. Pleasure this intense should be illegal, he thought, until she took away all thought and replaced it with a white-hot surge of pure feeling. He'd never trusted a woman enough to abandon himself to her. He'd always kept some measure of control.

But this time, all the barriers came down, leaving him open and vulnerable, hers to mold.

She brought him to the very edge of the precipice. Had she decided to hurl him over it, he couldn't have stopped her. But as he balanced there, she rose to her knees and kissed his mouth.

He closed his eyes and held on tight, tasting the passion on her tongue, growing dizzy from wanting her. Mindlessly he grasped her hips, urging her toward him.

"Wait," she murmured against his lips.

When she moved out of his arms he remembered they had one more step to follow. He'd been so crazed from passion that it hadn't even crossed his mind. He held out his hand for the packet. "Here. I'll—"

"No, I will." She was breathing hard, her breasts quivering, her hands shaking as she straddled his thighs and ripped open the foil.

He tried to help her, but he was trembling as much as

she was. Their breathless laughter turned into moans of frustration, but they finally managed to get the condom on. The moment it was secure he cradled her hips and guided her over him. As she settled slowly down, he gasped and clenched his jaw against the urge to pour himself into her.

She clutched his shoulders, closed her eyes and tilted her head back. "Oh, Zeke."

That gesture of surrender nearly did him in. "Don't move yet," he said, his voice raspy.

"I have to." She lifted her hips.

He fought the pressure rising within him as she began a seductive rhythm. When she whimpered and quickened the pace, he lost the fight with a moan of pure ecstasy. Her cry of release echoed his as she shuddered and sagged against him.

Feeling more complete than ever in his life, he gathered her close. *I love you.* His lips silently formed the words as he pressed his cheek against her hair.

KATHERINE HEATED TOMATO SOUP over the fire for their very late lunch. Amanda continued to sleep as she brought a tray of soup and crackers to bed. "*Bon appétit,* ranger man."

He surveyed her and the tray. "Shouldn't there be a flower or something on there?"

"You want a flower?" Setting the tray down, she walked over to the door.

"Hey, I was kidding."

"You want a flower, I'll get you a flower." She was feeling wonderfully reckless as she stepped outside wearing nothing at all. At least she wouldn't get her clothes wet!

"Katherine, forget the flower."

She flashed him a grin over her shoulder and closed the door behind her. But damn, it was cold, and raining like crazy. She glanced around and saw a drenched and rain-flattened daisy near the edge of the clearing and not too far from the porch. If she stepped just right, she'd be able to jump from one tuft of grass to another and not get her feet muddy.

She braced herself for the deluge of rain as she went down the steps. Leaving the shelter of the porch felt exactly like stepping under the shower, except, of course, that she was outside. And naked.

She stood there for a second adjusting to the idea that Katherine Seymour was standing outside a Wyoming cabin in the rain in her birthday suit. Then she began to laugh as the downpour soaked her hair and cascaded over her body. Finally she let out a whoop, threw her hands in the air and lifted her face to the rain, opening her mouth to swallow the drops as they pelted down.

But as exhilarating as the experience was, the air was pretty damn cold. She located the daisy again and hopped from one grassy spot to another until she could lean down and pluck it. "A flower for m'lord's lunch tray," she said, straightening.

That was when she saw the bull moose.

The breath seemed to leave her body as she stared at him and he stared back. He was huge, bigger than the biggest draft horse she'd ever seen in a New York City parade. He stood less than twenty feet from her under the shelter of the trees, his magnificently curved antlers dripping with rain, his coat dark and wet. Even his muzzle dripped.

Fully clothed, Katherine might have felt more secure about meeting a moose in the woods. Naked, she was a little less confident. She backed up one slow step at a time. The ooze slid between her toes as she made her gradual retreat without taking her eyes off the moose.

Glancing over her shoulder, she saw that she was almost on the porch. The moose hadn't budged. He was probably as startled to see a naked woman running around in the yard as she was to see a bull moose in the midst of her flower-gathering trip.

When the back of her heel bumped the bottom step, she turned, hurried up the steps and across the porch. Yanking open the door, she stepped inside, and closed it quickly behind her. Adrenaline poured through her system. She felt wildly primitive, but also half-frozen.

She crossed to the bed and climbed in, wet hair, muddy feet and all. "I'm f-freezing to d-death."

"Can't have that. Although I could say I told you so." Zeke gathered her close.

"B-but you won't."

"No." His tone was amused. "I won't."

"Good." After a while his warmth calmed her and her teeth stopped chattering enough for her to talk. "You'll never believe what happened. While I was in the midst of picking flowers, I looked up, and I was practically nose to nose with a big ol' moose."

He began to chuckle.

"Easy for you to laugh. You weren't standing there stark naked twenty feet away from him."

"That's Elmer. He probably wanted the daisy you picked."

"Oh. The daisy. Wonder what I did with it."

Zeke peered over the edge of the bed. Reaching down, he scooped something up and held it in front of her face.

The daisy was pretty well mangled. She glanced up at him. "Sorry."

He smiled. "It's the thought that counts."

"But I messed up the sheets and the pillowcase."

He gave her a long, slow kiss before leaning back and surveying her appreciatively. "I have other sheets. Don't let being muddy stop you from climbing into my bed."

"You know what? I liked it. I liked running around naked in the rain, and even coming face-to-face with Elmer."

He looked into her eyes. "That's a good sign."

"If this keeps up, you're going to turn me into an exhibitionist."

He grinned. "As long as the exhibit's only open when I'm around."

She realized they were both talking as if they had a future, when in fact they had none. Sobering, she gazed at him. "I guess there isn't much chance I'll turn into an exhibitionist, is there?"

Quietly Katherine disentangled herself, and the exuberance that had lightened her heart turned to despair. She reheated the soup and they sat together on the bed, their backs propped against the headboard while they ate, but they remained silent throughout the meal. Katherine knew she was negotiating her way around the tricky subject of their relationship and figured he was, too. Then they spoke at the same time.

"You first," Katherine said.

"No, you."

She set down her empty bowl on the tray between them and took a deep breath. "Have you ever heard of a movie called *Same Time Next Year?*"

"No. It must not have played the Isis, and since then I haven't seen many movies."

Katherine picked up a cracker and broke it in two. "The man and woman in it each have different lives, even different partners, but they meet once a year, make love and get reacquainted. Then they separate and agree to meet again the next year, and so on."

He put his bowl on the tray and looked at her, his face devoid of expression.

"I hate it when you look like that. Inscrutable. I suppose you're going to say that's your Sioux blood coming out in you."

"No." His voice was very quiet. "It's the orphan coming out in me."

"Oh, Zeke!" She dropped the cracker and reached for him, nearly overturning the tray. Her throat tightened as she cradled his face in both hands. "Zeke, I—" She paused. *I love you. I'll always love you.* And once she said those words, what else would she say? That she would give up everything for that love?

He turned toward her and laid his hands gently on her shoulders. The mask fell away as he looked into her eyes. "I know what you're trying to do, Katherine," he said softly. "I've thought about this, too. You're hoping we can work out some sort of compromise where we can both have what we want, what we need, and yet still…" He massaged her shoulders and his voice grew husky. "Still stay connected to each other."

She nodded.

He sighed. "I wish I could be that kind of man—strong enough to see you once a year, make love to you and let you go away again. Strong enough to believe that in a year, you'll be back."

"Maybe…maybe a year's too long. Maybe every six months we could—"

"No." He shook his head. "Don't kid yourself. Six months would become three. Three would become one, and pretty soon we'd be flying across the country every weekend. You can't function that way and neither can I."

She swallowed the lump in her throat. He was right. Her body still hummed from his caresses, and she wanted him again. "We shouldn't have made love. We should have kept things platonic, so that we wouldn't make this any worse."

His smile was sad. "God knows I tried. I don't know about you, but I ran out of resistance early in the game." He slid his hands down over the tops of her breasts and then cupped them lovingly. "I still don't have any."

"Neither do I," she said in a choked voice. "But this… this is it, isn't it?"

"Yeah." His gaze searched hers. "This is it."

She wiped the tears from her eyes and dredged up a watery smile. "Then if this is all we're ever going to have, what are we doing with a tray of dirty dishes between us?"

"Beats the hell out of me." He released her, scooped up the tray and plopped it down on the floor on his side of the bed. Then he gathered her into his arms.

"I suppose we should change the sheets," she murmured. "I did get things messed up with my wet hair and muddy feet."

"Why bother?" He slipped his hand between her thighs and boldly caressed her as he nibbled on her lower lip. "Now that I know running around naked in the rain like some wood sprite gets you hot, I'll probably try to get you to do it again."

ZEKE COULDN'T REMEMBER the last time he'd spent so many daylight hours in bed, or when he'd enjoyed it as much. And he'd have at least one more night with Katherine before he had to pay the piper and give her up for good. The rain had stopped at dusk, but the phone was still out and he was sure the creek was still impassable. Funny that he'd never been marooned here before, and he might never be marooned again. Yesterday he would have called it damned bad luck. Today he called it a miracle.

He would have preferred to be marooned without a bum ankle, but he was managing to get around a little bit with his walking stick. The pain always increased when he was vertical, though. And with Katherine sharing his bed, he was perfectly happy to stay prone most of the time. In fact, with Katherine "in charge," as she called it, making love hardly seemed to bother his ankle at all.

As darkness gathered outside the windows of the cabin, he lay in bed watching Katherine change Amanda after nursing her. He was really going to miss that tender, arousing scene of Amanda at Katherine's breast. Hell, he was really going to miss everything about this weekend, but he might as well not dwell on that now. Right now he still lived in paradise.

Katherine leaned over the table as she talked to Amanda.

She used the same happy singsong voice, but Zeke no longer felt left out of the charmed circle, especially when she would turn and include him in the conversation.

"Are we going to give her another bath?" he asked.

Katherine glanced over at him. "I'd love to. I'd love to give myself a bath, now that you mention it, before we put clean sheets on the bed."

"I wouldn't mind one myself. Of course, I could always take a shower."

"Come on, Zeke. That cold shower you took couldn't have been much fun."

"Okay, it wasn't much fun."

"How about if I heat up enough water to fill the bathtub? You can go in with Amanda."

"Or we could all go in together. I think we'd fit." He knew there had been a reason he'd bought that old antique tub that had come out of some silver tycoon's mansion in Casper. It was so huge that his buddies had expected him to start entering bathtub races.

"I don't want to take a chance on reinjuring your ankle."

"I'll be careful."

"I don't know, Zeke. It seems a little risky."

"No risk. I'll get in the tub first and you can hand the baby in. Then you can climb in." He had a compelling urge to have them all cradled together in the big tub, and he couldn't say exactly why. He just wanted it to happen.

"If you say so. Sounds like teenagers cramming into a phone booth to me."

"It won't be."

"Then I won't bother putting her sleeper on her yet."

"No. Just bring her over to me while you take care of heating the water." He was amazed at how eager he was to hold Amanda again. She'd slept most of the afternoon away, and when she'd woken up, she'd needed Katherine to feed her. Now at last he could get an armful of that precious little bundle.

Katherine walked over and deposited Amanda in his arms. With only her diaper on, she seemed more active, waving her arms and legs happily in the air.

He gathered her against his bare chest, enjoying the feel of her soft skin against him. "Hi there, sunshine," he said, smiling at her because he couldn't help himself. On schedule, she smiled back. Zeke glanced up at Katherine. "You can't tell me that's gas."

"No. It's not gas." Her voice sounded funny, and her eyes were moist.

"Are you okay?"

She sniffed and nodded her head. "Yeah," she said with a smile. "I'm okay."

CHAPTER SIXTEEN

ZEKE FELT GUILTY that Katherine had to carry the kettle of hot water back and forth to the bathroom, especially when she could only use one hand to do it, but she insisted the thought of a warm bath was worth the effort. The cabin grew dark enough to light the kerosene lanterns, and she placed one in the bathroom, making the room glow invitingly.

Finally she took the last kettle of hot water in and returned, looking eager. She held out her arms for Amanda. "The water temperature is perfect. Let me put her into her bassinet while I help you in there."

He handed the baby over before leaning down to unwrap the bandage from his ankle. "I can manage with the walking stick."

"Sure you can." She deposited Amanda in the bassinet. "But I'm here, so why not make use of me?"

He glanced up at her. "Because you've already had to lug all the water in. It's embarrassing to be such an invalid."

"Or is it embarrassing to be dependent on someone else?"

He looked away. She was too close to the truth for comfort. Depending on someone else wasn't only embarrassing, it was dangerous. In fact, in his experience the ones you needed the most were the ones who ended up leaving you. "I guess fending for myself is a habit after all this time."

"I can understand that," she said softly.

The tone of her voice prompted him to glance back at her. When he saw the compassion in her eyes, the solid door to his heart opened a crack. Maybe she did understand, at least a little bit. Being understood was something new to him. The ranch had been a bustling, happy place, a haven that had saved his life. But with so many boys, no one got lots of individual attention. He'd always felt he had to wrestle with his private problems alone. Looking into Katherine's eyes, he didn't feel quite so alone anymore.

But her understanding wasn't a luxury he'd have much longer. He reached for the walking stick leaning by the bed. "I'll use your help getting into the tub. God knows I don't want to fall climbing in. But let me make my own way into the bathroom."

"Zeke, for heaven's sake. I—"

"You'll be leaving soon." He gazed into her hazel eyes and thought how much he would miss being able to do that.

She studied him quietly for several seconds. "I get the point." She stepped back.

"Thank you." Standing was an effort, and without crutches he couldn't manage it without putting at least some weight on his bad ankle. He grimaced at the pain as he began the slow hobble into the bathroom. It was a symbolic gesture, and maybe an empty one, he thought. Katherine had already breached his defenses in a hundred places, and when she left he'd have to spend years repairing the damage. Considering that he'd be reminded of her whenever Amanda paid him a visit, he might never recover completely.

He stepped inside the bathroom, which looked a hundred times better in lantern light than in the light from the ordinary bulbs he'd installed over the sink. In fact, the whole cabin looked better this way. Maybe he'd forget about electric light and just go with kerosene from now on. Except the cozy glow might remind him too much of Katherine.

"*Now* will you let me help?" she said, coming in right behind him.

"Yeah." He unclenched his jaw and ran a hand over his sweaty forehead. This was one nasty sprain. He'd probably be riding a desk at work for a while until he healed. "This ankle is a damned nuisance," he muttered.

"But you saved the mother raccoon and her babies."

"Yeah, that's true." He surveyed the situation with the old-fashioned claw-foot tub. "This seemed like a great idea at the time, but I don't know how in hell I'm going to get in there without putting all my weight on my bad ankle at some point."

She pointed to the closed toilet seat. "You could sit there, put your good foot in and ease over into the water while you held on to the edge of the tub and me. You can get out the same way."

He sent her a dark look. "Sounds pretty undignified, if you ask me."

"Yeah, but it'll work."

He sat down and leaned his walking stick against the wall. "Here goes nothing." When he put his foot in the warm water, he sighed with pleasure.

"See? It'll be worth it. Now start sliding over, and I'll hold on under your arms." She moved in close. As she slipped her hands under his arms, her breasts swayed against his chest.

"I'm beginning to like this plan better." As he slid sideways, she moved sideways with him, and the friction of her body was very arousing. "Lots better," he added.

"Now is not the time to get frisky. Grab the side of the tub. Lift your other leg in. That's good. Oof. You're heavier than I thought. I—oops!"

He landed with a splash as Katherine lost her balance and tumbled against him. He caught her around the waist so she wouldn't fall headfirst into the tub, but she ended up with one breast pressed against his cheek. That sweet circumstance made up for the way the sudden movement had jolted his recent injury. Ignoring the pain in his ankle, he turned his head and nuzzled her. "Great plan," he murmured.

She braced herself by putting one hand on his shoulder.

"If I weren't hanging on the edge of this tub in an incredibly awkward position, I might enjoy what you're doing."

"But you don't?" He drew her nipple into his mouth. Nectar of the gods.

She sighed. "Okay, maybe I enjoy it a little bit. But I hear Amanda fussing in there. This started out as her bath, remember?"

"Mmm." He loved having the baby around, mostly. But the idea of fondling Katherine in a tub of warm water had definite appeal. With one more tug on her nipple he drew back and placed a quick kiss on the puckered tip. "Okay. Go get the baby."

As she pushed herself upright, he saw with some satisfaction that her cheeks were pink and her breathing unsteady. She was as agitated by the encounter as he was. After she left the bathroom, he wondered for the first time how she'd take their separation. From what he'd heard, New York had plenty of distractions. Maybe she'd throw herself into the fast pace of the city and barely give him another thought.

But he didn't think so. And while she'd filled this cabin with reminders that would never go away, he'd left her with a baby, a baby with many of his features. She wouldn't easily put him out of her mind and her heart. Selfish though it might be, he didn't want her to.

KATHERINE TOOK OFF her elastic bandage. Then she unfastened Amanda's diaper and carried her into the bathroom. "Here we are, our own little nudist colony," she said. She handed the baby to Zeke.

"Hey there, sunshine! Swim time!" He cradled her against his damp chest.

Amanda responded with a loud crow and waved her hands at his face.

Laughing, he leaned down and brushed his nose against hers while she patted his cheeks and gurgled.

Katherine stood transfixed by his expression as he played with Amanda. The face that often looked as if it were carved in stone was now animated with love. And so very, very vulnerable.

Katherine wondered what she'd done.

He glanced up at her with a smile. "Coming in?"

"Are you sure there's room?"

"You bet." He moved to the far side of the tub. "You can put your feet up by my hips. Climb in. It feels great."

"Okay." She stepped, wincing slightly as the warm water made her blisters sting.

"What was that for?" he asked.

Two could play the macho game, she decided. "Nothing."

"Hmm."

"Really. It's nothing." Holding on to the edge of the tub with her left hand, she eased into the narrow spot Zeke had provided, making sure she didn't bump his sprained ankle in the process. Once she was settled, she leaned back against the enameled surface and sighed with pleasure. "Where did this monster tub come from?"

Zeke swished Amanda through the water. "Some guy who made a fortune back in the days of the silver mines. They decided not to keep the tub when they turned the mansion into an office building, so I bought it." He swirled the baby around in the water until she wriggled with ecstasy.

"Good move." Katherine relaxed as she enjoyed the effects of the warm water, the feel of Zeke's leg aligned alongside hers, and the shared joy in their baby girl. "Look at her kick. She loves that."

"She's going to be a regular little tadpole, aren't you, sunshine?"

Amanda slapped her hands against the surface of the water, and Zeke laughed. After playing with her some more, he looked over at Katherine. "Ready to take the kid for a while, or will that be too much pressure on your wrist?"

"I can manage." She leaned forward and took the slippery baby, using mostly her left arm and hand to grip her. "Enough playtime, Mandy. Mommy's going to wash you now."

"Got her?"

"Yep." Katherine tucked Amanda in the crook of her right arm and reached for the washcloth she'd draped on the edge of the tub.

"Okay. Now I can take a look at your feet."

He'd obviously had that in mind ever since he saw her expression when she stepped in, she thought. So much for putting one over on him. He seemed to miss nothing.

He gently lifted her right foot out of the water. "Holy Toledo, Katherine. Why didn't you say something?"

"It's just a couple of blisters." Katherine washed Amanda's face while the little girl blinked and sputtered.

He lowered Katherine's foot into the water and picked up the other one. "This happened when we hiked down to the creek, didn't it?"

"Well, yeah."

"Damn it to hell." Then he glanced at Amanda. "Sorry, sunshine. But your mommy is an idiot."

"Nice talk."

He leaned over to examine her foot more carefully. "This must have really bothered you."

"Some."

"Yeah, right." He kissed her toes. "More than some. You should have said something the minute your feet started to hurt."

"And then what?" She methodically worked the washcloth over Amanda's pudgy little body. "You would have made me stay in the cabin, right?"

"Which is where you should have stayed, instead of walking all that way in those shoes."

"It was worth it. Believe it or not, I loved being out there, and besides, I thought Amanda and I should be with you."

He grew very still.

In the deafening silence, she glanced up to find him gazing at her, his dark eyes intense. When he spoke, his voice was husky. "Better be careful, Katherine. The next time that urge takes you, you might hurt more than your feet."

Her mouth grew dry. "Sounds like you're warning me away."

"That's exactly what I'm doing. Don't even think of giving up everything so we can be a family. I don't want that responsibility."

Pain sliced through her. He'd been so loving and relaxed with Amanda that she'd imagined she was the one preventing them from forming a family unit. She'd been wrong. Her throat was tight, but she forced the words out, anyway. "Don't worry," she said. "I have no intention of saddling you with responsibility." The water had begun to chill. "If you'll hold her until I get out, then I'll take her and dry her off."

"I have some first-aid cream we can put on those blisters."

Katherine climbed out of the tub. She didn't want to cry, so she settled on anger. "Never mind. I've had blisters before. They'll heal." But she might never heal from the wound he'd just given her. He didn't want her. Although she doubted she could ever sabotage Naomi by choosing a life with Zeke over her career at the magazine, it was pointless to even think about it now. He didn't want the full-time responsibility of a wife and child.

ZEKE ACHED WITH the pain Katherine was feeling, but he'd had to say what he did. Better that she feel the pain now rather than ruin her life. Of course she wanted them all to be together. He wanted that, too, and he'd known that the emotion between them was growing stronger with every minute they spent in each other's company, in each other's arms.

But when he'd seen the blisters she'd endured without

complaint, he had a horrible picture of her giving up the career opportunity of a lifetime and alienating her god-mother just to hold them all together. And that was what he didn't want responsibility for.

If she interpreted his comment to mean that he didn't want the responsibility of having her around all the time, that was okay. That would keep her on track better than the other, more complicated truth that he didn't want to be the reason she abandoned her dreams. He wasn't worth it.

She took Amanda and wrapped her in a towel. "Don't try to get out of the tub without my help. I'll be back as quickly as I can after I've put a diaper on her." She hurried out of the bathroom.

He damn well would get out of the tub without her help. A nursemaid wasn't his style. He took some time to survey the situation. Finally he decided he could get his good foot under him, push on the rim of the tub with both hands and lever himself out. In theory he shouldn't have to put any weight on his bad ankle.

In theory.

In fact, his anchor foot started to slip, and the only way he could keep from falling and possibly cracking his head against the edge of the tub was to put weight on his sprained ankle. He muffled his groan of pain behind tightly com-pressed lips and heaved himself onto the toilet seat.

"And you have the nerve to call me an idiot." She stood in the doorway wearing his blue flannel shirt. Her legs were bare, probably because she hadn't had time to pull on a clean pair of his sweats. She'd obviously been in the process of covering up when she heard him get out of the tub.

Panting, he pulled a towel from the rack and started dry-ing himself. "I never said I wasn't one, too. Did you get Amanda settled in?"

"She was out like a light almost before I got her diaper and sleeper on."

He glanced at the shirt she was wearing. "Are we dressing for dinner?"

She shrugged. "It's your house. Do what you like."

He'd thought he could handle her hurt and anger, that it wouldn't tear him to bits. Maybe he was wrong. "Look, I know I didn't say what you wanted to hear, but—"

"Maybe it was exactly what I needed to hear. You've made life easier for me, Zeke. For a while there, I was confused about what I should do. Now I'm not."

"Giving up your chance at the magazine would be a terrible mistake on your part, no matter what your reasons."

She gazed at him across the short space separating them. She'd accused him of hiding his emotions, but she was doing a great job of it herself. "Of course you're right," she said tonelessly. "It's a huge opportunity, and Naomi's been planning this for years. I wouldn't dream of throwing her generosity in her face. And then there's the money to be considered. With the salary I'll be making eventually, I'll be able to afford all sorts of extras for Amanda. And there's the foreign travel. Once she's old enough I'll take her with me to Paris and London for the shows. I'm sure she'll love it."

"I'm sure she will." And the two of them would move further and further away from him, he thought. Once Amanda had become used to mingling with the rich and famous of the fashion world, she wouldn't want to spend time in a backwoods cabin like this. And that went double for Katherine. She'd been seduced by the sexual tension between them, the temporary appeal of the landscape and the romantic concept of turning him into a daddy. But none of that would last long enough to replace what she'd be giving up in New York.

"I saw a can of chili in the cupboard when I got out the soup for lunch," she said. "Would you like me to heat it up for our dinner?"

"That would be fine."

"Um, about the sleeping situation." She cleared her throat. "I don't want you on the floor, considering your ankle."

"I don't want you on the floor, either." Actually, he wanted her on the floor, or the bed, or the dining table. He just wanted her, period. But it appeared that part of the weekend was over.

She ran her hand nervously up and down the door frame. "There's no reason we can't both sleep in the bed. But I don't think we should...make love anymore."

"If you say so." Black despair moved through him. He'd known the moment would come, the moment when they'd never make love again, but he hadn't expected to have to face it until she'd left the cabin.

"I do," she said softly. "You see, I think a relationship should be about more than just sex."

If he hadn't been hurting so bad inside, he might have laughed at that. "So do I," he said.

Little did she know that when their relationship had been about sex, he'd managed to control himself. When he finally admitted to himself how much he loved her, his control had disappeared.

"I'll go put the chili on to heat."

"Okay."

He finished drying off, which took a while. Finally he wrapped the towel around his waist before hobbling out of the bathroom. Sure enough, by the time he got into the main room, Katherine had put on another pair of his sweats. She stood by the fire stirring the chili in the kettle.

If he remembered right he had one pair of sweats left, which meant they could both be decently covered for the evening, damn it. He made his way painfully over to the dresser and took out a T-shirt and the last pair of sweats. That would have to do. Considering how tough it would be getting the pants on, he didn't want to bother with underwear.

God, he was going to miss the sight of her sweet body. Sure, he became aroused watching her walk naked around the cabin, and that was part of what he enjoyed. But he'd also loved the chance to memorize intimate details that the rest of the world wouldn't ever know about her, like the tiny mole on her right breast, and the faint birthmark on her fanny. He was just getting familiar with the line of her back-bone, the curve of her thigh and the spun-gold color of the curls covering her sex.

As he stood by the dresser balanced on one leg, he figured out that in order to get dressed without offending her new-found modesty, he'd have to hobble back to the bathroom. The hell with that. If his nakedness bothered her, she'd just have to look the other way.

With his clothes tucked under his arm, he arrived back at the bed and noticed she'd changed the sheets. So they'd both be squeaky-clean, sleeping on nice clean sheets, and they weren't supposed to touch each other. Maybe he'd have to take the floor, after all. He'd be damned if he'd beg, and lying next to her all night, he might be reduced to that.

He pulled off the towel before sitting on the bed. Getting the sweatpants on was a trick, but he managed. Then he pulled the T-shirt over his head.

"I can rewrap your ankle, if you need me to."

He glanced over to where she stood by the fireplace. He had a strong suspicion she'd watched his entire perfor-mance. "I'll manage."

"Yes, but I'm sure it would be easier if I did it."

"There wouldn't be anything easy about it, considering how close you'd have to get." He watched the awareness build in her eyes. "So unless you know a way to wrap my ankle without touching me, or unless you've changed your mind about making love, you'd better keep your hands to yourself."

CHAPTER SEVENTEEN

THIS WAS ALL FOR THE BEST, Katherine told herself as they ate their dinner. Zeke was in bed, a tray balanced on his knees, and she sat at the table, deliberately putting distance between them. If she thought Zeke wanted her to stay, she would have had a difficult decision to make. Now that she knew he didn't want her to, life became very easy. Or so she tried to tell herself as she forced the chili past the lump in her throat. She would have preferred not to eat, but that wouldn't be good for Amanda.

Okay, so life wasn't easy now, with Zeke less than ten feet away and the memory of their lovemaking freshly imprinted on her mind and her body. But once she was back in New York, the pain would grow less until one day she'd barely feel it. Her job and Amanda would fill her days with satisfaction and creativity. Then she remembered that Naomi had suggested she use her time in Wyoming to generate some concepts for future issues, concepts that she'd be proud to implement.

Now, there was a forward-thinking project, one that should point her in the right direction. She glanced over at Zeke. "Do you have some paper and a pen I can use?"

"Far right drawer in the kitchen. Help yourself. Oh, while you're up, would you please bring me that paperback mystery on the far end of the bookshelf?"

"Of course." She took the book down from the shelf and walked over to hand it to him.

"Thanks." He gave her the briefest of glances, but his expression was closed.

"You're welcome. If you don't mind, I think I'll open one of the porch windows a bit. It seems stuffy in here."

"Fine."

She wanted to scream. They were treating each other like polite strangers. No, more like civilized enemies. Polite strangers would make more of an effort to be pleasant. But she was better off this way, she reminded herself again.

In the kitchen she found the unlined sheets and a collection of ballpoint pens. She chose a black one and took several sheets of paper back to the table. Then she opened the window a couple of inches to let in some fresh air.

She took a deep breath and felt her brain revive. Yes, this was more like it, she thought, sitting down at the table. No wonder she'd been in a total funk about Zeke. She hadn't given herself anything challenging to think about, focusing instead on what she was giving up—the comfort of having Zeke help with Amanda and, of course, incredible sex.

And it had been incredible. She stared off into space for a minute before bringing herself back on task with an impatient shake of her head.

Taking her cue from Zeke, she'd insisted on wrapping her wrist herself this time, and although the job wasn't as neat as his, it would do. Writing gave her some pain, but it was better than sitting there doing nothing, so she kept it up in spite of the throbbing in her wrist.

Fifteen minutes later she had a page full of ideas, all of them crossed out. She stared into the fire in frustration. Everything she came up with seemed so trivial, a waste of the staff's time and talent. Besides that, she kept glancing over at Zeke. He seemed engrossed in his book, but she wondered if he was as serene as he appeared. She fought the urge to go crawl into that bed and...nope. Bad idea.

Finally she tossed the pen down and cradled her chin in both hands as she stared at her abortive attempt to get some work done. Maybe this wasn't the time or place to brain-storm. Zeke's presence would make concentration difficult for any woman with a pulse. She'd do up the dinner dishes and then follow Zeke's example and lose herself in a book.

She picked up her dishes and walked over to the bed to get his.

"Thanks," he said again in that monotone that drove her crazy. Then he returned his attention to his book.

It bothered her that he could ignore her so easily. She should have walked away with his dishes, but she didn't. "Is there anything else you need?"

His head snapped up and his eyes looked as if someone had tripped a switch, bringing them to full wattage. He tossed the book aside. "Yes, as a matter of fact, there is."

Heart pounding, she backed away. "I'm...sorry. I didn't mean..."

His voice rumbled low. "Then don't ask, Katherine. Not unless that's exactly what you mean."

"Right," she said breathlessly. Clutching the dishes, she walked over to the kitchen. She set the dishes in the sink and leaned against it while she hyperventilated. Good Lord. And she'd thought she was holding herself on a tight leash. Her body warmed and throbbed as she imagined what loving him now would be like. It would be very good.

But she'd announced to him not two hours ago that she thought a relationship should be about more than sex. She really believed that, and going to him now would allow him to think that sex was enough for her. And it wasn't. Of course not. But when she thought about the look in Zeke's eyes just now, she had the urge to forget her principles.

She managed to wash the dishes without breaking them, although her hands trembled. When she was finished, she went through the motions of taking a book from the shelf and sitting in the rocker with it open in her lap. In the distance a wolf howled, and then another, their cries drifting in through the partially open window. The sound affected her as much as it had the night before, stirring the lusty side of her nature so recently awakened by Zeke. It promised to be a very long night.

ZEKE CONSIDERED HIMSELF a master of self-control. He prided himself on being able to hide his emotions from even those closest to him if he chose to do so. Self-preservation had taught him that lesson early, and he'd polished his skills over the years. But he'd never been tested like this.

His whole body felt drawn into a knot as he tried to keep himself from asking Katherine to reconsider. He'd been reduced to examining her every movement, her every word for some sign that she was weakening in her resolve not to make love again. Surely he was too proud to beg. He'd never lowered himself to do that for any man, woman or child since the day he'd pleaded with his mother not to make him get out of the car.

But when Katherine had asked if he needed anything else, he'd come very close to pleading with her. Very, very close. He of all people should know that it wouldn't work and he'd humiliate himself for nothing. Yet as they sat together in the silent cabin, he grew desperate to hold her in his arms one more time.

When Amanda woke up for her next feeding, Katherine nursed her so discreetly that it nearly broke his heart. How he'd loved the moments spent in the big bed with a shamelessly unclothed Katherine holding the baby to her breast. He gripped his book and resolutely turned the pages he wasn't reading while she finished and changed the baby's diaper.

From the corner of his eye he saw her approach the bed, Amanda in her arms. He glanced up into her golden eyes, and his heart beat faster.

She swallowed. "Would you...I wondered if you'd like...to hold her for a while before she goes back to sleep."

He laid down the book immediately. "Yes, yes I would.

Thank you.'' As she placed Amanda in his arms and he adjusted to the now-familiar sensation of holding a tiny human being close to his heart, his throat tightened. The next time he saw her she wouldn't be a baby anymore. Her face blurred slightly as he gazed down at her. "Hey, sunshine."

She stared up at him in the wise way she had. During her nap she'd slept on her hair so a tuft of it stuck up from her head, making her look even cuter. Gently he pressed his thumb against the tiny dimple in her chin. "There. Now it'll stay that way for a while longer." His heart ached as he smiled at her.

She flashed him her toothless smile and polished it off with a hiccup.

"Uh-oh. Katherine?" He glanced up and discovered she hadn't moved from the spot where she'd stood to hand him the baby. "She has hiccups."

"Try putting her on your shoulder and burping her."

"I've never done that." He looked down at Amanda as she hiccupped again. "What if I do it wrong?"

"You won't. Just hold her against your shoulder. That's right. And pat her back lightly."

He tapped Amanda's back a few times, but she continued to hiccup, her small body jerking each time one hit.

"Well, pat her a little harder than that," Katherine said. "She won't break."

He increased the pressure some. "It's not working."

"A little harder. You're being too gentle."

"She's a little kid!"

"I know, but pat harder."

So he gave her a couple of harder taps and hit pay dirt. She barfed all over his shirt. And the hiccups were gone.

"Oh, dear," Katherine said. "I'm sorry. I should have given you a towel. Give her back to me. I'll get you a clean shirt and—"

"In a minute." Zeke wanted to bask in his success. He lifted Amanda away from his shoulder and tucked her into the crook of his arm. "Got rid of those hiccups, didn't you, sunshine?" He used the hem of his shirt to wipe her tiny mouth. "That's the important thing. Who cares about a little barf on the shirt? Not me. Got a smile for Daddy?"

Amanda grinned at him.

"That's it. A big smile and no more hiccups. Good combo."

"Zeke, don't you want to change your shirt?"

"Not yet." He glanced over at her. "In fact, not for a while. Amanda and I have some playing to do."

She gave him a long, thoughtful look. "Okay. I'll be over in the rocker reading my book. Call when you think she's ready to go back to sleep."

"I'll do that."

TRY AS SHE MIGHT, Katherine couldn't hear much of what went on between Zeke and Amanda. He kept his voice low while he talked to her. Every once in a while he'd laugh softly, and the sound was so intimate that Katherine got goose bumps. His whole routine with Amanda gave her goose bumps, in fact. She didn't think many men would react with such nonchalance after a baby spit up on them, let alone continue wearing the shirt while they played with the baby. Zeke was quite a daddy.

Too bad he had no interest in being a husband. Because if he did, she'd—no, there wasn't any point in thinking about that. He'd made himself clear. They would take different paths from this point on. But at least Katherine would know that when Amanda came to Wyoming to visit Zeke, she would be in the hands of a real superdad. She told herself to take comfort in that.

But weak woman that she was, the only comfort she could imagine finding at the moment was in Zeke's strong arms.

"I think she's getting sleepy," he said at last.

Katherine put down her book and went over to the bed. "Would you like me to get that shirt now?"

"No, you take care of Amanda. I'll get it. I want to go into the bathroom and wash up a bit, anyway. I think there's a little of it in my hair."

"I would be glad to—"

"Help?" A dangerous light shone in his eyes. "Do you really mean that?"

"Uh, no." She reached for Amanda and held her close to stop the sudden trembling that overcame her. "I'll tend to the baby."

"I thought so."

Katherine walked slowly away from the bed and knelt down next to Amanda's bassinet. Gently she nestled the baby inside. Amanda's eyes fluttered once and closed. She was asleep, but Katherine needed some time to collect herself. She also didn't want to leave the bassinet while Zeke was up and around, so she stayed beside it and pretended to be coaxing the baby to sleep.

When the water started running in the bathroom she relaxed a little. "You know, your daddy is a very sexy man," she murmured to the sleeping baby.

Amanda's eyelids flickered and her tiny mouth pursed.

"I wish I knew what he was talking to you about," Katherine said. "I can just picture what will happen when you're older and come out for a visit. I'll quiz you unmercifully when you get home." At least Amanda could bring her news of the man she loved.

Katherine sighed and glanced through the window that looked out on the porch. The sky must be clearing. Moonlight washed the porch and sparkled on the raindrops clinging to the pine branches overhanging the roof. Just her luck, it was probably very romantic out there tonight.

Then a shadow blocked the silvery light.

Katherine's chest grew tight as she stared out the window. The shadow moved, turned toward her. Dark eyes glittered in the light spilling through the glass.

Instinctively Katherine wrapped both arms around the bassinet. "Zeke." Her voice was faint and raspy.

Water ran in the bathroom. He couldn't hear her.

She started to call again and stopped. What was she doing? Zeke could barely hobble, yet if she alerted him, he'd come charging out here as best he could. Then he might think he had to be a superhero and go out to confront the bear, never mind the danger of facing a wild animal when he had a bad ankle.

Maybe, if she stayed perfectly still, the bear would go away. Zeke seemed to think she wouldn't try to break in. If only he could be right. Heart pounding, she watched the bear's nose twitch. Damn, she'd had to open that window a couple of inches, hadn't she? Now Sadie could get a good whiff of whatever was inside the cabin, like food, and a little baby. Katherine's arms tightened around the bassinet.

Then, to her horror, Sadie rose on her haunches. With one swipe of her paw, she ripped through the screen.

Pure instinct took over as Katherine carried the bassinet quickly over to the dresser and yanked open the bottom drawer. In less than a second the gun was in her hand.

Years ago a boyfriend had taken her to a pistol range. She'd hated it, but at least she'd shot a handgun once in her life. Fortunately Zeke's gun was similar to the one she'd used on the range. Breathing heavily, she watched Sadie drop back to all fours and stick her nose through the open window. Katherine forced herself to check and see if the gun was loaded. It was.

She stood, the gun in her right hand. Sprained wrist or not, she had to use that hand or risk a wild shot. Eons seemed to have passed since she first saw the bear, yet it had to be less than a minute. Zeke was still in the bathroom with the water running. Her heart beat at a frantic pace, but her hand on the gun was steady.

As she walked toward the door, Sadie pulled her snout free and looked at Katherine.

"I don't want to hurt you," Katherine murmured. "But I want to scare you so much you go away. And stay away." She cocked the gun.

Mouth dry, she cautiously opened the door a few inches, enough to get her right arm through. The rank scent of the bear assailed her. Both outside and in, silence fell, as if the world were holding its breath. Terror licked at the edges of her self-confidence. Refusing to give in to it, she concentrated hard on her love for Amanda and Zeke, pointed the gun away from the bear and pulled the trigger.

The blast rocked her back from the open door. The bear roared and Zeke yelled at the same time. Pure reflex caused her to lurch forward and slam the door shut just as Amanda started to scream.

"What the hell are you doing?" Despite his injury, Zeke was standing in front of her in no time, the color leached from his face.

She leaned against the door, shaking violently. "S-Sadie" was all she could say.

He took the gun from her nerveless fingers and stared at her. "You shot her?"

Katherine shook her head. Her lips felt frozen as she tried to form words. "Is she…gone?"

Zeke hobbled quickly to the window. "I don't see her." He shut the window and laid the gun on the table before limping over to Katherine. The starkness of fear had given way to a blaze of anger in his eyes. "Damn it, Katherine, why didn't you call me?"

Still trembling, she gazed at him. She longed to say she didn't call him because she loved him and wanted to protect him because he was injured. "I thought I could handle it." Her voice quivered.

"You had no idea what that bear might do! How dare you put yourself in danger like that? My God, Katherine, anything could have happened! You have no idea. No idea." He sputtered to a stop and stood there shaking his head.

Katherine watched the muscles work in his jaw and the anger simmer in his eyes, and slowly the reason for his tirade sank in. He was furious with her because she'd risked her safety, which could only mean... Maybe their relationship was about more than sex, after all. After considering that for a moment, she had another thought. Her heart beat faster as she realized what she wanted to do.

"I don't know what the hell you were thinking," he muttered. "You just took the biggest damn chance in the universe."

She pushed away from the door. "I'll get your walking stick."

"I don't give a damn about my walking stick. Amanda needs attention."

"I'll take care of her in a minute." She retrieved his stick from the bathroom and walked over to hand it to him. Gazing into his eyes, she no longer tried to disguise her emotions. Maybe he needed to know that her feelings for him were pretty damned intense, too. "Please go over and lie down."

He met her gaze for several long seconds before he took the stick. "Okay." He winced as he started back across to the bed.

Scooping Amanda up from the bassinet, Katherine sat in the rocker and cuddled the baby until her eyes began to close. By the time Zeke had climbed back into bed, Amanda was asleep. Katherine tucked her back in the bassinet. Then she turned down the wick on the lantern she'd used to light her reading and walked over to the bed.

Zeke glanced at her. "You know, maybe I'd better take the floor tonight, after all."

"I'd like you to stay." Katherine started unbuttoning her shirt.

"Katherine..."

"I know we'll go our separate ways after we leave here." She took off the shirt and untied the drawstring on the waist-

band of the sweats. "And that's why I want you to make
love to me tonight."

His voice was strained. "Look, you're probably not
thinking straight. Adrenaline can mess with your mind, and
the incident with the bear has probably caused you to—"

"I'm thinking perfectly straight." She stepped out of the
pants and got into bed.

"Katherine...." He held her gaze. "God knows I'm not
strong enough to talk you out of this."

She reached up and touched his cheek. "I don't want you
to."

He took a shaky breath. "Then we need the box of condoms."

"No." She moved into his arms. "If this is the only time
we'll have together, I want it to count. I want another baby,
Zeke."

CHAPTER EIGHTEEN

ZEKE LAY VERY STILL, his heartbeat drumming heavily in his ears as he held Katherine's gaze. "You're sure?"

"You were an only child. I was an only child. We both know what a brother or sister would have meant to us."

"Everything."

"Yes."

Once again he had the feeling of looking into the depths of a clear mountain stream, and he knew that she was at peace with this decision she'd made. She wanted this for herself and for Amanda. And best of all, she had confidence in him as a father.

And he couldn't deny her, not when the urge to mate rose so hot and strong. But there would be conditions this time. "If it happens—"

She nodded. "I have a feeling it will."

He thought so, too. The certainty of it made him tremble. "You'll call me the minute you know."

Her eyes were luminous with anticipation. "Yes."

"These will probably be the only two children I'll ever have." He knew beyond a shadow of a doubt that he'd never have a child with another woman, but if he started speaking in absolutes, she might not believe him.

"Me, too, Zeke."

He closed his eyes as relief and joy flooded through him. "God, how I needed to hear you say that."

She reached up to stroke his cheek. "I didn't know I was choosing you for the father of my first child," she said softly. "But you're the only choice for the father of my second."

"I want to be there this time." The more time he spent with Amanda, the more he resented missing so much in the beginning. "I want to watch you give birth."

"You will."

"And if there are…problems, I want to be there for those, too."

She combed her fingers through his hair. "The doctor said I shouldn't have problems next time."

He captured her hand and placed a kiss on each of her fingers. "Doctors can be wrong, and I don't want you to be alone if…something goes wrong." He wanted this so much he could barely breathe, but they wouldn't go through with it unless he had her word that he wouldn't be shut out. Not again. His voice was strained as he held her hand very tight. "Give me your promise, Katherine."

"I promise, Zeke." She swallowed. "I promise to let you be part of this pregnancy. I promise that you will be by my side when I give birth to our son or daughter. I promise to honor your rights as the father of our ch—"

His kiss transformed her final word into a moan of pleasure as he drew her close. Deliberately he guided her down and started to move over her, but she struggled in his arms. He lifted his head. "What's wrong?"

Her reply was breathless. "Let me be on top. Your ankle—"

"My ankle can take it. And this time, my love, I need to be in charge."

Her sigh of surrender was all the encouragement he needed. He covered her body with his.

He wanted to memorize her, absorb her into his pores, drown in the scent and taste of her. And then, when they'd flowed so completely together that they would never be separated, no matter how far apart they traveled, he would spill his seed into her, bonding her to him forever.

He'd never kissed like this, touched like this, wanted like this. He lifted his head and gazed into her eyes to find the same intense purpose shining there.

"I'm going to love making you pregnant," he said.

She gave him the smile of a seductress, then she went still. "Do you hear the wolves?"

"No. Just my heart pounding like a freight train."

"Listen."

He paused and tried to quiet his ragged breathing. Yes, there they were, louder this time, singing their haunting tribute to the moon. "I hear them."

"I love that sound. It makes me think of you." An untamed emotion burned in her eyes. "Love me while the wolves howl, Zeke."

And he'd thought he couldn't be more aroused. Heat surged in his groin as he began an intimate exploration of her body in tune to the rhythm of the wolves' song. The wild sound wove its way into his subconscious, driving him to a primitive sensuality as he reveled in her taste, her scent, and her wordless whimpers. He longed to carry her outside in the moonlight, lay her on a bed of pine boughs and take possession of her with the swift instinctive stroke of a forest creature. He wanted to howl his triumph to the world.

Yet a part of his civilized mind still functioned, leaping ahead to a time when he wouldn't have this woman stretched beneath him, writhing with pleasure, and he longed to make this moment last forever.

But instinct seemed to rule Katherine. She tugged at his sweats, pushing them down over his hips. Then she reached for him and guided him to her, spreading her thighs, arching against him. "Zeke, now," she pleaded with choked urgency.

He felt the call of her body, the insistent pull of her womb, and he followed that call, rising above her to look down into her flushed face.

"Give me another baby," she whispered.

His erection throbbed in response, but he slipped just barely inside her and paused. "Our baby," he murmured, looking into her eyes.

"Our baby."

As the wolves' howls built to a crescendo, he held her gaze and pushed deep.

ZEKE INSISTED THAT THEY make love all night to guarantee success, and Katherine didn't argue with him. But finally even their passion for each other couldn't keep them awake. Entwined in each other's arms, they slept.

Dawn had not yet found the clearing when Katherine woke to an unusual sound, one she'd never heard in the cabin. It took her several long seconds to realize the phone was ringing, but the meaning of the ringing phone came to her more quickly. Their isolation had ended.

Zeke started to climb out of bed, but she laid a restraining hand on him. "I'll get it. I can move faster." She hurried to the phone as Amanda woke up and started to cry. Katherine picked up the receiver. "Hello?"

"Katherine?" Naomi sounded worried. "Are you okay?"

"I'm fine." Katherine stretched the cord until she could reach Amanda's bassinet.

"Is that Amanda I hear?"

"Yep." Katherine cradled the phone against her shoulder and picked up the baby.

"Is *she* okay?"

"She's fine, too, Naomi. Just a little hungry at the moment."

"I am so relieved. When I hadn't heard a word from you, I called the lodge this morning and they said they hadn't seen you since Friday. The maid reported you didn't seem to be staying there, although your clothes were still in the room. I was frantic. So I made some inquiries through Lost Springs Ranch and got this number and some idea of where this cabin might be. Apparently it's quite remote."

Katherine jiggled Amanda against her shoulder. "Yes, and the phone was knocked out. It must have just been reconnected."

"I thought you two were going to stay at the lodge."

"Well, it…didn't work out that way, Naomi."

"Good heavens. He didn't kidnap you and drag you to his lair, did he?"

"No. There was a flat tire, and a bridge that was out, and—I'll explain when I get back." She swayed with Amanda, but the baby wouldn't quiet down.

"You poor woman. You sound exhausted, and Amanda doesn't sound happy, either. What an ordeal. I understand from the people at Lost Springs that this cabin of his is quite primitive. I had no intention of putting you and Amanda through something like this."

"It really hasn't been so bad." She glanced up as Zeke left the bed.

He'd put on his sweatpants, as if the telephone call from Naomi had restored his modesty. He limped over to the rocker, sat down and held out his arms.

Stretching the phone cord, she crossed to him and leaned down so he could take Amanda. "In fact, it's been fine."

Zeke rocked the baby and murmured to her.

"Well, you're very brave to say that, but I've sent a helicopter. They should be there shortly, but I decided to call and see if I could get in touch with you to let you know they were on the way."

"You've sent a *helicopter?*" Katherine glanced at Zeke in horror. Naomi meant to snatch her away from him in less than an hour.

"Of course. They'll fly you to the airport. The lodge can ship your things back here. Believe me, it's the least I can do after subjecting you to the weekend from hell."

Katherine gazed at Zeke holding Amanda. The baby had stopped fussing and was waving her arms at Zeke. The weekend from heaven was more like it. "Can you cancel the helicopter?"

"Well, probably not, but if you're worried about the expense, don't think another thing about it. The main thing is to get you and Amanda back safely to New York. I don't mind paying a little extra to accomplish that. I hope that at least you were able to tie up your loose ends with this man."

For the first time Katherine faced the fact that she would not be in Wyoming at all if Naomi hadn't paid a lot of money to arrange for this weekend. First Naomi had bought Zeke at the bachelor auction, and then she'd paid Katherine's airfare and reserved rooms at the lodge. For that outlay Naomi expected Katherine to tidy up her life so she'd be free to run *Cachet*. Instead, Katherine's situation with Zeke was anything but tidy, considering she'd spent the whole night trying to get pregnant again.

"You *have* worked things out with him, haven't you?" Naomi asked. "I expect there's nothing much to do in that little cabin except talk."

Despite her turbulent emotions, Katherine almost laughed. Fortunately she controlled the urge. She gazed at Zeke, and looking at him took away all the laughter and replaced it with deep sorrow. They would see each other again, but they would never share another experience like this one. They would never allow themselves the luxury of a passionate embrace or the temptation of being completely alone, because their love could go nowhere. Zeke didn't want a full-time wife and child, and Katherine couldn't turn her back on Naomi.

"We've worked things out," she said.

Zeke glanced up at her. She caught her breath at the grief in his eyes. Then his expression closed down.

"Thank God for that," Naomi said. "Well, I'd love to see you immediately when you get back, but if you'd like a day or so to rest up, feel free. Maybe we can do dinner tomorrow night. I know a lovely little place where they'll be happy to have Amanda and you won't be expected to dash into the women's room to nurse her.''

Katherine forced herself to speak around the lump in her throat. ''That...that sounds great.''

''Good. Then we'll do it. I can hardly wait to see you. I know it hasn't been that long, but I already miss you both terribly. You're the daughter I never had, and now that Amanda's here... Well, let's just say I've come to need that cute little baby face of hers to make me happy.''

Katherine swallowed. Naomi couldn't have put it any plainer than that. ''We'll see you soon, then. Bye, Naomi.''

''Goodbye, dear. You're a brave little soldier.''

ZEKE ROCKED QUIETLY as Katherine hung up the phone and leaned her forehead against the wall. ''How long do we have?'' he asked finally.

She turned, her eyes brimming with tears. ''Not long. She's already dispatched a helicopter.''

Zeke nodded and kept rocking. He couldn't let her see that he was being slowly torn apart by their inevitable separation. ''Funny how quickly a woman with money can arrange things, isn't it?''

''I could send the helicopter away.''

He gazed at her, wishing she'd do exactly that, knowing it wouldn't happen. ''No, you can't,'' he said softly. ''This woman is your ticket to achieving your dreams. She thinks she's saving you from a fate worse than death. You said yourself that you couldn't throw her generosity back in her face.''

Katherine wrapped her arms around her stomach. ''I don't think I can, but I don't know if I can stand to leave, Zeke.''

It took more strength than he thought he had, but he shoved aside his feelings of loss and concentrated on her. She had a brilliant future in front of her. He couldn't let her jeopardize it. ''If I thought you couldn't stand it, I wouldn't have made love to you. Maybe it was a big mistake.''

"Don't you say that!" She was crying hard now. "Making love to you last night was the best thing in my whole life! No matter what happens now, I'll never regret that!"

He wanted to cry with her, but he couldn't. She needed him to be strong. "That's good, because we can't take it back. And I'd be willing to bet my last dollar you're pregnant."

"I hope to God I am." She kept sobbing.

"You're going to need to be tough to break that news to Naomi when the time comes. She won't like it. One kid was a mistake. Two looks like a habit."

She started to laugh through her sobs, but there was a touch of hysteria in her laughter. "Some habit. We'll never make love a—"

"Don't. Don't go down that road, Katherine." His heart twisted in anguish, but he forced his voice into a steady, soothing rhythm. "We can't think about that now. We've both made our choices. We both know those choices are the best for everyone concerned." He stood, deliberately putting pressure on his ankle. The pain helped. "Go get dressed while I change Amanda. Then maybe you'll have time to feed her before the helicopter arrives."

She stared at him, her eyes red. "Ask me to stay. Ask me to stay and I will, Zeke."

Oh, God. He struggled with the raging desire to ask her, to beg her to stay with him. Finally he won the battle. "No."

She went limp and turned away.

Stay, he screamed silently. But he kept his jaw clenched and said nothing.

She walked over to the cold, sooty fireplace, picked up the blouse and underwear she'd left draped over a chair to dry and started putting on her clothes.

WHEN KATHERINE FINALLY walked up to her apartment door late that evening, laden down with a sleeping Amanda in the canvas sling, the diaper bag and the car seat, she felt as if she'd been gone a million years instead of only three days. A huge bouquet of colorful flowers sat beside the door. Careful not to disturb Amanda, she set down the diaper bag and the car seat, walked over and plucked out the card. Her heart pounded with the hope that Zeke had—but no, the flowers were from Naomi, with congratulations for going above and beyond the call of duty.

Katherine thought she'd squeezed out every possible tear in her body, but more threatened to fall as she gazed at the flowers and wished they were from Zeke instead of Naomi. She needed some token, some sign that he was thinking of her, that he was as torn apart by this parting as she had been.

The helicopter had arrived quickly, and once it had landed, there had been no time for tender goodbyes. The last thing she'd seen as the chopper lifted off over the trees was Zeke standing on the steps of his porch, arms crossed, as he watched her leave. The sight of him there all alone had nearly killed her.

Besides, she'd rather not have flowers from Naomi. Naomi shouldn't be congratulating her. Someday Katherine planned to repay Naomi the cost of everything, including the bachelor auction. It would take years, no doubt, but Katherine needed to clear her conscience. She hadn't really operated in good faith with her godmother, and guilt lay heavy on her heart.

With a sigh she fit her key in the lock, picked up the flowers and walked inside. She returned for the car seat and the diaper bag, shut the door and secured all three locks. Zeke hadn't needed three locks, she thought. He blended with his environment instead of erecting barriers against it. While she'd been with him she'd felt that sense of unity soothe her soul. The constant sadness of losing her parents had eased, and the world had seemed more balanced.

She tucked Amanda into her crib. The baby had her own

pink-and-white bedroom, one that Katherine had been proud of until now. But she couldn't help thinking how lost the little girl looked in such a big bed with so much furniture around. She'd seemed cozier in the copper kettle bassinet Zeke had created for her.

And when Katherine left the room, the separation of walls between her and her baby felt wrong. Her apartment seemed to have far too many rooms, in fact, and the noise from the street bothered her for the first time in the years she'd lived there.

Maybe she'd buy some nature music, she thought. Something with wolves howling in the background. She clutched her stomach as a wave of anguish passed through her. Zeke.

ZEKE HOBBLED OVER to the pile of wood by the fireplace and picked up another log, a log that Katherine had brought in.

After tossing it on the fire, he sat down in the rocker and picked up his beer. He still had the empty bottle from when she'd had a beer during their first lunch together. And their second lunch... He sighed and leaned his head against the back of the rocker. He'd had a total of three nights with Katherine, counting last summer. Three nights of memories to last him a lifetime.

He was probably an ungrateful son of a bitch to want more than that. He wasn't the right man for her, and he should count himself lucky that she'd been willing to love him for a little while. And she'd given him a gift. For a solitary, gruff man like him to have a sweet little daughter like Amanda was nothing short of a miracle.

Time to let Katherine go. Time to face the fact that he was who he was, and no woman would want to shut herself away in the woods with a guy like him, least of all a sophisticated lady like Katherine. She'd hooked the brass ring when she'd been born the goddaughter of Naomi Rutledge, and no way would he ever drag her down.

He wondered if she was home by now. It frustrated him that he couldn't imagine her there because he'd never seen her apartment. He didn't know where Amanda would sleep, where Katherine would sleep. He didn't know what pictures she had on the walls or what her furniture looked like. That seemed important, somehow.

Maybe one day he'd see her apartment...or maybe not. They might decide it was safer if they met in neutral territory. He'd have to be very careful not to do anything that would cause her to leave her New York job just because of their strong need for each other, which meant never, ever being alone with her again.

Naomi would not be happy when and if Katherine announced she was pregnant again. Zeke wished he could be there to give Katherine support when she made that revelation. But he'd probably only add to her stress. For the thousandth time since she'd left that morning, he worried about whether he'd done the right thing by making love to her with no protection. And whether at this very moment, their child was growing within her.

AS WOLVES HOWLED in Katherine's apartment, Amanda smiled and gurgled in delight.

"Like that, don't you, Mandy?" Katherine said as she finished changing the baby's diaper. The nature CD was Amanda's favorite, and Katherine had gotten into the habit of playing it every night when she and Amanda came home from *Cachet*. It soothed them both.

And it brought Zeke closer.

Katherine carried Amanda to the rocker in her living room and nursed her while the sounds of rushing water and the cry of a hawk brought back memories of the wilderness and the man she'd left behind. She'd traveled to Wyoming twice, and each time she'd learned more about herself, gained more confidence in her ability to handle any situation.

The rugged Wyoming countryside, she realized, made her strong in ways that the city could not. To be a whole person she needed that connection with nature that had been fostered when she was a child, and although she'd probably never become a wilderness guide as she'd once fantasized, she wasn't happy living in a high-rise in Manhattan, either.

She still wasn't sure how to reconcile this latest self-knowledge with her obligation to Naomi, but she would reconcile it somehow. So much depended on whether she was pregnant again. She prayed that she was. Far from dreading the prospect of telling Naomi that news, she welcomed it as a way to start revealing her true self to her godmother.

Katherine smiled. She was definitely a braver woman these days. She had Wyoming and Zeke to thank for that, but she also owed a debt of gratitude to Sadie. Without the bear's late-night visit, Katherine might never have discovered the courage to face her worst nightmare.

She longed to confide all this to Zeke, but he hadn't contacted her, and she didn't think she should call him until she knew definitely about the pregnancy. She missed him painfully and constantly, but she worried that excessive contact with her might make their separation worse. She'd disrupted his life enough as it was, and now he needed to return to the comfort of his normal routine. She'd no doubt be doing him a favor if she exercised some restraint.

As HE DID MOST nights, Zeke walked out to the front porch and settled into a chair. He wasn't limping much these days, but he almost hated to have his ankle heal because the injury kept him connected to those two incredible days with Katherine. He hadn't been able to make himself wash the clothes that she'd borrowed even though her scent was very faint now. Somehow they'd become "Katherine's clothes," and he didn't want them disturbed.

He'd never been on a sea voyage, but he felt like the

survivor of a shipwreck. Night after night he sat on his porch, searching for the peace that he'd always been able to find there, but it was gone. Everything reminded him of her—the empty Adirondack chair, the soulful howl of the wolves, the grazing deer, the hoot of an owl.

Then there was the ache that wouldn't leave, the hollow place inside that called out for his daughter. Two damned days he'd had, and she was imprinted like a brand. Once he'd accepted her presence in his life, he'd learned to hate the two months of growing he'd missed before he knew she was alive. Now that he'd come to know her smiles, her babbling and even her cries, he resented every hour that went by because it was another hour that Mandy was growing. And he wasn't there to see it.

He'd promised himself that he wouldn't interfere in Katherine's life, but he hadn't had a clue what he'd been promising. He hadn't known that she and Mandy had become as essential to him as breathing. He hadn't known that as the days stretched out before him with no prospect of seeing Katherine or Mandy, a part of him would slowly die.

KATHERINE WHIRLED AMANDA up in her arms and danced around the living room. "I'm pregnant! I'm pregnant," she sang. "You're going to have a baby sister, or a baby brother, you lucky little kid!"

Amanda grinned back at her. Now that she'd passed three months, nobody doubted that her smiles were really smiles, and she even had a start on honest-to-goodness laughter.

"Time to call Daddy!" Katherine planned to honor her promise. Zeke would be the first to know that the home pregnancy test was positive. Well, not counting Amanda, who wouldn't tell on her. She glanced at the clock. It would be very early in the morning in Wyoming.

As she allowed herself to think about Zeke, her jubilation faded a little. She'd had no communication from him, none at all. She hoped his reasons for not getting in touch were the same as hers. She'd tried many times to send a letter herself, but in the end she hadn't been able to figure out what to say. The emotions between them had been so intense that a letter seemed incredibly inadequate.

Even the phone call she was about to make seemed like the wrong way to tell him the news. She wanted to be able to see his face, see the light come into his eyes.

God, how she missed him. He was on her mind before she went to sleep at night and immediately after she awoke in the morning. He filled her dreams, and even her daydreams. She'd had some close calls at work when she'd been distracted by thoughts of Zeke and had nearly missed an important part of a meeting.

She kept hoping that the excitement of the job would kick in again and the time she'd spent with Zeke would fade somewhat in her memory. Instead, the job didn't seem able to hold her interest as it once had, and she found herself constantly reliving her days in Wyoming and wanting to be there.

She wondered if Sadie had come back and if the Adirondack chairs were still in one piece. She wondered if Zeke had rebuilt the bridge, and if Elmer the moose had come calling. Sometimes she tried to pretend the sirens on the streets were wolves howling, but the sound wasn't really the same. So she'd bought some more nature music and played it over and over, even if sometimes it made her cry.

She sat on the couch and gazed into Amanda's eyes. The older the baby was, the more certain it became that her eyes would be hazel, like Katherine's. Maybe this new baby would have Zeke's dark eyes. Katherine wondered if the dimple in Amanda's chin inherited from Zeke's mother would show up again in her baby brother or sister.

"I can't tell your daddy something this important over the phone, Mandy," she said at last. "And I promised he'd be the first to know, so I guess we'll keep this between us until I figure out what I'm going to do about that."

She tried to picture asking Naomi if she could take another trip to Wyoming without telling her why. It wouldn't wash. Naomi was already very curious about exactly what had taken place that weekend, because Katherine hadn't given out very many details. Naomi probably suspected that a flame still burned in Katherine's heart for Zeke, and an unexplained trip to Wyoming would confirm her suspicions.

Worse than that, it wasn't a good time to be jetting around the country. Naomi was turning over more of the magazine's responsibilities every day, and Katherine didn't have a lot of free time aside from the hours she spent taking care of Amanda. She even worked weekends, although that was supposed to be temporary until the change-over was complete.

Now that the rest of the staff understood Naomi's plan, Katherine had to be careful that she appeared responsible enough to take command. Running off to Wyoming when so many projects needed her attention wasn't going to inspire confidence in her co-workers. Announcing the pregnancy would be shock enough to everyone's system, especially considering how the last pregnancy took her out of the action.

Katherine looked down at the baby in her lap. Amanda had mirrored her mother's changed mood, and her chubby face wore a solemn expression, as if she carried the weight of the world on her baby shoulders.

"We'll figure this out, Mandy," Katherine said. "Don't worry. We managed with that bear. We will definitely figure this out. Just give me some time."

CHAPTER NINETEEN

ZEKE TRUSTED KATHERINE. He believed she would keep her promise. Yet she'd been gone six weeks and she should have called him by now to let him know if she was pregnant. Home pregnancy tests were all the rage these days, and he figured she'd use one the minute she missed her period. They hadn't established that she'd call him if she *wasn't* pregnant, but somehow he thought that she should, as a courtesy.

Hell, he just wanted to hear from her. The loneliness was excruciating. He'd been a loner all his life, but he'd never felt as if he existed in a vacuum before. He was so desperate to relieve his agony that he'd considered selling the cabin and building another somewhere else, somewhere that wouldn't remind him of Katherine every time he turned around.

But he couldn't do that until he heard from her, one way or the other, about the baby. Sure, she could contact him at work, but he thought she might try the cabin first. He couldn't always be there because of work, but whenever possible he hung around the place, hoping that she'd call. Of course, that meant he was faced with memories of her and the baby constantly.

When the waiting and wondering and remembering threatened to drive him crazy, he decided there was only one thing to do.

WALKING ALONG FIFTH AVENUE took Zeke's breath away. He kept looking up at the buildings towering above him, which meant he was constantly bumping into people hurrying down the sidewalk. So many people, all of them in a rush. He'd nearly been run over twice by taxis.

"Hey, cowboy, watch where you're going," muttered a guy Zeke knocked with his elbow.

"Sorry." Zeke tipped his hat. He'd decided against the flannel shirts he usually wore when he was out of uniform. For this trip to the big city he'd put on a western shirt and his best jeans. At the last minute he'd added the Stetson that Shane Daniels had bought him for the bachelor auction. He could use a dose of luck. There was a nip in the air on this October morning, but he'd left his jacket in the hotel room because he thought it was too scruffy to wear to the *Cachet* office.

He'd called, and without identifying himself had asked a receptionist to direct him to the place. Now he finally stood in front of the building, heart pounding. Somewhere in that tall gray mass of stone Katherine was working. She'd have Amanda with her. Zeke was so eager to see his baby he could almost taste it, but *eager* didn't begin to describe how he felt about meeting Katherine again. His breath hitched and his palms grew sweaty.

Well, he'd come this far. Pulling the brim of his hat low over his eyes, he pushed through the revolving doors and walked into the building. The heels of his boots clicked on the marble floor as he crossed to the bank of elevators. He consulted the directory. *Cachet* took up three floors—the top three.

An elevator opened in front of him and several people got off. Others waiting with him got on and turned to stare at Zeke as he stood there and debated whether to go through with this, after all. The elevator doors closed.

He was out of his element here, a stranger in this land of skyscrapers and crowds of people. This was Katherine's territory. She probably wasn't pregnant, and so she'd decided they shouldn't communicate again until Amanda was old enough to visit him by herself. She wouldn't welcome his intrusion into her busy workday.

But the fact that she was so close drove him crazy. A ride up the elevator and he'd be able to see her again, talk with her, even if only for a few minutes. And he was damned sure going to see Amanda. To leave without quenching his soul's thirst for a glimpse of his child would probably kill him. If Katherine became upset with him for showing up like this, he could take it. After all, she'd been upset with him before. He'd endure her anger for a chance to see his daughter.

He punched the elevator button.

Moments later he stood in the reception area. He looked around with a sense of doom. Everything from the glass-and-brass receptionist's desk to the white upholstered chairs lining the wall spoke of money and sophistication. He'd known his world and Katherine's were very different, but he hadn't realized just how different.

But by God, he'd get what he came for. By the time he left this slick world of hers he'd see how Mandy had grown and he'd know whether he'd made Katherine pregnant that night or not. If he had, she might even be regretting it by now. Ice surrounded his heart at the thought that she might have changed her mind about the baby, might have…no. She wouldn't do that. He believed in her more than that. He had to.

"May I help you?" The receptionist, a well-manicured brunette wearing a telephone headset, looked friendly enough.

"I'd like to see Katherine Seymour."

"Do you have an appointment?"

"No, but…I think she'll see me."

The receptionist gave him a long look. "And your name?"

"Zeke Lonetree."

"If you'd like to have a seat, I'll buzz her office, Mr. Lonetree."

"Thanks. I'll stand." He couldn't sit still if someone paid him to do it, he thought.

The receptionist punched a number into her phone. "Ms. Seymour? Oh, yes, Ms. Rutledge. I didn't expect to find you there. I see. Well, I have someone here who wants to see Ms. Seymour. His name is Zeke Lonetree." The receptionist fiddled with a gold pen while she listened. "All right. I'll do that. Thank you, Ms. Rutledge."

The receptionist cut the connection and glanced up at Zeke. "Ms. Seymour is in a meeting, but Ms. Rutledge will see you. She's in Ms. Seymour's office watching Amanda." She smiled, and her professional mask slipped a little. "That's Ms. Seymour's baby."

"I know." Zeke just bet Naomi would see him. She'd probably tell him to get the hell out of town. But Naomi didn't have that kind of power over him, despite her money and her connections. He'd stay until he saw Katherine, but in the meantime, he could get a look at his sweet baby girl.

The receptionist now gazed at him with frank curiosity, as if she had begun to put two and two together. "Do you know how to get up to Ms. Seymour's office?"

"No, I don't."

"Just go down that hall and take the elevator all the way to the top. Her office is the door on the left. Her name is on it."

"Thank you." Zeke walked down a hall carpeted in a black-and-white pattern he thought was called herringbone. The walls were lined with framed *Cachet* covers. The place was a maze, he thought as he rode the elevator to the building's top floor. And standing guard to make sure he didn't penetrate it and find Katherine was Naomi Rutledge. Well, he'd open every door in the place, if necessary.

Once he stepped off the elevator he saw Katherine's office door immediately. It was partially open. A similar door with Naomi's nameplate on it was right across the hall. Cozy.

He tapped on Katherine's door.

"Come in, Zeke."

He opened the door and stepped into one of the most elegant offices he'd ever seen, but then, he didn't spend much time in elegant offices. A wall of windows looked out on Fifth Avenue, and when he stepped through the door, his boot heels sank into thick cream-colored carpeting. Naomi sat behind a delicately carved cherry desk, but he didn't waste much time looking at her. His glance went immediately to a small crib in the corner of the office where Amanda lay fast asleep. Next to the crib were a rocking chair and a changing table.

He crossed the room to gaze down at Amanda. He couldn't believe how much bigger she seemed and how much more hair she had. His throat tightened as he watched her sleep, his beautiful daughter, growing so fast. And he'd missed all those days. He wondered if she still loved to play when she took her bath, if she'd learned how to roll over, and when she'd get her first tooth.

"Hello, Zeke."

He'd forgotten anyone else was in the room. With an effort he returned his attention to Naomi. "Hello, Naomi." She was about as he'd expected, polished and attractive in her black suit. Although she might be in her sixties, she carried her age well. Not a silver hair was out of place and her skin was in excellent condition.

"I wondered if you'd show up," she said.

"And why is that?"

She motioned to a chair in front of the desk. "You can sit down, you know."

"Thanks, but I'm just here to see Katherine for a minute." He didn't want to leave his position by the crib, just in case Mandy woke up.

Naomi's eyebrows lifted. "You came all the way from Wyoming to see her for a minute?"

"I—there's something we need to discuss." Amanda stirred and he turned back to the crib. If only she would wake up, then he could hold her.

"Try not to wake her up," Naomi said. "Katherine managed to feed her and get her to sleep before the meeting, which is a small miracle that doesn't always happen."

"I won't wake her." He was bothered by Naomi's attitude, as if he couldn't be trusted around Amanda. He was the father of this kid, and if he accidentally woke her up, he knew what to do about it.

"Katherine tells me you want visitation rights," Naomi said.

"Yes." He gazed down at the sleeping child. She was so perfect. Still. The tiny dimple in her chin made her even more perfect. He thought of it as the Lonetree stamp. She made a little sucking noise in her sleep, and the sound took him back to those magic moments in the cabin when he'd watched Katherine nurse her.

"Of course, she wouldn't be able to come out and stay with you for quite a while yet," Naomi said.

"Not until she's weaned," Zeke said. He wasn't sure how long that was, but he hoped not too long.

"Oh, I'd think you'd want to wait much longer than that. I'd say when she's four or five, then she might be ready."

Zeke turned to face Naomi as a slow-burning rage seared his gut. "I have no intention of waiting four or five years to spend time with my daughter."

Naomi regarded him quietly for several long seconds. "I see. It seems you became quite attached to her while the three of you were trapped in that little cabin."

Zeke glanced around Katherine's office. "You know, traps come in all shapes and sizes."

"And what is that supposed to mean?"

"Nothing. I—" Whatever he'd been about to say disappeared from his mind as Katherine walked in the door.

"Zeke!" Her face lit up with surprise and delight, but she quickly doused the light of those emotions and glanced nervously over at Naomi. "I wasn't expecting you," she said with more composure.

He held on to her first reaction and ignored her second. She looked great, charcoal business suit and all. "I know this is a surprise. I thought about telling you I was coming, but then I just...came."

"It's good to see you." Her eyes held a special glow as she gazed at him.

He lifted his eyebrows, silently asking the question. When she smiled back, he knew. Pleasure washed over him in a wave and he started grinning like a kid with a ticket to a major league baseball game. Hot damn. Another baby.

"Zeke said he had something to discuss with you, so I should probably leave you two alone." Naomi stood and rounded the desk.

Zeke glanced at her. Once again he'd forgotten she even existed. Good thing he hadn't followed his impulse to swing Katherine up in his arms and twirl her around the room. Of course he wasn't supposed to be doing stuff like that anyway. They were officially off limits to each other now. He'd said he wanted it that way, as a matter of fact.

"Oh!" Katherine seemed similarly surprised to find Naomi still in the room. "Well, maybe that would be best."

Naomi held out her hand to Zeke. "I'm glad I finally had a chance to meet you."

He took her hand. He'd never held one with so many rings on it. "Thank you again for your contribution to the ranch. I stopped by there not long ago and construction's started on the new bunkhouses for the boys. You made that possible."

"Actually I think you made that possible. I hope you enjoy your stay in New York."

"I'm leaving this afternoon."

"Really? What a shame. It's a great city." She withdrew her hand and turned to Katherine. "May I see you when you're finished here? There's a detail that's been nagging at me concerning the layout we approved yesterday."

"Certainly. Thank you for watching Amanda."

"As always, it was my pleasure. She's the light of my life." She left with the graceful air of a queen taking leave of her subjects.

Zeke waited until she'd walked across the hall and into her own office before he turned back to Katherine. "When did you find out?"

"A week ago."

His gut tightened.

"Don't look like that. I had my hand on the phone to call you, and then it seemed so impersonal."

"Damn it, Katherine, I've been practically living by the phone!"

Katherine glanced across the hall, where Naomi's door remained open. She nudged hers shut. "I'm sorry." Her eyes pleaded for understanding. "But I wanted to tell you in person. I tried to figure out a way to get out there, but I couldn't see how I could leave again, so I mailed you a plane ticket yesterday. Believe it or not, I talked your boss into telling me when you'd have a few days off."

"I switched those days so I could come now. I couldn't stand it another minute."

She clasped her hands in front of her. "I'm really sorry. I'll be glad to reimburse you for—"

"Not on your life." He cleared his throat. "You look terrific."

Self-consciously she tucked a strand of hair behind her ear. "Thanks." She blushed. "You, too. I've never seen you so..."

"Clean?"

She laughed, but her laughter had a nervous edge to it. "Don't you think Amanda's grown a lot?"

He couldn't seem to stop looking at the color of her eyes, the texture of her hair, the shape of her lips. "I can't believe how she's grown. She's going to be a big girl."

Katherine nodded. "Tall. Like you."

"And you. Both of them will probably be tall." Excitement churned within him and he couldn't help looking down at her stomach. "And you're absolutely sure?"

"Yes. I had it confirmed by a doctor yesterday. So you're really leaving this afternoon?"

"I only came to find out. Now I know, so I can get out of your hair."

"Oh." She looked disappointed. Turning away from him, she walked over to her desk. She drummed her fingers on it a few times before wheeling back to face him. "I'm going to resign."

"You *what?*"

"I've been thinking about it all week, which is why I finally decided to mail you a ticket. I wanted to warn you that I was doing this, so it wouldn't come as a shock."

Panic rose in his chest. "Katherine, no. Don't do this. I shouldn't have made love to you again. It was selfish of me, and—"

"Look, you don't have to change any of your plans. Well, you might have to make a little more time in your life for your two children, because they'll be living in Jackson with me, instead of here in New York, so naturally I hope that you'll spend more time with them."

"What are you saying? You can't throw all this away. My God, you have a window overlooking Fifth Avenue! Do you know what that means?"

"Yes." She lifted her chin. "Not much anymore. I have a lot to work out with Naomi, and it won't be easy. I'll hate letting her down, but I need to make…other plans. I'm not asking you to marry me, or take care of me. But I will be near enough that our two children can know you, know you really well. I will find something creative and challenging to do there, something that will involve the outdoors. It's—''

"No!" He'd ruined everything for her. Ruined everything with his selfish, greedy desire to give her another child.

Amanda started to fuss, but Katherine stayed where she was, her expression filled with pain. She put a hand to her chest. "Are you saying you...don't want me to be that close to you?"

Standing in this expensive office and knowing what she'd be giving up, he decided to lie. But he had to look away to do it. "That's what I'm saying." He knew he had to get out of there, and damned fast. "Goodbye, Katherine. Keep me posted on...everything." He flung open the door and practically ran down the hall.

The elevator opened just as he arrived, and he stepped inside. He had to put as much distance between him and Katherine as he could before he got down on his knees and begged her to spend the rest of her life with him. But what he had could never compare with all of this. Never in a million years.

KATHERINE STOOD WITHOUT moving. If she moved she might break. Soon she'd go over and pick up the baby, soothe her and get her back to sleep. Soon.

"What the hell was that about?" Naomi burst into the office. "Where was he going in such a hurry?"

Katherine blinked. Her voice was strangely calm. "Away from me, I believe. I scared him to death." She gazed at Naomi. "I didn't mean this to be so abrupt, and I hate that I'm messing up everything you've planned for, but...I need to resign. I had planned to move to Wyoming, but..."

"Because you love him."

Katherine felt as if she were enveloped in some sort of thick fog. "Yes, but I didn't tell him that. Listen, Naomi,

I'm so sorry about this. You've been the most supportive, most loving, most wonderful—''

"Never mind that. Why haven't you told him you love him? It's true. And he loves you.''

Katherine gazed at Naomi in confusion. "That's just it. He doesn't.''

"The hell he doesn't! He's giving up everything so that you can keep the job of your dreams!'' She shook her head. "Young people are so dense these days.''

Katherine stared at her. "You really think he loves me?''

"I would bet my fortune on it. In fact, I think I will. I've had a pretty good idea this would happen, and I've started looking into selling the magazine.''

Katherine's mouth dropped open.

"Oh, for heaven's sake, don't look so shocked. I've known from the minute you came back that you were gaga over this ranger of yours. So go get him. Chase him down before he gets out of town.''

"But, Naomi, you're going to sell *Cachet?*''

"Lock, stock and barrel. Well, maybe I'll keep some stock. Then I'll travel, come to Wyoming to visit my god-grandchild and have a life. That's something you have a chance to build, by the way. Create your own dream, Katherine. Don't chain yourself to mine. Now go, go get him!''

Still Katherine hesitated. "But what about Amanda? She's fussing and probably needs to be fed.''

"I'll deal with her until you come back. And don't come back without that gorgeous hunk of man. He's worth twenty jobs like this one.''

"Oh, Naomi, I don't know if he really wants me.''

"Have I ever steered you wrong?''

"No.''

"Then let me advise you one last time. Chase that man down. Use the express elevator at the back of the building.''

"Okay.'' Katherine began to grin. She ran down the hall and through a double door that led to the express elevator.

Rumor had it that the original owner of the building had had the elevator installed so that he could slip away with his mistress if his wife was spotted coming in the front of the building. The elevator plummeted her to the ground floor quickly enough to make her stomach jump, if it hadn't already been doing cartwheels at the prospect of blatantly throwing herself at Zeke.

Once on the ground floor she dashed out another set of double doors, through the lobby and into the street. Thank God he was tall and wearing a Stetson. She spotted him a block away.

Dodging pedestrians, she ran as fast as her tight skirt and designer shoes would allow. "Zeke!" she shouted.

He turned. The minute he caught sight of her he started making his way back toward her. "What is it?" he called as he drew near. "Is Amanda okay?"

"Amanda's fine." She leaned over and put her hands on her knees while she caught her breath.

"Then why are you here?"

She straightened. Maybe she'd been too coy. Maybe, in spite of her newfound courage, she'd been too cowardly when it came to Zeke. Well, she'd do her damnedest now. "Because I love you."

He stared at her.

"Naomi seems to believe the feeling's mutual, and that the only reason you've been pushing me away is because you're thinking of me, and this job I would be giving up." She looked into his dark eyes and her courage began to falter. "I'm here because I'm taking the chance she's right."

With a groan he gathered her close and pressed her head against his shoulder. "She's right, and damn it, Katherine, you have to stay here. You'll have everything here, while with me you'll have—"

"Everything," she murmured, lifting her head to look into his eyes. "All I want is you and our children. I want to live in the wilderness with you. I love it there, Zeke. I always have, but I lost track of that when my parents died, and then Naomi kept urging me to be a journalist and work for her. Please don't push me away because you think you know what's best for me."

"All I have is a one-room cabin!"

She smiled. "I dream about that cabin every night. I dream about it in the daytime, too."

"Just the cabin?"

"No, I dream about the man in the cabin. And I wonder if he loves me as much as I love him."

Fierce emotion blazed in his eyes. "More. I love you more than I ever thought I would love another person. Oh, God, Katherine, could you really be happy out in the woods with a guy like me?"

Her heart swelled with joy. "Not just a guy *like* you, but with the one and only Zeke Lonetree? I think it could be arranged. Of course I want the whole package—the ring, the ceremony, the honeymoon."

He tightened his grip. "And where would you like to go for this honeymoon? I could probably swing Hawaii, or maybe San Francisco, but then some people like—"

"I was thinking about a little cabin in the woods."

"But you've been there."

"Yeah, and I wasted far too much time, and wore far too many clothes."

"Ah, New York lady." He cupped her chin in his hand. "I'm going to kiss you right in the middle of your precious Fifth Avenue."

"Kiss me right in the middle of my mouth, ranger man. You'll like the taste better."

People eddied around them, jostling them in their haste to get on their way, but Zeke held her tight. And as his mouth found hers, she imagined she smelled wood smoke, pine trees and rain-soaked earth. She could even swear she heard, somewhere in the distance, the proud song of the wolves.

EPILOGUE

"JUST A LITTLE MORE." Zeke crooned. "That's it. Breathe...breathe. Now *push*. That's it."

In the muted light of the hospital birthing room, Katherine ignored the murmurs of her doctor, Eva, and the attending nurses. Her world had narrowed to the pain and Zeke. She focused intently on his calm, patient voice and his dark warrior's eyes made even more dramatic by the pale green surgical mask he wore. With each contraction she clutched his hand with the same urgent grip as when he'd pulled her from the rapids. He was her key to survival.

He touched a cool cloth to her forehead. "Almost there. Big push, sweetheart."

She could do this. She'd faced a bear, damn it. She could do this.

"One more push." Above the mask, his eyes seemed to glow. "Give us our baby, Katherine."

Our baby. Fighting exhaustion and pain, she closed her eyes and bore down with a loud groan.

For the first time, his voice quivered. "The baby's coming. That's it. That's it! God, how I love you, Katherine!"

She opened her eyes as a lusty wail filled the room.

"It's a girl," Eva announced as she laid the warm, wet baby on Katherine's chest. At the contact, the baby's cries slowly subsided.

"A girl." With a soft smile Katherine cradled the child they'd created. Then she gazed up at Zeke. "I'm glad."

Zeke leaned over them, his voice choked. "Yeah, me, too. I'm starting to get the hang of little girls."

"Yes, you are." She couldn't imagine ever loving him more than she did at this very moment. Yet she knew she would. Every day the bond between them grew stronger.

He swallowed and cleared his throat. Then he laid a gloved hand on the baby. "Welcome to the world, Naomi..." He paused and glanced at Katherine. "We never decided on a middle name, did we?"

"I did." Katherine had been saving her idea until this moment, hoping and praying the baby would be a girl. "I want to name her Naomi Suzanne."

He sucked in a breath and stepped back, clearly taken by surprise. "After my mother?"

Katherine nodded.

Zeke lowered his head and turned away as a tremor passed through his massive body.

At his reaction, Katherine's chest tightened with anxiety. Maybe she'd made a mistake. "Unless you don't want to," she said softly.

His head came up. His dark lashes were spiked with the tears he'd fought unsuccessfully to control. When he finally spoke, his voice was rough and unsteady. "I want to," he said. He crouched down so that he could gaze into the baby's face. Slowly he settled his big hand over the tiny body. "Welcome to the world, Naomi Suzanne."

continues with

HIS BODYGUARD

by

Muriel Jensen

Bodyguard Meg Loria had never before drawn such an
assignment from her family's security firm: successfully
bid on a gorgeous guy at a charity auction, hole up alone
with him in a secluded cabin so she can protect him from
his rivals without his knowledge, and then try—just try—
to keep her mind strictly on her work!

Available in October

Here's a preview!

"Don't move a muscle!" she threatened, "or I'll blow you away." He didn't *have* to know he was in danger from a twenty-two caliber finger.

To her complete surprise, her captive didn't move except to draw a labored breath. "Good morning, Meg," he said in a strangled voice.

For an instant she couldn't move. Then she silently called herself all kinds of stupid names and got up on her knees astride his waist.

"Amos?" she demanded, as angry with him as she was with herself.

There was another labored breath. "You were expecting maybe a rapist or a murderer?"

She leapt to her feet and went to the light just inside the kitchen. The glaring track lights over the counter revealed Amos supine on the floor in khaki shorts and a white T-shirt. He grimaced against the light as he got to his feet.

"What are you doing up at this hour?" she demanded. "Why didn't you put a light on? Why is the back door open? You've never heard of identifying yourself when you're attacked?"

He winced as he stood, then bent over, his hands braced against his thighs as he drew deep breaths. "It's almost five," he replied, pausing to blow out a breath. "I'm always up at this hour. I didn't...put a light on because I didn't want to disturb you." He straightened as he blew out another breath. "The back door is open because I love the smell of morning.'' He focused on her, his expression wry and amusedly critical. ''When you're being punched in the solar plexus or kicked in your...pride, it doesn't occur to you to say, 'Hey, there. I'm Amos Pike. You got anger issues you want to talk about?'''

Embarrassed and still annoyed, she glared at him. ''I'm sorry. I heard noises.''

He spread his arms. ''It didn't occur to you that it could be me and not an intruder?''

''I...forgot you were here,'' she fibbed instead of admitting that sometimes, alertness could be honed to too fine a point.

He folded his arms and shook his head. ''Well, that hurts my feelings. I thought about *you* all night long.''

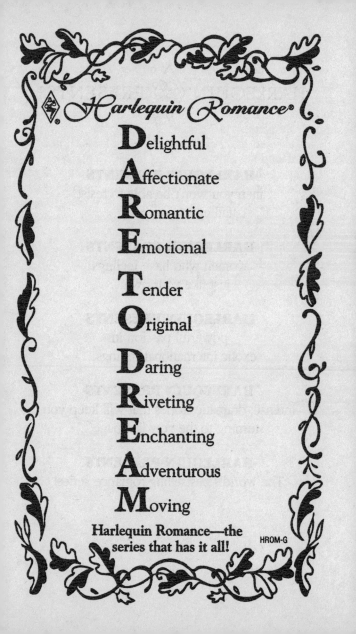

Harlequin Romance®

Delightful

Affectionate

Romantic

Emotional

Tender

Original

Daring

Riveting

Enchanting

Adventurous

Moving

Harlequin Romance—the
series that has it all!

HROM-G

HARLEQUIN PRESENTS®

HARLEQUIN PRESENTS
men you won't be able to resist
falling in love with...

HARLEQUIN PRESENTS
women who have feelings
just like your own...

HARLEQUIN PRESENTS
powerful passion in
exotic international settings...

HARLEQUIN PRESENTS
intense, dramatic stories that will keep you
turning to the very last page...

HARLEQUIN PRESENTS
The world's bestselling romance series!

Harlequin® Historical

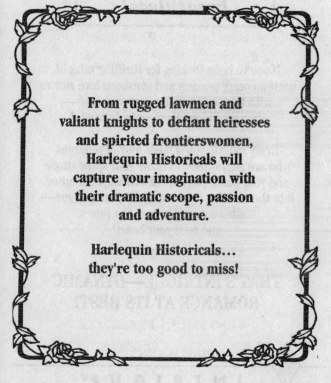

From rugged lawmen and
valiant knights to defiant heiresses
and spirited frontierswomen,
Harlequin Historicals will
capture your imagination with
their dramatic scope, passion
and adventure.

Harlequin Historicals…
they're too good to miss!

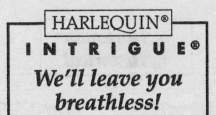